Eye on You - Murder in Biloxi
By Joe Hamilton

Text Copyright @ 2014 Joe Hamilton

All Rights Reserved

This is a work of fiction. Names, characters, and incidents are the product of the writer's warped imagination and are used fictitiously. If anyone thinks there is a resemblance to actual persons then they are wrong…dead wrong. Any resemblance to people, living or dead, businesses, companies, or events are entirely an illusion. The writer has chosen the city of Biloxi as a backdrop, because of its rich, dynamic culture and history.

I would like to dedicate this book to my loving wife Anita, who tirelessly supported me, emotionally and financially throughout.

Table of Contents

Chapter 1 7
Chapter 2 9
Chapter 3 15
Chapter 4 23
Chapter 5 28
Chapter 6 33
Chapter 7 41
Chapter 8 51
Chapter 9 56
Chapter 10 63
Chapter 11 70
Chapter 12 77
Chapter 13 86
Chapter 14 90
Chapter 15 95
Chapter 16 102
Chapter 17 110
Chapter 18 122
Chapter 19 127
Chapter 20 134
Chapter 21 138
Chapter 22 147
Chapter 23 152
Chapter 24 158
Chapter 25 164
Chapter 26 167
Chapter 27 172
Chapter 28 177
Chapter 29 181
Chapter 30 186
Chapter 31 190

Chapter	Page
Chapter 32	198
Chapter 33	207
Chapter 34	211
Chapter 35	215
Chapter 36	218
Chapter 37	223
Chapter 38	227
Chapter 39	235
Chapter 40	240
Chapter 41	244
Chapter 42	250
Chapter 43	254
Chapter 44	261
Chapter 45	266
Chapter 46	271
Chapter 47	277
Chapter 48	279
Chapter 49	283
Chapter 50	289
Chapter 51	298
Chapter 52	303
Chapter 53	311
Chapter 54	315
Chapter 55	319
Chapter 56	324
Chapter 57	330
Chapter 58	335
Chapter 59	339
Chapter 60	342
Chapter 61	344
Chapter 62	352
Chapter 63	356

Chapter 1

Saturday Morning, May 19th, 1979

The steam was already rising from the black asphalt under the early morning Biloxi sun. It was going to be a hot one, or as his father used to say, hot as horseradish. The parking lot was surrounded by clean white sand beaches. It was too early for the usual joggers and sun worshippers. He couldn't see a soul, but the feeling of being watched came over him. You could almost taste the salt in the warm sea breeze. The ocean was calm today, its waves gently licking the shore like a kitten lapping up milk. A squadron of brown pelicans was perched on the wooden pilings of the pier, looking down like judges as he made the short walk to the solitary car in the parking lot. It was a navy blue Chevrolet Caprice, exactly as expected. A sense of foreboding came over him, sending shivers up and down his spine. As he approached the car, a sporadic pattern of bullet holes in the trunk was the first indication that something was wrong. The clinging, smothering smell of whatever was in the trunk was overwhelming. He moved to the driver's door and found it unlocked. The car was empty, except for some papers left on the black leather passenger seat. Empty that is, if you didn't count the black revolver sitting on the driver's seat. Opening the door, he picked up the gun and sat behind the wheel. He smelled the gun and examined the barrel for copper and lead fouling. Someone had used it recently. Maybe the same person who also left the left the keys in the ignition?

Taking both the gun and the keys, he decided to check out who, or what, was in the trunk. Before he could move, he heard the sirens. Looking into the Caprice's side mirror, three police cars appeared on the boardwalk with lights flashing.

Chapter 2

Gabriel-Monday morning, 18 days earlier

My name is Gabriel Ross, and I was running late for a client meeting. That's what prompted the mad dash for the elevator. Holding the doors apart, I wrestled my way in like I was Samson. A pimply kid of about sixteen was standing next to the panel. He smiled, having enjoyed my predicament rather than holding the door. I asked him to press the button for the 7th floor. Just to irritate me he pressed #6. I huffed in frustration and reached over a couple of people, and pressed the correct floor.

I looked around the old and poorly maintained elevator. Whatever carpet it had was now threadbare, its color long since faded away to nothing. One bulb flickered on and off, in its last throes, working hard to illuminate the tiny elevator. A lens covering the bulb had become a mausoleum for hundreds of dead flies. Rose colored wallpaper hung from the walls. Near the ceiling the paper started to curl, with one section hanging down like the pink tongue of a salivating dog. A scratchy version of Barry Manilow's "At the Copa" crawled out of the ancient speakers. Like some sick joke, the speakers only ever played "At the Copa" over and over again.

As the door closed, I saw everyone looking up at the floor indicator, no doubt praying to the God of Elevators that the ride end as quickly as possible. I made a mental note to talk to my partner about relocating our struggling detective agency to better premises. The elevator made a clunking sound, signaling its slow and painful climb. The air was stagnant with the fan having long quit the job.

While everyone else was looking up, I decided to look down. Apart from my sneakers, I saw a selection of loafers and dress shoes, some sandals and a pair of Winnie the Pooh bedroom slippers. The latter worn by a little girl, no more than four, playing peek-a-boo behind her mother's tree trunk of a leg. I thought there was an old Chinese proverb that signaled playing peek-a-boo with a little girl this early on a Monday morning was a good omen. The girl was probably there to help plead her mother's case to the welfare people on the 4th floor. I also spied a pair of red ladies pumps, the kind with the stiletto heels. Further, the shoes were attached to beautiful legs, which were attached to... a fine looking Asian-American brunette, wearing a tight fitting red dress that hugged her body like a Ferrari on the coastal highway. I wondered what a dish like her was doing in this dump. As if reading my thoughts, she turned and eyed me suspiciously. We made eye contact; her eyes shielded behind thick lenses. I smiled, which prompted her to look away in disgust.

Everyone had exited by the time the elevator climbed past the 6th floor, leaving just doll face and myself. I found this to be a bit odd since the 7th floor was the top of the building. The only other room being a broom closet that Larry the cleaner liked to call his office. My mind scrambled trying to remember the client I was scheduled to meet. The elevator finally creaked to a stop on 7. I looked over, and said with my most suave, gentlemanly tone, "After you, Mrs. Cooper."

I made a show of holding the elevator door for her. She was standing back at the rear of the elevator eying me suspiciously. While we looked at each other, the doors repeatedly tried to close. Open-close-open-close. Finally, an alarm sounded. Embarrassed, I retreated down the hall to my office. I looked back and saw Mrs. Cooper walking towards me down the hall. She had a signature walk, feline and graceful. Her stride measured; one stiletto placed delicately in front of the other, like a prowling tigress stalking her prey. Behind her glasses, her eyes met mine.

"What are you looking at?" she challenged, interrupting my reverie. After mumbling something unintelligible, she hit me with a triplex of questions. "Are you some pervert? How did you know my name? Do you work for Gabriel Ross, the private detective?"

Taken aback for a brief moment, I calmly extended my hand, "Nice to meet you, Mrs. Cooper - my name is Gabriel Ross, and I own the "Eye on You Detective Agency. As for how I came to know your name, I saw a Caddy parked in the lot as I drove in. The personalized plates read, "I Cuff Um". I put two and two together, once I remembered seeing your picture in the local rag last week."

She tentatively allowed me to shake her hand, which was small and dainty, her grip limp like an uprooted weed. "Well, you're smarter than you look." she said dismissively.

"Uh, thanks," I replied, unlocking the door. A flick of the switch illuminated a small office devoid of unnecessary things like a waiting room, secretaries, paintings, coffee, diplomas... My silent partner Ben O'Shea and I had rented this space about three months ago and let's just say business was as slow as a hot summer day here in Biloxi.

"Couldn't find a smaller office?"

"I'm currently negotiating for a much larger space in the new Drayton Tower," I lied.

"Sure," she said with a look that left no doubt she didn't buy it for a second.

"Please have a seat?" I said pointing to one of the two chairs adjacent to a small wooden desk.

Ignoring me, she moved about the tiny office looking out the window, inspecting the spectacular view of the red brick of the apartment building next door. "Nice" she said sarcastically. "Do you know you have a cat on your fire escape?"

"Yes, that's Bourbon. He came with the place," I replied, opening the window to let in the orange tabby. "He thinks he works here. I pay him in tuna fish."

"Cute, Mr. Ross," she said, continuing to stand. She was almost as tall as a 6 foot street light, overshadowing me by the better part of twelve inches.

"Call me Gabriel," I replied, offering her a cigarette from the pack of Camels I kept in my desk. I don't smoke; I kept them around as a courtesy. I figured it might help people relax and open up.

"No, thank you Mr. Ross, smoking stunts your growth; didn't your momma tell you?"

Bourbon jumped up on the desk purring as I put the pack away. "Have a seat Mrs. Cooper, and tell us what "Eye on You Investigations" can do for you."

She finally sat down and crossed her legs, causing her red dress to rise up mid-thigh. Bourbon and I were riveted.

"It's a strange name for a detective agency? It sounds more like you're some …stalker." I smiled, wondering how many more shots Bourbon and I would have to endure.

"So what exactly do you do as a "Private Detective," Mr. Ross?"

I didn't care for her accentuating "Private Detective." She struck me as a spoiled brat. I had half a mind to put her over my knee and give her a spanking, but I didn't think our relationship had developed that far yet.

"It's Gabriel, and I do a variety of jobs ranging from finding missing people, stalking... I mean surveillance, investigating insurance fraud, doing background checks, that type of thing. Were you referred to me?"

"I called the local police about my... situation and a gentleman there said you were the best in town."

No doubt she was referring to my silent partner Ben. "Great! I love referrals, how can we help?"

"We?" she said, looking around the office as if some associate might have snuck in behind us.

"I have a partner, but he's more of a silent partner. Of course, there's always Bourbon." As I said this, I noticed Bourbon had already chosen sides. He had jumped down and was doing his normal "rub up against a beautiful girl's leg" routine.

"Mr. Ross, you obviously know who my husband is. He's a very powerful man in Biloxi and has a reputation as someone who gets what he wants. I'm here to ask you to expose the affair he's having." I was momentarily distracted. To think anyone would cheat on the doll sitting across from me was as big a stretch as a fat lady in ski pants.

"Mr. Ross?"

"It's Gabriel. What makes you think he's having an affair?"

"Let just say I have my suspicions. I need you to follow him, and get me some proof."

"So what happens if I get you proof? Will you ask for a divorce?"

"I won't be asking for anything, and divorce is the least he can expect," she replied putting emphasis on the word asking.

I made a note on my pad; *speak to Ben about the quality of his referrals*. The potential for disaster here was enormous; William Cooper was more than just a man who got what he wanted. In his position as Sheriff of Harrison County, he was rumored to be involved with some pretty shady characters. If he was crazy enough to step out on doll face, then he was crazy enough to get rid of a nosy detective.

Bourbon was now perched on her lap, making a purring noise like a 67 Ford Mustang. I put a lot of stock in Bourbon's opinion. Even so I had decided to send her packing. I had just opened my mouth to give her my decision when I saw a tear fall from those beautiful brown eyes. I put all reason aside and fell for her like a blind roofer.

Before I could say anything, she recovered. "Is a $2000 check sufficient as a retainer?"

I was right, the Winnie the Pooh slippers were a good sign. "So tell me, how did you meet your husband?"

Chapter 3

Jacqueline −7 years earlier…

"I REALLY, REALLY need this trip Jackie," said Chevon, her excitement bubbling over. "Wait until you try some down home southern cooking." Catherine shook her head and rolled her eyes. Chevon, who Catherine and I met at Oberlin, was raised in New Orleans and was the catalyst for our upcoming road trip.

"If we take turns and drive straight through, we should be there in about 20 hours," offered Catherine, the self-appointed navigator. Catherine and I have been best friends for as long as I can remember. I couldn't help but notice a bit of rivalry between Catherine and Chevon. I was hoping the road trip would draw us all closer together.

"Don't worry, we'll make it before that, I know some of the back roads," replied Chevon.

"Yeah, can't wait to visit Bumblefuck Alabama, and Hootersville Mississippi," said Catherine.

My parents were a little wary of the trip, but at 19, they knew I had to find my way in the world. For all of my life growing up in Chicago, I led a sheltered life. My father, Frank Chen emigrated from Hong Kong and had gotten a good job as a math teacher at a local high school. My dad was fond of telling me my logical side came from him. Not long after relocating, he met my Mom Celeste, who was working in the school cafeteria. As a French Canadian, she liked to tell me I got my looks and temper from her.

"So, looking forward to partying in the French quarter, Jacqueline?" asked Catherine, breaking through my thoughts.

"You bet. Just don't expect me to get you out of trouble." I replied, starting my 1968 Chrysler Newport. It was a clear Ohio morning, a little chilly, but there was no snow in the forecast, and that was all that mattered. We got the car loaded and then we set off on our grand adventure; little did I know my life was about to change forever.

We made great time on I-75, only stopping for gas, bathroom breaks and for Catherine to buy smokes. The radio was getting a workout as we tried to find decent channels driving through the mountains of Kentucky. Whenever we were lucky to find a top 40 AM station, we made ourselves hoarse by singing along to tunes like "War" by Edwin Starr, and Diana Ross' "Ain't No Mountain High Enough".

We crossed into Tennessee, and the conversation turned to boys. I had my share of admirers, but I was reluctant to let anything get in the way of school. I looked over at Catherine, who was taking a turn up front with me. She was busy polishing her nails for the five hundredth time. Catherine gave the impression of being much more "experienced," but I sometimes wondered if all of those graphic details were just a fantasy. Chevon, on the other hand, seemed to have the hots for one of her professors.

"Do you guys know Wilson, the art teacher? I just think he's the best prof at Oberlin," said Chevon, leaning forward.

"I heard he's a pretty good lecturer. They say he's a pretty accomplished painter too." I replied.

"Yeah Chevon, I bet you'd like to check out his etchings." Catherine chipped in, trying to get a rise out of Chevon. As a black woman with a strict Baptist upbringing, Chevon could be a little naïve. This was something Catherine loved to exploit. I quickly changed the subject.

"Have you guys thought about what you might do for the summer?" I asked. We were all in the 3rd year of a Liberal Arts program. My major was Art History, while Catherine was working towards an English degree. Chevon was getting top marks in Music.

"I imagine I'll go back to Orleans and work in my uncle's restaurant, maybe play a little horn for one of the bands," said Chevon.

"I was thinking about dating a sugar daddy." said Catherine, "What about you Jacqueline, going to pump the hose again?"

I'd had a series of meaningless summer jobs ranging from flag girl on a road crew to gas station attendant. "No, I've had enough pumping gas to last a lifetime. I've been offered a job tutoring new immigrants from China in English. I'm looking forward to doing something worthwhile for a change."

Things started getting interesting when we got off the interstate, and took one of Chevon's "can't miss" short cuts. The two-lane country road took us through rural Alabama, and then crossed into Mississippi. It was 2 in the morning, driving down a deserted country road, when the engine light came on. Moments later, it was all I could do to coax the car to the side of the road. It died with an ominous death rattle.

"Now what Jacqueline?" Asked Catherine. "There's not a car or house anywhere." I desperately tried to restart the car, getting nothing but a click for my efforts. For a long moment, no one said anything. Here we were, three young, attractive college girls stuck out in the middle of nowhere. It was like a scene at the beginning of a B horror movie.

"Hey, did I ever tell you about the family from up north, whose car broke down along the road like this?" asked Chevon. Neither of us wanted to say anything that would encourage her. Not to be put off, Chevon continued, "The story goes that the cops found their abandoned car along the side of the road. The next morning, some farmer found their dismembered bodies out in the hayfields. It was the work of some crazed half man, half wolf."

"Thanks for sharing," Catherine said sarcastically. I looked around and grew concerned. The night was like a blanket of darkness. There was no moonlight, just a million stars looking like diamonds on black velvet.

"What was that town we passed 10 miles ago? I asked.

"Fucksville," replied Catherine.

"Thanks, can you look at the map, and try to figure out where we are?"

Catherine used her Bic lighter to illuminate a small portion of the map. "This road is not even on the fucking map!"

"I'm sorry guys. The short cut was my idea," offered Chevon with a frown in her voice.

Ignoring the apology, Catherine continued in a passive aggressive way, "It's anyone's guess; you could walk miles without coming across anything. This road is way off the beaten path, away from any civilization, stuck in the middle of nowhere."

It had been five minutes, and we had not seen a single car. The temperature had fallen and the mood in the car was getting as dark as the night sky. "If Chevon hadn't told us that story I would have voted we stay put; now I think one of us should venture up ahead to look for a farmhouse or something," said Catherine.

"Are you volunteering?" I asked.

"No, but I think Chevon should go, she's more familiar with the area, and it was her idea to take a short cut."

"I think we should stay together," replied Chevon.

After a moment of silence waiting for one or the other to cave, I said, "Oh, I'll go. It was my crappy car that died,"

"Jacqueline, just go a little way. If you don't see lights come back. I'm sure a car will be by sooner or later," said Chevon, her voice full of concern.

"Do the four-way flashers work?" asked Catherine, as I opened the door to get out.

"No, I tried them. The battery must be dead. I'll just go half a mile ahead, and see if I can see anything."

"Do you have a flashlight?" Asked Catherine.

"That would have been a good idea."

"A flare?" She had a smirk on her face.

"Fuck off." The night air was cool, probably low 50's. I couldn't see my hand in front of my face. After about 10 feet I looked back and could no longer see the car. I had ventured forward for another 100 yards before I heard a noise off to my left. It sounded like a dog barking, but then came a long howl. The sound froze me in my tracks. I did an about-turn and started back to the car. I picked up the pace as the howling continued. I broke off into a hysterical run, imagining a wolf nipping at my heels. I breathed a sigh of relief as I made it back to the car only to find it empty. Oh my god! Where did those two go? Getting in, I tried starting the car again only to curse as the ignition continued to click. I slammed on the horn, getting only a low whimper which slowly died out, like a tuba player running out of breath. Rolling down the window, I screamed, "Catherine, Chevon!" I must have jumped a foot in the driver's seat when the two of them started howling from behind the seat. "Don't do that!" I screamed at them. "Did you hear the man-wolves out there?"

"Don't get all scaredy-cat ….that was probably just a regular wolf," Chevon laughed. It had been close to an hour by that point; we were all getting a little edgy. We were about to start yelling for help, when Chevon noticed a set of headlights off in the distance slowly coming our way. We debated whether we should lay low rather than signal for help. If they were backwoods psychopaths, we would be at their mercy. As the vehicle neared I could make out it was a truck.

"Maybe they won't see us, and just drive by," said Catherine.

I took matters into my hands, getting out. I climbed up on the roof of the car and used Catherine's Bic lighter at the highest setting to cast a flame. When the headlights were about 20 yards away, the driver pulled onto the shoulder of the road facing us. The truck's headlights were illuminating the car, making it impossible to see inside the truck. The driver seemed to take forever getting out. After what seemed like five minutes, we heard the driver's door open, creaking like a rusty spring. Chevon and Catherine let out a collective gasp as they called for me to get back into the car. From my vantage point, I could see the silhouette of a large man standing watching us. He finally approached the car with a flashlight shining in my face.

"What y'all doing sightseeing this late at night?" said the shape. When we didn't respond, he used his flashlight to illuminate the inside of the car. He then shone his light up at me. "I'm County Sheriff William Cooper; y'all ok?"

I worked up the courage to say something, only the words came out fast like air escaping from a balloon, "Our car broke down an hour ago - won't start - lights and horn won't work – we're from Oberlin College going to New Orleans for the spring break - there are wolves out there!"

"Yeah, well not too many folk travel these country roads at night 'cepting maybe the back woods people trucking their shine. You should be happy I came down this way. Word is that a family ventured this way a few years back and wasn't nearly so lucky when their car broke down."

As the Sheriff came closer, he looked to be in his mid-twenties, tall and very handsome. He wore a leather bomber jacket over his brown uniform and held his Smoky the Bear hat in his hand. He held out a hand to me with an impish grin and said, "You can get off the car now."

"I'm Jacqueline Chen, and these are my friends Chevon and Catherine."

He gave us a friendly nod and asked me to press the hood release. After having me try the ignition, he attempted to boost the battery. With an air of resignation, "Sounds like your charging system." He shone his flashlight on the engine and shook his head as if my car had let him down. After a few minutes, he ambled back to his truck and spoke into the radio.

"Bobby, this is Sheriff Cooper, there's a car stranded out on old route 15. Can you roust Boone and have him tow it into town; it's about 2 miles north of Lamey Bridge Road?"

"Right away Sheriff."

The Sheriff then went over to our car and said, "Best you gals squeeze in with me and come into town, I'll get you all squared away for the night. A good friend of mine owns The Trade Winds apartments. There's also a good mechanic in town that'll look at your car in the morning."

Chapter 4

Gabriel- Monday Morning, Day 1

I listened intently to Jacqueline's story, interrupting when only necessary. "He sounds like quite the southern gentleman; what happened next?"

Instead of continuing the story, she handed me the check and said, "Perhaps some other time, I need to run to another meeting. Do you have what you need to start the surveillance?"

"Yes, I'll get right on it, Mrs. Cooper." As she got up and walked to the door, Bourbon and I were again captivated.

She suddenly turned, sensing our eyes. With a tired look, she said, "I'm counting on you Mr. Ross."

She closed the door behind her. "It's Gabriel," I said under my breath.

I picked up Bourbon and put him on my lap. I sat back in my chair with my feet up on the desk looking at the check. Since opening the Agency, I'd learned a lot about being a detective from Ben. He was a veteran on the Biloxi Police force. He not only took me under his wing, but also bankrolled the business. With his help, I'd been busy solving a couple of missing person cases, which turned out to be runaways. I'd also done a few background checks for local employers. Doing surveillance on the local Sheriff represented a much bigger challenge. Ben must have felt I was ready.

Starting the business had all of the usual challenges. I signed a lease, arranged for a phone, and bought an answering machine. I ordered stationery and business cards with our tag line "When you Really Need to Know." We were trying to be economical, so the sign on the door was simply a piece of paper with "Eye on You Detective Agency" written in my best penmanship, my handwriting gradually rising up at one end like the foothills of the Rockies.

Getting up from the chair, I went to the cabinet and put some tools I had assembled over the past few months on the desk. One of my first purchases was a Kodak 35 Millimeter camera. It came with a detachable telephoto lens. I had practiced using the camera by taking shots of Bourbon in various action shots. There was a shot of Bourbon wearing a little fedora, one where he was wearing a trench coat, and yet another with him curled up in front of a bottle of bourbon.

Another item came from Ben. I'm not sure where he got it from, as it was not readily available at the local Wal-Mart. It was a Vibro-Acoustic Microphone, a listening device similar to what was used by the CIA a few years ago to eavesdrop on the Russian embassy. Originally designed as an earthquake detector, this bug picked up the vibrations of human conversations as they hit the concrete wall, causing it to vibrate. The bug enabled technicians to easily pick out the sound of voices from other types of vibrations in the room. The unit itself was no bigger than a dime and came with a slim wire antenna, no more than a few inches long. The unit had a maximum range of a city block, with a signal that could be picked up by multiple receivers and recorded on tape.

I decided to call Ben to thank him for the referral. I figured he could fill me in with background material on Sheriff Cooper. He answered his office line with his normal, I wish I was anywhere but here, voice. "Biloxi Police Department, O'Shea."

"It's Gabriel. I just met with Mrs. Cooper. Pretty heavy stuff."

"Did you accept the case?"

"Of course, have you seen her? She's as sultry as a summer heat wave in Biloxi."

"Gabriel, when you get to be as old as me, you'll realize that women are like roads, the more curves they have the more dangerous they are."

"I don't understand why Sheriff Cooper would step out on a doll like that."

There was a pause on the line as if Ben was distracted. A moment later he came back on the line and said, "Listen Gabe, be careful with this. Cooper's not just another cop. Rumor has it; he's involved with some nasty people. He might not take too kindly to you investigating him. Then he added, "I wouldn't make a point of talking to very many people about this. He has lots of friends. Word will get back to him that you're asking questions. Hopefully, you can follow him, take a few pictures of him banging some other broad, and then get the hell out of there."

"You make it seem so easy."

"Listen Gabe, I have to go, remember what I said and let's grab lunch in a couple of days."

I no sooner hung up, when the phone rang again. It was Edith Glaswell. She was a client with a runaway child, a 16-year-old teenage girl named Rebecca. She'd vanished this past Friday afternoon, and no one had seen her since.

"Hello, Mr. Ross, it's Edith Glaswell. I was wondering if you uncovered any clues about Rebecca?"

Rebecca was the right age for partying down on Biloxi beach. I'd spent the weekend checking with her school friends, and neighbors. Rebecca seemed to have run away without a trace.

"I'm still working on a few leads, Mrs. Glaswell. I'm sure something will turn up."

"Rebecca's been missing for more than two days!" she said, trying her best to hold it together. "I reported this to the Sheriff's office like you told me. They said to go back home and wait. The party will eventually end, and she'll come home."

"I can't imagine how you must feel Mrs. Glaswell." I struggled for something else more encouraging before adding, "I haven't given up."

"What about these leads you referred to?"

"I was planning on coming by the house to take another look at her room. Sometimes teenagers hide stuff from their parents." I waited a moment for a reaction.

"Alright Mr. Ross, I'll see you this afternoon, but I doubt you'll find anything hidden. My Rebecca is not that kind of girl."

The other lead was a bit of a long shot. Mrs. Glaswell had mentioned earlier that Rebecca had an account at Sun Trust Bank. I was going to ask the Manager when the account was last active. Mrs. Glaswell had hung up before I had a chance to say anything else.

I decided to swing by the Biloxi Sun Herald after grabbing a quick lunch. I put Bourbon back on the fire escape, and gave him the rest of the day off.

Ben had given me some good advice the other day. He said I was trying to do the job sitting behind my desk, and making phone calls. He'd looked at me with his deadpan expression and said, "Gabriel, you're too good to be cooped up here. To be effective a detective needs to look people in the eye." As I made my way across town to a small diner near the Herald, I reflected on my progress as a private investigator. I was wrestling with my private detective persona. Should I be a tough guy like Bogart and slap people around like his character in the Maltese Falcon? Should I be more laid back like Jim Rockford in the Rockford files? Should I play an unassuming, clever detective like Columbo?

I now had two active investigations - Rebecca Glaswell and Jacqueline Cooper. Not bad considering it'd only been six months since I left Detroit. As I got in the elevator, I couldn't get Mrs. Glaswell and her missing daughter out of my mind. Looking at my reflection in the elevator door I made a mental note to clean up my image; new shoes, a haircut, and maybe I should get back into jogging. My thoughts slipped back to my first days in Biloxi, when I first met Ben at a local watering hole.

Chapter 5

Gabriel- 6 months earlier...

We'd struck up a conversation while sitting at the bar together. Ben was dressed in a yellow sports jacket with a plaid shirt and a striped tie. I later learned that this was one of his more fashionable outfits. I guessed he was north of fifty. When he asked me where I pahked my cah, I knew he was from New England. We looked at each other in the reflection of the mirror behind the bar. I had allowed my brown hair to grow into a bit of a mop. The bags under my green eyes had bags of their own from lack of sleep. In contrast to my three day beard, Ben was clean shaven. He had the dominant, veined nose of someone who liked to drink. He must have noticed me staring at his reflection, "My Doctor told me to watch my drinking. Now I always drink in front of a mirror."

I laughed at the joke and saw that he had more of a smirk than a full blown smile. Sort of like he had a secret.

"So what brought you to Biloxi, Gabriel?" he asked as we drank our beers. The Charlie Daniel's Band was on the jukebox wailing about the Devil going down in Georgia. The bar, a popular spot for off duty cops, was nothing special. There were a dozen tables resting below the glow of tiffany lamps. Paintings of the harbor decorated most of the walls. The place was about half full with a mainly middle class crowd.

"Do you want the Coles notes version, or all of the gory details?" I replied

He answered by signaling the bartender for two more Ballantines, "I want to hear all of the dirt, don't leave anything out."

We'd been at the bar since I arrived in town a couple of hours ago. He'd introduced himself as Ben O'Shea, a police detective with the Biloxi PD. He was a good listener with a charismatic personality, or maybe I just needed to tell the story.

"I graduated from the University of Michigan in '76. My Dad, who worked for the Ford Motor Company for 30 years, arranged an interview with the head of the accounting department. I ended up getting the job and initially, things were going well. I was working in a little cubicle, surrounded by a wall of printouts and reports. After about 3 months, I uncovered a little scheme in one of the dealerships where they were misrepresenting sales numbers and altering the inventory through some creative accounting. My boss was pretty happy with the discovery, so happy he took all the credit. He was a little weasel, or as my Dad would say a person like him couldn't get laid in a monkey whorehouse with a bag of bananas. I was never quite sure what that meant. I started to realize that with Ford, I was just a small cog in a big wheel."

"Good old Ford, they put the K in Kwality," volunteered Ben, who seemed engrossed in my story.

"Trying to add personality to my cubicle, I put up a little statue of Lee Iacocca and some posters in my office. But in the fall of '78 things started to turn sour at Ford. The energy crisis, earlier in the decade made a big impact on our product line. Iacocca responded by coming out with the Pinto. It was a disaster, and touched off lawsuits followed by bad press, and then declining sales. Next of course, came the layoffs. It hit me about a week ago, when the weasel called me into his office."

"I was sitting in his office waiting for him, fearing the worst. Rumors had been rampant about cost control. When he eventually walked in, he gave me a look of disappointment, like finding your fortune cookie with no fortune."

"So what does the word loyalty mean to you?" He'd asked me, leaning back in his chair with his big feet up on his desk facing me. From the sole of his shoes, I could see he'd stepped in something. I spent a moment trying to Rorschach the image. I decided it looked like a pony.

"I don't know, I guess being faithful."

"Do you think YOU have been a faithful employee here, Ross?"

"Sure," I said, knowing I would never pass a polygraph.

Weasel just stared at me for a few moments before he pulled out the statue of Lee Iacocca from his desk. With a quick touch of his finger, he set the head bobbing up and down. "Really?"

After a moment of us watching the head going up, down, up, down, "Is that what this is about? A plastic toy?"

"Do you think having a poster of a broken down Ford in your cubicle with the caption "Fix, or Repair Daily" is casting the right image? Or, what about the one with a broken down Pinto with, "Found on Road Dead"?"

"I didn't mean to suggest...."

"What kind of car do you drive Ross?" He asked, cutting me off with a wave like he was scaring off an annoying fly.

"A VW...But my Dad drives a Pinto."

"Listen, Ross, I've covered for you for almost two years now, and helped you learn the business. Sales are off, and I've been asked to make some cuts. You need to gather your stuff out of your office. There will be a guard to escort you out of the building Mr. Ross," he said with a sigh. "I hope you're thankful for the lesson I'm giving you, loyalty to one's employer is Job One." At this point he'd taken his feet off the desk, and put his focus on a file in front of him, obviously signifying the meeting was over.

"You have dog shit on your shoes; and do you know what Pinto means in Spanish?" I asked, getting up to leave.

"No, what does it mean?"

"Little Balls" and with that I flipped him the bird and left.

"Atta boy," Ben said, laughing so hard he almost fell off the stool.

Ben and I had a good laugh and then I added, "I tried to get back in, realizing Weasel had not returned my bobble head, but the guard said I was no longer allowed in the building."

"So you came down to Biloxi to find yourself?" Asked Ben, in between handfuls of peanuts. There was something about his tone that suggested that this was a conclusion and not a real question.

"I met up with one of my buddies from school, who suggested I not dwell on the past. To take what happened as a gift, and rebound into something that would give me more satisfaction.

Until I can figure that out, he suggested soaking up some sun and working hard on the oil rigs in the Gulf would make me feel better."

"Sounds to me like you have a smart friend there," said Ben.

"We were practically brothers and grew up across the street from each other. He taught me to stand up for myself."

We hung out for another round, and he introduced me to some of the regulars. "Listen, what are you doing tomorrow?" he asked, finishing his beer.

"I guess I'll be talking to the guy who hires for the oil rigs."

"I know the guy, and I can put in a good word for you if you want. But why not give yourself another day? You can do a ride-along with me. I can show you some sights that will never be part of any tour package. I also have an idea about something that might give you the satisfaction you're seeking." When he saw the indecision on my face he added with a smile, "Oh, and, by the way, I don't drive a Ford."

I gladly accepted the offer, not knowing the trouble that was yet to come.

Chapter 6

Gabriel-Monday Morning, Day 1

It was a typical May Day in Biloxi as I made my way to the parking lot after my meeting with Jacqueline Cooper. The sun hung in the morning sky like a fireball. The high temperature today was going to exceed a humid 80 degrees. I found the local rag on Debuys Road, pretty much the outskirts of Biloxi. The building was a sprawling one story affair, built earlier in the seventies. I needed some background information on Sheriff Cooper. I also needed a plan on how to expose the affair his wife was so sure he was having. Since Ben suggested I use discretion, I figured the best bet was to catch up with my reading of the local paper.

I entered the building and saw that they had divided the office into the press room, as well as administration and production departments. Approaching the counter, I tried to catch the eye of a lady sitting at a desk talking on the phone. She looked to be in her sixties and was clacking away on her typewriter. She was dressed neatly, wearing her graying hair up in a style popular with that age group, and bumble bees. A flavored cigarette dangled from her lips; she looked over at me and held out a finger signaling she would be with me in a minute.

"I wonder if you could help me," I said, violating the one-minute embargo.

In response, she rolled her eyes in frustration. She told the caller to hold on, and looked over at me with tired eyes, "Well, what y'all want then?"

"I was hoping to do a little research on the town, the local crime scene, the police, and Sheriff's Department, etc."

"You're not from around here, are you?" Picking up that I wasn't mispronouncing every second word, like her.

"I'm originally from up north, but I live here now. My name is Gabriel Ross."

She got up from her chair, and looked me up and down. "Kinda fancy aren't you Mr. Ross?"

"Look, I could come back if this is a bad time."

"You a cop or somethin'?"

"No, nothing like that. I just want to get to know my new home."

"That so? You're much too short to be a policeman anyway." She turned and called to her beehive friend across the office. "Anna Belle, ain't he too short to be a policeman?"

I noticed Anna Belle and a couple of other ladies had stopped working, and were looking over at us like a bunch of hyenas. I guess I was the day's entertainment. I looked back at the exit and contemplated leaving.

"Nah it's ok, Mista Ross, just funning with ya." She pulled over a large manual. "We've converted most of our archives into microfilm going back to 1970; that's when we opened up this location. Seeing as the old one was damaged by Camille. We keep the last two weeks of newspapers on the shelves in the library to our right. Anything further back you need to look at the film."

I knew she was referring to Hurricane Camille. "Is there a way for me to pinpoint what issue would have particular stories?"

"It wouldn't take long to scan the headlines, but if that don't suit ya, you can look in the index in this book. You see if you want to know what the major stories were in 1972, you look it up in the index, and then go to that particular date."

"Thank you, I think I have it. Can I borrow this book and sit in the library?"

She took a large drag from her cigarette, blowing the smoke in a crooked smirk up towards the ceiling. "This here book ain't leaving this counter. Ya want to do research then you're free to look at the book right here."

"Thank you for all your help Ma'am, I'll do just that." I pulled out a notepad out of my brief case, and started to look in the index for stories that might help me get a handle on crime in Biloxi. Beehive, however decided she should stick around in case I needed more help. Fearing she could read upside down, I made a show of looking for stories about oil drilling in the gulf, jotting down dates of various articles.

"Don't you have someone on hold?" I reminded her.

She gave me a look, one that said "mind your own business". After a brief staring contest, she put out her cigarette in the ashtray and went back to her desk.

I changed the focus of my search to the Sheriff's department, and copied down some dates. Once I had a dozen, I headed for the library and the microfilm area. The first article I uncovered was from the Herald edition dated November 15th, 1971. The headline captured my attention right away.

Harrison County Elects One of Their Own

By Alex Dermody

Yesterday the voters of Harrison County overwhelmingly voted to elect Mr. William Cooper from nearby Gulfport to be Sheriff of Harrison County. Mr. Cooper, who graduated from Ole Miss before interning with the Gulfport Police Department, ran an effective campaign on a platform of cleaning up crime in the county. Cooper is replacing Sheriff Dan Harper, who opted not to run for re-election under a cloud of suspicion for bribery and corruption. "It's time for the citizens of Harrison County to take back our towns, away from the criminals who have been allowed to operate right under the nose of law enforcement," Sheriff-elect Cooper proclaimed in his acceptance speech. Cooper, backed by local interests, is a member of the Baptist Church, and he credits his strong family values as a lighthouse for him in the sea of depravity that has been allowed to fester in Biloxi. Cooper bested two other challengers for the position in an election that was far from close.

The second article was dated January 21st 1972:

Sheriff Cooper Ushers in the 20th Century to Local Department

By Alex Dermody

Since his election this past November, Sheriff Cooper has been working to revamp the local Sheriff's Department. He is committed to building a strong team, dedicated to the protection of the citizens of Harrison County. "I've been fortunate to be able to attract good, young talent from as far away as Jackson and New Orleans. We have had a number of very experienced deputies opt for retirement, or relocate. While you hate to see good men leave, this provides an opportunity for the department to attract bright young minds to help the department make a leap forward. We who do police work need to embrace today's new crime fighting techniques. All of this goes towards protecting the good folks of Harrison County," said Sheriff Cooper at yesterday's press conference. Sheriff Cooper also introduced his most recent hire, Deputy Sheriff Barry Franklin.

The article contained a picture of Sheriff Cooper standing in front of a group of reporters. Standing at over six feet, with brown wavy hair and an infectious smile. You would have to call him handsome. Maybe I was reading between the lines, but I would bet Cooper didn't feel bad about certain experienced deputies leaving.

The next article appeared March 19th, 1972

Local Crime on the Run in Harrison County

By Alex Dermody

If you notice one less strip club along the coastal highway; if you see fewer prostitutes hanging around the street corners downtown; if you hear about fewer muggings and robberies, then a big thank you to Sheriff William Cooper and his department. "It's standing room only in our cells," said Sheriff Cooper. "The deputies are doing some fine work in making arrests. The word is getting out there. Harrison County is tough on crime." Since his election this past November, Sheriff Cooper and his Department have averaged a dozen arrests each week. "People will soon be able to walk the streets without having to worry about being mugged or propositioned," added Deputy Sheriff Barry Franklin.

Again, there was a picture of Sheriff Cooper standing in front of a crowded cell with his baton in his hand. The next date I had written down was May 21st, 1972.

No More Party Time for Local Business Man

By Alex Dermody

At yesterday's press briefing, Sheriff Cooper detailed the investigation leading up to the closure of the Party Time Tavern and the arrest of its owner Louis Monsour. An undercover operation going back six weeks identified "B drinking" prevalent at the Party Time. "B drinking" is the practice where waitresses, often doubling as strippers, sell liquor in return for table dances and additional tips. Sheriff Cooper also said they found instances of under aged drinking. "Establishments like this are a gathering spot for illegal activity, like gambling and drugs, and have no place in our city," said the Sheriff.

Once again, there was a picture of Sheriff Cooper and some of his deputies in front of the Party Time Tavern. The establishment was old and looked to be falling down. On July 10th, 1972 I found another article.

Drug Ring Busted at Local School

By Alex Dermody

Sheriff William Cooper announced today a raid was made on a local pot farm suspected of supplying the illicit drug needs of most of Harrison County. Speaking to the assembled reporters Sheriff Cooper vowed to put an end to the illegal drug trade. Sheriff's deputies raided the farm based on an anonymous tip. The deputies seized forty pounds of marijuana, along with an unspecified amount of cash and weapons. It is not immediately known who owns the farm. Sheriff's deputies made a number of arrests including Leroy Jackson from nearby Gulfport, Purvis Washington from D'Iberville, and Lamont Bradley from Biloxi.

Every other month there seemed to be an article, each written by Alex Dermody espousing the virtues of Sheriff Cooper and his department. In addition to presenting a picture of the effectiveness of the operation, there were also stories capturing Sheriff Cooper as more than just a Sheriff. There was a picture of him entering a fishing derby for handicapped children. Another had him participating in the community bake sale. The reporting continued along the same line until March 15th, 1974 when they came to an abrupt stop. I figured the reporter must have retired. So far, my research into Sheriff Cooper painted a picture of someone who was not only a pillar of the community, but someone with a strong moral compass. He appeared dedicated to keeping his campaign pledge of cleaning up the city. Coming from Detroit, where corruption was common place, it was hard to swallow that I had found the first truly honest elected official.

While searching for more articles written by Alex Dermody, I came across what looked to be the reporter's last story.

Local Girl Missing

By Alex Dermody

Anne Mullens, a local teen, was reported missing to the Gulfport Police Department yesterday. The 16 year old high school student reportedly left school at 3:30 on Tuesday and never made it home. Mrs. Janine Mullens, the teen's mother, said she originally thought her daughter had met up with friends and gone to the mall. Later that evening when her daughter had not returned home, she contacted all of Anne's friends. She discovered the last anyone remembered seeing Anne was when she left the school. Her husband Bryan Mullen contacted the Gulfport police when the girl had not returned home by midnight. If anyone has any information concerning Anne Mullens, you are to call the Gulfport Police Department.

I scanned the next month of microfilm, looking for a follow up on the girl's disappearance. Other than a couple of updates later in March the thread disappeared into the obscurity of country fairs and fishing derbies. On June 8th, 1974 I found a story detailing Jacqueline's wedding.

Local Sheriff Weds, in Down-Home Celebration

By Mark Fraser

"Sheriff William Cooper, do you take Jacqueline Chen to be your lawfully wedded wife, to honor and cherish..." This was the scene this past Saturday, as a record number of Harrison County's citizens came out to attend the nuptials of their favorite son to his betrothed. The couple met by accident last March when her car broke down along Route 61 and her Prince Charming came to her rescue. Sheriff Cooper, never at a loss for words, offered that he was "the happiest man in the county".

There was a picture of the bride and groom on the front page. She was beautiful in her full-length white wedding dress. They made a stunning couple. I was amazed things could have unraveled so quickly for them. I went back to the story about the disappearance of Anne Mullens and pulled out a photo of Rebecca Glaswell from my brief case. Anne Mullens and Rebecca Glaswell could have been sisters. On my way out, I decided to ask Beehive if she remembered the reporter, Alex Dermody.

"Sure, he was on the city desk up until a few years ago."

"Did he retire, move away...."

"No, he was in a bad car accident and couldn't work no more. He's up at Gulf Oaks."

"What's Gulf Oaks?"

She looked at me with the same scorn I had seen earlier. "It's a Looney Bin about 20 miles north of here."

On the way back to my car, I thought back to last November and the ride-along with Ben.

Chapter 7

Gabriel –6 months earlier…

The day had started early, meeting Ben at the diner. The relief you'd expect to come after yesterday's heat wave didn't materialize. It was just as hot, but now accompanied by a torrential downpour. It was like standing in a hot steamy shower. According to Ben, the storms along the coast were infrequent, but fierce. Hurricane Camille had hit the area in 1969, with winds around 175 miles per hour causing $1.4 billion in damages and flattening almost everything in its path. Despite authorities evacuating over 200,000 people inland, the storm cost the lives of 259 people.

Ben was wearing a blue seersucker sports jacket with a green shirt and an orange tie with yellow polka dots. Over coffee, he told me I was welcome to stick with him as he went about his duties. Today he planned to contact a local businessman about a suspected case of arson, followed by meeting with a girl who claimed she was a victim of a potential abduction. "I've pushed off my paperwork to another day, so you wouldn't fall asleep from boredom. If you ask any cop they'll tell you that 90% of this job is paperwork. My paperwork has its own paperwork!" he said, rolling his eyes.

"So how long have you been a cop?" I asked him. I was conscious that I had shared a great deal the previous night and that he hadn't said much about himself.

"I joined the force in 1972, after I relocated from Providence."

"What were you doing in Providence?"

"It's a bit of a story. After about five years as a beat cop I made it to detective and joined the Narcotics Squad. I met a girl, and we ended up living together in a one bedroom apartment over a Chinese restaurant. At first things were pretty good. We both wanted the same things. You know, a career, home, making a difference in the world. Things started to change after we had been living together for a year. She wanted to get married, she wanted a family, she didn't like me working nights, she didn't like eating Chinese food every night…We worked on it, didn't give up. Meanwhile at work my squad made a big bust. Lots of wise guys were charged. That's when the threats started. There were bricks thrown through my window; my girlfriend was hassled at the supermarket by some local assholes. I got the impression that the agenda had changed in the department. The DA dropped some solid cases, and the department shifted manpower away from Narcotics. A lot of it was bullshit and I was tired of the politics."

"I wasn't happy at work and coming home to a scared girlfriend was no treat. One day she just packed up and headed home to Vermont. I have a cop friend who moved down to Biloxi in the late sixties. I spoke to him, and before I knew it, I was offered a detective position on the force."

"In a way it sounds like what happened to me." I offered.

"Well - except for the wise guys, the cheating wife and the Chinese food."

"So what's this opportunity you referred to yesterday? I think I'm too short to be a policeman." All my life I have had to deal with height jokes, so I thought it best to volunteer my acceptance of the issue.

"Let's leave that until later," he said as we climbed into his unmarked navy blue Caprice. "Our first stop is the Rockaway Bar. The Fire Department was called out last night to put out a fire in their kitchen. They thought the fire looked like it was deliberately set." Driving down the coast road the rain was so torrential we could barely make out the car in front of us. As if reading my thoughts, "If you decide to stay down here Gabriel, you might want to invest in a good raincoat."

As we drove along at a snail's pace, he filled me in on some local Biloxi history. "The town is mainly a tourist resort, a poor man's alternative to the beaches in Florida. Because New Orleans is 90 minutes away, this area became a summer retreat for people. A lot of cottages sprang up as well as motels and hotels like the place you're staying in." Last night Ben had made a call to a friend who owned the Trade Winds Apartments and got me a one bedroom suite.

"Biloxi spans across the coastal strip and ends at Debuys Road. The area past that is an unincorporated area and falls under the jurisdiction of the Harrison County Sheriff Department."

"Along with tourism, the fishing and cannery business became the major employers. To your left you can see some of the shrimp and oyster boats going out. To the right you can see Kessler Air Base. The air force built Kessler Field during WW2. It was a big boom for the city. The fly-boys liked to have fun in the downtown bars and casinos."

"I thought gambling was illegal down here?"

"Oh, it is. Just like prostitution is illegal, drugs are illegal…we have lots of things that are illegal. Let me tell you a bit about Mississippi. The people down on the coast are quite a bit different than the rest of the folks up north. The people down here are descendants of the French,

Spanish, and Croatians. They're mainly Roman Catholics. They like to relax and have fun. In contrast, the folks up North including most of the politicians in Jackson, are Baptists and Methodists. Do you realize that Mississippi was the last state to repeal the prohibition laws? That didn't happen until 1966."

"Folks along the coast have been drinking up a storm for decades. Back before the 1950s, gambling and drinking existed openly. The Biloxi Police Department and the Harrison Sheriff's Department kept a blind eye, letting folks blow off a little steam. Later in the fifties a bunch of Protestant ministers lobbied the state to crack down on the gambling. At the time, there was a Government Task Force to look into the link between gambling and organized crime. They ended up agreeing with the Protestant ministers, and closed down a lot of bars and supper clubs. I believe some vigilantes from up north even threw some slot machines into the Biloxi Bay. At the same time, there was a new Air Force Commander at Keesler and he felt that gambling and whoring were not appropriate pastimes, so he banned the fly-boys from frequenting a lot of places. After that, everything went underground or more importantly, into the unincorporated areas."

"So why doesn't the Sheriff raid those places?"

"Well, that's a great question Gabriel. There's an expression that some folks use to describe things down here. You pray in public and sin in private. The Sheriff and even local police forces are around to make sure that things don't get out of control. Believe me, no one wants to close everything down and ruin the local economy. Every once in a while, some politician will react to something. He'll demand the Mayor clamp down, and that brings a flurry of activity. So just like with anything else that's illegal, there's always an underworld that ensures those who want these things can still get them."

"What about the justice system, does anyone ever get arrested?"

"Sure, Biloxi is a pretty small community; everyone knows everyone else. Have you heard about the Clifton case?"

"Sorry, no."

"There was a big trial down here last year. It was a murder, so that's why I thought folks up North might have read about it. The prosecuting attorney called his first witness, a grandmotherly woman to the stand. When he asked her if she knew him, she responded "Why yes, I know you, Mr. Jackson. I've known you since you were a boy, and frankly, you've been a big disappointment to me. You lie, and you cheat on your wife, and you manipulate people, and talk about them behind their backs. You think you're a big shot, when you haven't the brains to realize you'll never amount to anything more than a two-bit paper pusher."

"The lawyer was stunned. Not knowing what else to do, he pointed across the room and asked, "Mrs. Clifton, do you know the defense attorney?"

"Why yes, I do, "replied the old lady. "I've known Mr. Graham since he was a youngster too. He's lazy, bigoted, and he has a drinking problem. He can't build a normal relationship with anyone, and his law practice is one of the worst in the entire state. Not to mention, he cheated on his wife with three different women. One of them was your wife. Yes, I know him."

"The defense attorney almost collapsed on the spot. That's when the judge asked both counselors to approach the bench and, in a very quiet voice, said, "if either one of you idiots asks her if she knows me, I'll send you both to the electric chair."

When Ben got to the punch line, he let out a hearty laugh, making his bulk jiggle like a mound of jello. I'd caught on that this was a joke midway through the story and laughed right along with him.

We pulled into the parking lot of the Rockaway Bar. It was nothing special. A one story clapboard structure, decorated in fisherman gear. As we got out of the car, he said, "The place doesn't open for a couple of hours, but the owner said he would meet us here. I'm going to ask him a few questions. See what he knows about the fire."

It took a few minutes for our eyes to adjust to the darkness when we first entered the bar. You could hear the pelting rain bouncing off the tin roof. They had drawn the window shades, and the lights were dim. As soon as you walked in, you saw a long oak bar facing you. To the right there was a small stage setup with some instruments and amplifiers, and to the left was a small dance floor. The owner, who I later learned was Bud Carson, must have heard the door open as he appeared from one of the closed rooms in the back.

"You the detective that called about the fire?"

"Yes, that's me," Ben said, showing off his gold badge. Nodding his head to me, "this is my associate Gabriel Ross. Can you take us back to where you had the fire?" We followed him to a fair sized room off the bar that opened up to a large kitchen. The equipment looked old but well maintained. By the looks of things, the fire had damaged about half of the room. "So what happened here Mr. Carson?" asked Ben, inspecting the stove.

"I don't know, but I suspect our night staff left the stove on. There's a lot of flammable stuff here, surprised there wasn't more damage."

"Who discovered the fire?" I looked at a couple of empty cans that might have held gasoline.

"It was some guy who just happened to be going down the street. He went to a pay phone and called it in."

"Don't suppose he left his name?" asked Ben, pencil poised over his notebook.

"No, I wish he did, I'd like to thank him."

"What time was this?" Ben asked.

"We close up at 1. I would say this must have been around 3 am."

"The fire chief thought there was a reason to suspect arson." Ben let the statement lie there. I watched Carson closely. The shifting of his eyes to the top left was a dead giveaway. What came next was going to be pure bullshit.

"Like I said, someone left the stove on. You know hot grease on a stove...." he said with attitude.

"That so? Are you the sole owner Mr. Carson?" Ben interrupted, in a tone that suggested he was getting tired of the horse-pucky.

"Yep, had the place going on 12 years now. Bought it soon after they repealed prohibition here."

"Are you up to date with your creditors?" Ben asked.

"I have bills like everyone, but I always make my payments."

"What about disgruntled employees, anyone think you're an asshole?" Ben asked, making a scribble in his notebook.

"I don't think anyone here would do this deliberately. Like I said, it's just an accident."

"What about protection. Are you paying someone for that?" asked Ben, making eye contact with Carson.

After an awkward moment, "I keep a clean place here." Carson said a hint of nervousness in his voice.

With that Ben handed me a Polaroid camera and asked me to take a few pictures of the damage.

"Is your place insured Mr. Carson?" I asked, taking a picture of the stove and the pantry where the damage was the worst.

"Yeah, listen is this going to take much longer?" Again with the attitude. When neither of us replied, he answered, "Of course, but there is a pretty big deductible, so it'll probably go unreported."

"Can I see the back door?" Ben put his notebook away. Carson escorted us to the back door. Ben opened the door and bent down to look at the lock. "You might want to invest in a better lock Mr. Carson," said Ben, now on his knees examining the door.

"I was thinking that myself." Carson mumbled, making a show of looking at his watch.

"You sure no one's putting pressure on you Mr. Carson? Looks to me like someone forced the door." For my benefit, Ben pointed out the groove in the door frame.

"No, like I said this was just an accident."

We left at that point, telling Carson we would need to file a complete report with the Fire Department. When we got back to the car, Ben asked, "What do you think?"

"I don't know much about arson, but the bullshit was pretty heavy in there."

"Well, here's a tip for you. All fires start someplace. You can usually tell by the burn marks where the fire began. Once it starts, it usually goes out in a V or U pattern. I looked at that kitchen; there's no way the fire started from the stove. The burn pattern was too random, like you would get if someone splashed gasoline and then lit a match."

"Any idea who that someone might be? I asked.

"No, but I'll talk it over with some of the guys, and head over to visit the Sheriff's Department and see if they heard anything. This area is their jurisdiction. Not sure what we can do since it doesn't look like Carson wants to cooperate."

"I thought he started to get nervous when you asked him about protection."

"On any given night, the word is there's a game going on in one or both of his back rooms. I was here once checking it out a few years back. I managed to get into a card game in one of the backrooms. There was a broad dealing cards. I couldn't tell which was more stacked, her or her deck. I'm sure there's more going on there as well, like underage drinking, drugs you name it."

"So why don't you bust his ass and close him down?"

"Again, this is outside of the Biloxi city limits. I know the question of raiding one of these places has come up before. The last raid, on a similar place, was a complete bust. We went in with as many policemen we could spare, as well as a bunch of Deputy Sheriffs. When we got there, we found nothing but a couple of old stiffs drinking at the bar. No girls, no drugs, no gambling."

"Sounds like someone knew you were coming."

"We thought so too. Even if it was in our jurisdiction, we walk a fine line. Unless there's an indication of underage drinking, or a suggestion of drugs, then we back off and let things run their course. As long as the hookers stay inside, and don't bother people, then we tend to put our limited resources towards other crimes." After a minute he added, "I believed him when he said he wasn't paying anyone."

"I think that's his problem." I said, wondering what part of this job was satisfying for Ben.

Chapter 8

Gabriel- Monday Afternoon, Day 1

I arrived at the Glaswell's around 3:30. The day hadn't cooled. It felt like being in a sauna, with a dozen heat lamps bearing down on me. They lived near the back bay of Biloxi, in a house on stilts. I hadn't seen this type of housing before but understood it had caught on after Hurricane Camille. It was a typical clapboard bungalow, except it rested on a series of wooden pilings approximately 8 feet off the ground. A steep, large wooden staircase extended out front, daring you to make the climb.

Mrs. Glaswell must have been waiting for me. The door opened as soon as I lumbered up the staircase. She had to be close to six feet tall. From her position on the step looking down at me, she looked like the Friendly Giant except she wasn't smiling. A small dog, later introduced as Gracie, barked an intruder alert. Mrs. Glaswell had to be in her mid to late fifties, judging by the dull brown hair streaked with grey. Her Edith Bunker-like face had wrinkles that ran like ripples on a lake. Looking around at a simple living room, it was obvious that Mrs. Glaswell took pride in her home. The walls were adorned with dozens of framed photographs, mainly of Rebecca growing up. When I originally caught the case I had asked about Mr. Glaswell. In her words the "scumbag" left a couple of years back, and was rumored to be living in California. According to Ben, cases involving missing kids usually came down to one of two things. The first and most common is the runaway, who ends up living with friends. In nice weather you can see them camping and partying at one of the bonfires on the beach. The second almost always involves an estranged parent. In Rebecca's case, I ruled out living on the beach. She wasn't the type to run away. She was a straight "A "student, not involved with drugs or booze.

Mrs. Glaswell asked me to have a seat in the living room while she made a pitcher of ice tea. "I was just making up some signs with pictures of Rebecca. I figure I'll put them up on the telephone poles," she said, continuing to talk while working in the kitchen.

The dog, a black and tan dachshund, had finally stopped barking and was busy giving my pant leg a sniff over. The dog probably smelled Bourbon….my cat. "That's a great idea, Mrs.Glaswell. I'll take some with me." I didn't want to discourage her, but I'd already spent last Sunday going up and down the street with the girl's picture and struck out.

"I take my ice tea plain, but some like a little sweetness in it; how do you like yours Mr. Ross?"

"Whatever way you're having it." The dog had dropped a little rubber ball at my feet. I wondered if Rebecca was the one who played with the dog. The dog was making little whining noises, backing away from the ball, waiting for the dumb human to throw it. I obliged, throwing the ball across the room. It landed under a Lazy Boy recliner. Getting up from the couch, I ignored the dog's whimpering and looked closer at the photos on the wall.

"I have some cookies somewhere; they'll go well with your tea." The dog meanwhile was tearing up the chair trying desperately to retrieve the ball.

"I went to Sun Trust and asked about her account before I came over. They were a little guarded, but confirmed the last time Rebecca used her account was last weekend, when she deposited $50."

"I wonder where she would have gotten $50?" She asked her tone confused. "She wasn't working, other than the odd babysitting job."

I made a mental note to ask Ben if he could pull some strings and check the account further for an explanation. While looking at the photos, I saw a picture of Rebecca standing beside a deputy sheriff. The deputy's main feature was his greasy orange hair, which was blowing in the wind. It reminded me of the stringy guts you pulled out of a pumpkin at Halloween. "This picture with the deputy sheriff, when was it taken?"

Mrs. Glaswell came in, putting a pitcher of ice tea and a small plate of biscuits on the coffee table. The cookies looked suspiciously like dog bones. "That picture was taken about three months ago. The school had a "Take your child to work day". Because Rebecca's Dad's a scumbag loser, she approached the sheriff's department for the work experience. She enjoyed herself and ever since then that's all she wanted to talk about…wanting to be some big hotshot, "Private Detective." She said using air quotes to suggest her disapproval of my profession. "Oh Gracie, how did your ball get under there?" Shaking her head, she got down on all fours to retrieve the ball for the appreciative dachshund.

I took a sip of the ice tea. Its bland taste made me wonder if, along with the ice, she might have forgotten the tea.

"Try one of those cookies; they're great with iced tea." she said, standing up.

I picked up a dog bone from the plate and held it in my hand. "Do you mind if I take a quick look at Rebecca's room?"

"It's the second door on the left. I'm not sure what you think you will find. Rebecca was not a secretive girl."

I made my way down the hall, finding a plant to dump the ice tea. The bedroom was tidy, like the rest of the house. The room was dominated by a double bed, covered with a pink quilt. The furniture was cheap, escapees from the local Wal-Mart. It was all veneer with the genuine wood look. A popular poster of Farrah Fawcett in a red bathing suit and big hair was on one wall. At first I thought it was an unusual choice for a young girl, but then it hit me. I picked up a framed photo of Rebecca from the dresser, realizing she had styled her hair to look like Farrah.

I checked the drawers in her dresser, and found nothing other than what you would expect a teenage girl to have. A search of the night stand yielded a couple of paperbacks and some pens and pencils for school. I lifted the mattress and checked underneath, but found nothing. Maybe the mother was right. Rebecca was the one kid in the world who didn't have a secret. I shifted over to the closet and looked through coat pockets and a weathered suitcase. A box on the top shelf contained pictures of Rebecca with various friends. My eyes were drawn to a bible sitting on the shelf. I picked up the book, and an envelope fell out containing a bunch of photos banded together. All of the pictures were of Rebecca, together with an older man.

I asked Mrs. Glaswell, who was standing in the hall, if she recognized the man. She was surprised by the photos and confirmed that this was "the scumbag". "When he left a couple of years ago, I took down all of the pictures of him and threw them in the trash. He was a useless creature. Rebecca must have rescued them." Once again she looked like she was about to start crying.

"Would you know if she kept a diary?"

"I don't think she did, but I had no idea she kept those pictures either."

The dachshund had followed Mrs. Glaswell into the bedroom and was now playing with something under the bed. I waited a moment and looked over at Mrs. Glaswell to see if she was going to get down on all fours again. When she didn't, she caught my look and said, "Well, you're closer to the ground."

Other than Gracie and her ball, there was nothing else of interest. I noticed that part of the veneer had come away from the headboard. On a hunch, I crawled under the bed. Gracie took the opportunity to give my face a thorough licking, like I was a meat-flavored Popsicle. I reached into my pocket and gave her the biscuit. I found a small scrapbook wrapped in a paper bag pushed up near the headboard. Retrieving my prize, I back crawled from under the bed and sat down. I opened the scrapbook and staring at me was a picture of Anne Mullens.

Chapter 9

Gabriel - 6 months earlier...

I was still wondering how Ben found satisfaction from his job, when he pulled out of the parking lot and headed uptown to the Sheriff's office. When we got there, he dropped me off at a coffee shop, saying it wouldn't be wise to have the Sheriff recognize his shadow.

I waited over coffee for about thirty minutes watching the torrential downpour puddle the road. Ben shuffled in after about 20 minutes. As he took off his wet coat, I reflected that with the funny walk, weird clothes he reminded me a loveable shaggy dog.

"The Sheriff's out on patrol. A Deputy Sheriff named Franklin was there, and he said they might have heard something about the fire but had no information. He also said he had never met the owner. He never even heard of the bar nor any mob activity. I felt like telling him that he was depriving some village of their idiot."

"Ok, where does that leave us?"

"We can check for fingerprints on some of those containers, but likely with that fire; it's probably a long shot. Usually in this situation, if the insurance company wants to pursue it, the company will assign it to one of their men. Since Carson isn't going to make a claim, this will end when I file a report."

We finished our drinks and headed out again. Ben had set up an 11 o'clock appointment to take a statement from a girl who had claimed she was almost abducted. An appointment was set with her principal, giving us permission to meet with the girl at the school.

Janice McVeigh, a grade eleven student of St Patrick's High School, was waiting for us in the principal's office with her parents when we arrived. After everyone had introduced themselves, Ben handed me his notebook and asked me to take notes for him. A signal that he wanted to take the lead.

"Janice, please take us through what a happened Friday," said Ben.

"It was around four in the afternoon; school was over, and I started walking home like normal. We only live a few blocks over, so I don't take the school bus. I was halfway home, when a white van pulled up along the curb, and the driver rolled down his window and stared at me. He drove along the side of the road, as I walked on the sidewalk. After a couple of moments, he told me he was looking for his daughter's cat. He had a photo of a cat and wanted me to come closer so I could see it. I just stayed where I was, and said I hadn't seen it. He got all nervous and said that he was in big trouble because he had let the cat out by mistake. His daughter was going to be upset when she found out."

"I felt badly for him, and I stepped up to the window to say I was sorry. At that point, the man put his hand on my arm and asked me if I would do him a small favor. I started to feel uneasy about the guy, but I didn't know what else to do, so I said, what do you want me to do? He put a firmer grip on my arm, and asked if I would be willing to drive around the neighborhood with him. He said he was sure together we could find the cat. I pulled my arm away from him and said I had to get home. He yelled after me, something about a reward, but by that time I was running home."

"You did the right thing Janice," said her father.

"What did the van look like?" Ben asked.

"It was white, a little rusty in front, and I think it was a Ford." I saw a grin run across Ben's face at the mention of a Ford.

"Did you notice if the van had a sign or any lettering on it, maybe a bumper sticker?" I asked.

"It was plain white van with no windows. I didn't see anything else." She confirmed she had not seen the license plate, even to tell whether it was from Mississippi.

"Did the van have an odor to it, like paint? I asked

"Not that I noticed, the guy had bad breath, sort of garlicky," She replied, scrunching up her face showing her dislike for garlic.

"Was anyone else in the van?" asked Ben.

"I'm not sure. I kind of sensed that there was. There was no one else up front. I suppose I could have leaned in to look, but I was getting scared."

"No, you did fine," replied Ben. "Did you recognize the man from around the neighborhood?"

"I've never seen him before."

"What can you tell us about him? You know age, build, features, hair color.....," Ben continued to dig.

"He was creepy. I would guess pretty old, kind of like your age. Maybe he was 40 or so. He had a baseball cap so that I couldn't see his hair. His beard was reddish and messy. Oh, and he was wearing brown coveralls."

Everyone else got a chuckle out of her saying that 40 was old. "Was there a name on the coveralls or the baseball cap?" I asked.

"Not that I noticed."

"How about eye color, or distinguishing marks like scars or tattoos?" asked Ben.

"No, I'm sorry; I guess I'm not a very good witness," Janice replied, looking over at her parents.

"What about an accent, did you get the feeling the guy was native to Mississippi?" I asked, grasping at straws.

"Yes, I think so, he said y'all, like y'all seen my cat?"

Ben had her run through the story a couple of times, the details remaining the same. We thanked everyone and reassured Janice that she did very well. Ben made an appointment for Janice to come down to the police department to sit with a sketch artist.

Back in the car, he asked what I thought of Janice's statement.

"I think she's a very brave girl. I supposed the missing kitty might be legit, but the guy sure sounds like a pervert."

"My gut tells me you're right. But without more information on the van, it would be pretty hard to run it down. Still, I'll put out a general stop and question for plain white vans in the area."

We drove in silence for a while, before I asked, "What's the skinny on this exciting opportunity you have in mind for me? "

"First let me ask you a question. Let's say that Janice hadn't been so smart, and ended up going for a ride with that guy. Just suppose she disappeared, and her parents reached out to you for help. How would you feel if you were able to find the guy and rescue Janice?"

"Obviously, I'd feel pretty good."

"Here's what I am thinking. I'm about five years from qualifying for my pension. What I would like to do when I retire is go into business as a private detective. There are virtually none around here, and the increased police rules and red tape will end up driving more people to go that way."

"Sounds like a great idea. How would I fit in?"

"I have a little money set aside. I figure I could set you up so that you can get the business up and running. I can refer the odd case to you, and we can split the profits."

"Is referring business to a private agency something that you're allowed to do?"

"Not exactly, I would have to be a silent partner until I retire. We'd have to keep any referrals between us," he winked at me.

"I don't know Ben; I don't know anything about being a detective."

"I've seen you ask questions all morning. You're smart, and I think you'd be pretty conscientious about getting to the bottom of things, like the guy in the white van. Besides, I can teach you anything technical you might need to know."

"Don't I need a license?"

"Not in Mississippi, anyone can call themselves a Private Detective."

"Why me Ben, you hardly know me?"

"I guess all my years as a cop has made me a pretty good judge of character. I think you'd be a natural. You found that fraud up in Detroit."

"Would we make any money?"

"I have enough to keep you going for a year, but I know there would be a steady flow of cases I can refer."

"Like what kinds of cases?"

"Proving adultery is a big one; cops aren't in that game. There's lots of work for companies wanting to do background searches. You'll get a lot of missing person cases, where the cops have given up. There's also plenty of insurance work. Most of the work would be routine, but occasionally you'd land a good case. It's the good cases that would give you that satisfaction you're looking for."

I'm not sure what possessed me to say yes. The work sounded interesting, but I think it had more to do with wanting to believe in Ben, especially after the Ford fiasco. I needed to trust there were decent people out there.

Chapter 10

Gabriel- Monday Afternoon, Day One

Mrs. Glaswell had been distraught at the discovery of Rebecca's scrapbook. My heart went out to her as she peppered me with questions, none of which I could answer. I told her I needed to take the scrapbook with me and would get back to her when I figured how everything fit together. "I have contacts within the Biloxi Police Department. I'll be in touch with you as soon as I have something concrete."

As I sat in the car outside the house I looked at the scrapbook. The first page had the same Herald story I had discovered earlier today. The second page had yet another article of a blonde teen missing from nearby Gulfport. This new article was dated February 27th, 1973, and detailed the disappearance of Shannon O'Shays. The girl apparently disappeared after her shift at the local McDonalds. On the third page, there was yet another article dated February 11th, 1975 from the New Orleans Times-Picayune. The article had a picture of a blonde teen girl named Lynda Morrison, who disappeared while on a local school field trip.

It was close to five pm when I arrived back in the office. I let Bourbon in through the window and poured us both a stiff drink. I like mine on the rocks, he takes his in a saucer. Bourbon was very vocal today, expressing his dissatisfaction about being outside all day. The light was flashing on the answering machine. There were two messages from companies I had approached about investigation services. I decided to follow up on these later. I tried Ben on his office line, hoping I hadn't missed him. He picked up after five rings.

I took a few deep breaths to contain my anxiousness, "Ben, it's Gabriel, I found out some stuff today I need to share with you."

"Great, let's get together sometime on Thursday."

"This is too important to wait, Ben."

"Is this about the client we talked about earlier?"

I got the impression Ben wasn't alone. "No, it has to do with a case I was working on myself, something about a missing teen."

"Okay, tell you what, how long has the teen been missing?"

"Almost two days."

"Has this been reported?"

"The mother tried to, but the Sheriff told her to wait until the party ends, and the kid would eventually come home."

"Not very helpful. Is the kid someone who likes to party all night?"

"No, and there's much more to this than meets the eye. There is a pattern of missing girls, all around the same age, all attractive blondes."

"There have been a number of cases involving missing teens. Most never get solved. I remember something a few years back, how many other cases are there?"

"There are three I know about."

"All from Biloxi?"

"No, one disappeared in Gulfport, another in New Orleans."

"New Orleans, huh? Were these by chance all around Mardi Gras?"

The connection had escaped me. I replied they all were from February to March, except for Rebecca who disappeared in May. Ben took the details for a missing person report on Rebecca and promised to get the word out before he left for the evening. As for the scrapbook, he said he would stop by the next day to look at it. I no sooner hung up from him when the phone rang again.

"Hello, Mr. Ross, it's Jacqueline Cooper."

"Hi Jacqueline, what can I do for you?"

"Mr. Ross, I was wondering when you might be able to update me on what you have uncovered."

"Well, you just gave me the case earlier today. Still, I've done a fair bit of research on your husband, and I'm going to tail him tomorrow."

There was dead air after I said this, prompting me to ask if she was still there.

"I asked what you have uncovered so far."

"I've barely scratched the surface Jacqueline. There are a couple of things I am checking into, but it would be too early to comment on whether your husband's been cheating on you."

Once again there was dead air, so I stupidly added; "I should have something more concrete to give you by the end of this week."

"You'll be able to tell me whether he is having an affair or not?"

"I hope to be in a position to do that."

"Okay, Mr. Ross, I will expect your call one way or the other by Friday."

As she hung up I said, "It's Gabriel," under my breath. I knew I had made a mistake. Offering up a Friday deadline was going to come back and haunt me. I needed to unwind, and the booze wasn't cutting it. It had been my most-eventful day since I started the agency. To clear my mind, I decided to head back to my Trade Winds apartment, and take a stroll along the beach.

That Sheriff Cooper had put Jacqueline and her friends up there seven years ago was an interesting twist of fate. The apartment building was right on the beach and prior to Camille it was a popular nightspot for partygoers. Getting out of the VW, I took off my shoes and socks, loosened my tie and rolled up my pant legs and headed for the beach. The shoreline was beautiful. There was something about the salt air and the majesty of watching the surf run up onto the sand that energized me. I took a deep breath and let the warm breeze refresh me. The anxieties that had been building up all day evaporated in the grandness of the scene. The sand was white and reminded me of Uncle Ben's White Rice. The ocean licked the shore, taking sand back to its watery home. A mob of people crowded the beach basking under the Biloxi sun. I dropped my shoes and socks and made a run for the surf, my face welcoming the afternoon sun. About 10 feet in, the hot sand was driving miniature holes into my feet. I bounced around like a hot potato. The sand was a scorching furnace searing the flesh of my feet. What kind of hell was this? I felt like one of those firewalkers moving across hot coals. Except I wasn't walking, I was hopping up and down screaming like a baby. Finally, I heard someone near say, "For Pete's sake stand on my blanket."

I looked over and saw an older, colored man reading Stephen King's latest novel, "*The Shining.*" Relief came in an avalanche as I stepped onto his beach blanket.

"Good way to burn your feet off," he said, handing me an icy coke from his cooler.

"Thank you, thank you!"

"Not from around these parts are you?"

I extended my hand and introduced myself as Gabriel Ross from the land of snow.

"The name's Arnie Sims. I recognized you as one of the renters staying at the Trade Winds." Arnie looked to be mid-sixties judging by his closely cropped gray hair and skin leathered from too many sunny days. "You can thank me by not telling Mr. Ahmed, my boss at the Trade Winds, that his caretaker is slacking off." A smile flashed across his face like a blooming flower.

Sitting down on the blanket, I thanked him again and assured him his secret was in the vault. "How do people stand the heat from the sand?"

"Just takes a bit of getting used to."

I pointed at the Trade Winds, "This is a grand old building, how long have you worked here?"

His eyes came alive, and he gave a little chuckle, I think he was chewing tobacco. "I'm so old; I can't rightly remember a time when I didn't."

I laughed and asked him how old the Trade Winds was.

"I don't rightly know. It used to go by the name, the Tivoli." He pronounced it Tivoooolliiiii, as if it had a couple of extra syllables. "I guess it goes back to the twenties. It used to be one of the grand hotels on the strip, just like the Edgewater and the Buena Vista." The latter he pronounced with added emphasis on Vistaaaaaaaa. Looking up at the apartment building, he shook his head nostalgically and said, "The place is just a shadow of the way it used to be. The owners renovated in the fifties and changed the name to Trade Winds."

"Was there ever gambling at the Tivoli?"

"At one time you'd be hard pressed to find a place that didn't have the slots. By the 1950s, though, the gamblin' was pretty much done round here. Then when Camille hit, the hotel was pretty much devastated along with much of everything else." "Ptooie," was the sound, as he spit a gob of something disgusting onto the sand near my feet. I could hear it sizzle. "The owner, he built it up again using Government money, but it'll never be the same."

"I guess at Mardi Gras it must get busy?"

"No, not really, being ninety minutes from Orleans and all. There are much better places to stay, if you want that kind of fun. People come to the Trade Winds because they're looking for a cheap apartment for a couple of months. What kind of line are you in Mr. Ross?"

"I own a detective agency in town."

"Really? Lots of calls for detecting are there?" I liked this man, not because he saved my feet, and gave me a coke. It was his down home, folksy way of looking at things.

"I'm working on a case involving a missing girl. She went missing last Friday, and her Mom is very upset."

I moved over a bit, as it looked like Arnie was going to hawk another loobie. He looked at me with a confused look. "If you're thinkin' she went to a Mardi Gras party, you're about a month late. Sounds to me like, 'stead of talkin' to you, her mama best be talkin to the pohlice."

"That was my advice too, except the Sheriff feels she hasn't been missing long enough."

"I don't know about that, but if your lady lives in Biloxi, she should go to the regular pohlice, rather than those jokers in the sheriff's department."

"What makes you say that Arnie?"

"Probably, said too much already. Just be careful of them deputies, they're not what they say they are."

We stayed for another 15 minutes and chatted about Biloxi and the Trade Winds. I saw my opportunity to leave when a family of heavy-set sun worshippers came walking by the blanket; I might be able to escape by walking in their shadow. I thanked Arnie again for everything and said I would see him around.

Chapter 11

Gabriel – Tuesday Morning, Day 2

After a restless night, I woke with the sunrise and the sound of birds chirping in the Magnolia tree outside my window. The weatherman on the local station was predicting a blazing, humid day. I gathered all of my tools; camera, telephoto lens, water bottles, notebook, and made sandwiches. Last month, my first surveillance assignment had not gone well. A local company asked me to confirm one of their employees was at home sick. I parked right in front of the employee's house with my camera at the ready. After about 30 minutes, the guy came out of the house sporting beach attire and wearing a snorkel, mask and carrying an inflatable duck. He jumped into his pickup while I started up the VW. The guy stopped at the first stop sign, got out of his car, and came back to my car screaming at me. I made a hasty retreat.

The positive from this incident was a change in my surveillance strategy. I parked the Bug further down Cooper's street and observed my suspect through holes punched into the newspaper. I knew I needed to do something about the blue VW. It stood out in the land of pickup trucks and muscle cars. It was on my list of things to do once the money started flowing better.

I decided to park down the street and observe the home at a distance. The Coopers lived in a very nice neighborhood on Bayview Avenue. Their house was a two story job with a wraparound balcony that encircled the whole second story. Palm trees adorned the front yard. There was a small knoll with a wooded area across the street giving a good view of the property. Jacqueline's Cadillac and a police cruiser sat in the driveway. I checked my watch and recorded no activity at 8 am.

I spent an hour reading the Herald. The front page covered a story about the 150,000 children that go missing every year in America, with roughly 48% running away voluntarily. Of this number, 80% of teenage girls who ran away were victims of abuse. I was surprised to see that Mississippi and Louisiana were leading all other states in incidences of missing kids. On page 2, the story continued with an update on an abduction of Rose Marie Levandoski, whose naked body was discovered on February 21st, six years earlier near a bridge in Biloxi. A high school student, Rose Marie disappeared when she left class to go to the washroom. Her body was recovered 20 days after she went missing.

It was close to an hour before I saw Sheriff Cooper leave in his cruiser. Luckily he pulled out and turned right instead of towards me. Thirty seconds later, I put the Bug in gear and followed a hundred yards back. I tailed him through town, always conscious of leaving a car or two in between us. He led me to the town of Gulfport, turning onto 23rd Avenue and parking in front of a long, one-story building. A sign on the lawn identified the building as the Harrison County Sheriff's Department.

I continued on down the street and pulled into a People's drugstore parking lot. I watched as Sheriff Cooper got out of his car and proceeded to walk in my direction. Jaywalking across 23rd, he started making his way towards my car. Memories of my last botched surveillance haunted me. I desperately looked for an escape route. If I got out of the car now, he would surely see me. I watched in my side view mirror, as he approached the parking lot. I put the newspaper up to shield me from view. I kept the paper like this for 30 seconds. I heard a commanding knock on my window. Damn, maybe I just wasn't cut out to be a private detective. When I put the paper down, I was staring at the face of a heavyset, middle-aged woman wearing a uniform. She was gesturing for me to roll down my window. I saw out of the corner of my eye that Sheriff

Cooper had proceeded down the street, and had gone into a donut store. I rolled down the window,

"This is private property; the owners of People's Drugstore only allow cars to park here if they're shopping in the store." I gave her a blank look. When I didn't reply, she added with a touch of attitude, "It's not for people to park and read."

"I was just looking for specials in the paper before I go in." I blurted out, keeping an eye on the donut shop.

"Alright mister, you do that." She gave me a smile and pulled out a small binder from her pocket. Surely she wasn't going to write out a ticket? From the binder, she pulled out a colorful flyer and said, "When you go in, there's a great special on Ajax, it's going for 35 cents. If you want J Cloths, they're 25% off the regular price." She was going on about Kraft salad dressing, when I got out of the car and went into the store. I was able to stand at the front of the store with a full view of the street. A few moments later, I saw Sheriff Cooper as he walked by carrying coffee and a bag of donuts.

I continued to watch as he went into the Sheriff's office. I was going to go back out to my car, when I spied the old lady watching me from the parking lot. I grabbed some Cokes from the cooler, and for good measure picked up some J Cloths.

After paying for my items, I made my way to my car. I waved the J Cloths at the guard with a big smile, mouthing the words "Screw You." She took it to be "Thank You", and gave me an "it was nothing" wave. I pulled the car out of the parking lot and drove back onto 23rd. I was able to find a parking space along the street.

There was no shade, so I spent the next hour slowly melting under the midday sun. Unfortunately, when I purchased the VW up in Detroit, air conditioning was an expensive option. The other issue is the Bug's engine doesn't have much power when the air is running. But now, sitting here under the hot Mississippi sun, I was starting to curse my decision. Thank goodness for the cokes I picked up at People's.

At noon, Cooper and one of his deputies, the guy with the pumpkin hair, left the office. I watched them from behind my paper as they headed to a diner down the street. My ass was starting to get sore, so I got out and walked around the car. Leaning against the car, I ate a ham sandwich that was hot and tasted like an old rubber tire. It hadn't occurred to me to bring a cooler.

From where I was standing I could see the entrance of the diner. After about an hour of melting under the midday sun and silently cursing about taking this job, Cooper and his deputy came out eating ice cream cones. Bastards! I think Pumpkin hair had strawberry while Cooper was licking a double-decker chocolate swirl. Double bastard!

I watched them as they leisurely strolled down the street. Cooper stopped to talk to shopkeepers, laughing and slapping them on the back. At one point, he stopped to talk to a woman as she pushed a baby stroller. I noticed that old Pumpkin hair didn't have his boss' amiable disposition. They split up when they got back to the sheriff's building, with Cooper finishing his cone and getting into his cruiser. Ok, here we go! Showtime.

I pulled out and tailed the cruiser for about two miles to a municipal park in the northern part of Gulfport. There was a celebration going on, with approximately a hundred people milling about a bunch picnic tables and a small stage. I watched as Cooper made his way through the crowd shaking hands and slapping people on the back. A banner strung between two trees announced "Welcome Home!" The banner had the initials NVOA. Given the number of people in uniform I guessed it stood for the National Veterans Organization of America. A small band of musicians to the left of the stage played, "I Wish I was in Dixie." I wondered who they were honoring, as the Vietnam War had ended six years ago. After a few minutes, an older gentleman dressed in an army uniform took the stage. I could make out most of what was being said. He was talking about the sacrifice that soldiers fighting in Rhodesia had made. He droned on about bravery and fighting for freedom.

My ears perked up after five minutes when the soldier said, "I would like to call on one of our own very special soldiers who are fighting a different kind of war. A war just as perilous as was fought overseas. A war where there's an enemy every bit as dangerous as the rebels in Rhodesia, I give you Biloxi's own.... Sheriff of Harrison County, William Jefferson Cooper."

I watched as the Sheriff made his way to the stage amidst enthusiastic applause from the crowd. This guy was pretty popular. For something to do, I took a few photos. As I scanned the crowd with my telephoto lens, the few women in attendance all looked to be older and hardly a likely girlfriend. Cooper was a natural orator and seemed to know how to work the crowd. His message was a simple one. In order to catch today's modern criminals and safely put them behind bars, the Sheriff's department, as well as other local law enforcement, need to embrace new tools and procedures. As the Sheriff, he remained committed to public safety and the belief that citizens were entitled to feel free to enjoy all that Biloxi had to offer, without the fear of being mugged, or propositioned to buy drugs.

It sounded like a campaign speech to me, but it connected beautifully with the mainly older, military crowd. Ten minutes into his speech I had the urge to pee, probably from too many Cokes. I looked over at Cooper and wondered how much he had left to say. With my luck, I'd head to a service station only to come back and find him gone. Cooper couldn't possibly have more to say. Rather than risk leaving, I reached for an empty coke bottle. Unzipping, I positioned myself and started using the bottle. There isn't much room in a Bug, and my leg started cramping up. I tried to straighten my leg while continuing to pee into the bottle. I was concentrating so much on the task at hand, I only noticed the old lady at the last minute. I looked up to see the woman standing directly in front of my car. She approached my open window. I tried to stop the procedure, but as any man will tell you, once you start…. Well, it would be like "Wile E. Coyote" stopping at the edge of a cliff. She was at my window now. Her garlicky breath flowed into my face as she exhaled. Her teeth were either chipped or missing; the remaining few were yellow with age. Her old wrinkled skin sagged down her face. She wore her graying hair, tucked under a military style beret. In her right hand she clasped an old mahogany walking stick.

"Whatcha doing in there little man? Are you a Nazi, in this here little Nazi car?" She asked, pronouncing Nazis as if it had a dozen "Z"s. She looked into the car, catching me… exposed.

"I'm sorry ma'am, I was listening to the speeches, and you know it's been so hot, and well the Cokes…and I just had to go."

She poked me in the face with her walking stick, a look of disgust on her face. "You pervert."

I bit my lip and tried not to cry out in pain. She started to reach into the car. She was momentarily distracted by the crowd, cheering Cooper's speech. I took that moment to turn the ignition and slam on the gas. As I peeled out of there, I looked back in the rearview mirror and saw the old lady wavy her walking stick in the air, hollering about Nazzzzzzzzis.

I reached for the J Cloths to clean up, realizing that like the J Cloths, my surveillance skills had holes.

Chapter 12

Gabriel - Tuesday Afternoon, Day 2

I arrived at my office by 3 pm, wishing for more than a fan to cool the place down. I opened the window to let some fresh air in, and listened to Bourbon complain again about having to wait all day on the fire escape. A little tuna shut him up, and once again he was my best friend.

Going through the day's mail, I found some unwanted solicitations, an unwanted rent bill and an unwanted magazine offer. Checking voicemail messages, all but one were equally unwanted. My mother had called earlier in the morning, around the time I was battling with the parking lot lady. Her message was not urgent. My dad's back was bothering him again, and my 74 year old Aunt Justine had announced a date for her wedding. It would be her sixth time to the altar, and I think even my mother was getting a little bored. She ended the call with her well wishes, and a demand that I should call home more often now that I had landed a cushy accounting job.

Getting the call from my Mom was bittersweet. They had always been there for me, especially that fateful day when I lost my job at Ford. I think Dad was a little disappointed, seeing he originally hooked me up for the interview. But in typical Dad fashion, it didn't take him long to rally. He soon started cursing Ford, and bemoaning how much the company had gone downhill since he retired. Mom had welcomed me home with open arms and helped me get settled in my old bedroom. Growing up, Dad helped decorate my room with mementoes from Ford including model cars, marketing posters, and of course a Ford Pinto bedspread. Small wonder I needed to get out of there.

I hadn't been completely honest with my folks since coming down here. I had told them I'd scored an accounting job at a company specializing on finding missing kids. Had I told them the truth about being a detective, my Mom would have been up at night worrying?

Despite the embarrassment at the park today, I felt I was making progress. Inexperience aside, I had seen enough episodes of "Streets of San Francisco" to know there had to be a connection with these missing girls.

Ben arrived just before four. I was sure the police department building had air conditioning, but the massive sweat stains under his arms were witnesses to how uncomfortable it was outside. He was carrying a grey sports jacket and wearing a western denim shirt with a red string tie. He looked as tired and rumpled as an unmade bed, dropping on my poor chair like a sack of rocks.

"Anything to drink in this place?" He pulled his shirt collar loose.

"I stopped at the store, and bought us a six pack of cold Michelob's."

"Thanks partner, beer is the reason I wake up every afternoon," he said, uncapping the brew and taking a big swig and looking around. "This place is a dump."

"I meant to talk to you about that, when business picks up, how would you feel about a classier location?"

He shook his head, "We signed a lease for a year. We've only been in business for less than six months. Let's keep things building, maybe in the fall we can start looking." He changed the subject by asking, "Have you been tailing our boy?"

I brought him up to date with the surveillance from the morning, leaving out the pee episode. "The guy looks like a Dudley-Do-Right," I reported.

"I never trusted ole' Dudley. Did he spot you?" He uncapped his second Michelob.

"I was invisible; you could say I melted into the scenery."

"That's my boy, finding anything else?"

"I spent a good part of yesterday at The Herald reading news stories all praising Dudley and his band of deputies for ridding this town of scum."

"I figure most people would say they feel safer in Biloxi now than ever before. I bet they would swear on a stack of bibles that the crime level is down," he replied, taking a long swig of his beer.

Bourbon jumped up on the desk and was sniffing my beer. I picked him up, and put him on the window ledge, "Sounds like you have a different opinion."

"From my point of view, I think the crime is just as bad, just a little less obvious."

"Like hookers who no longer have to hang out on the street?" I asked finishing my beer.

"Yeah, I think you got it. Did you notice that the stories died off after a while?" remarked Ben.

"I noticed that someone named Alex Dermody did almost all of the reporting. The stories came to a sudden stop a few years back."

"At that time, Dermody was the city reporter at the Herald. Talk was he must have had a problem holding his liquor because they found his car wrapped around a tree up near D'Iberville. I don't know all the details, because it was the Sheriff's turf, and they were on the scene. Apparently he almost died, and now he's pretty much a vegetable."

"Is there a connection between Dermody and the Sheriff?" I asked.

"I don't know. Why?"

"There must have been a dozen or more articles that were more like television commercials, talking up the Sheriff and his Department and their success in making Biloxi crime free."

"You are not the first to have had that thought. Some went so far as to say that Dermody might have been hired, among other things, for that purpose."

"What relationship exists with the sheriff's department and the Biloxi PD?"

He took a huge swallow followed by a belch so loud it shook the windows. "Pretty good. There are a few deputies over there that are willing to share information and work together. You have to remember that the sheriff's position is political. He's up for re-election every four years. He hires deputies he believes will help his cause. When Cooper was first elected, he got out the broom and cleaned house. There was a lot of speculation, at that time, some of the more experienced deputies weren't willing to play ball in making him look good. So they packed up and went to work either up in Jackson, Natchez or even Hattiesburg. Keep in mind that the Biloxi Police Department has had their share of scandals too. In 1973 there was what became known as the Blue Flu. Thirty-Five of Biloxi's finest were canned, transferred or asked to retire."

"What was behind that?"

"Well, there's a cultural tendency down here to do things a certain way. Sometimes that might mean looking the other way, for the right people."

"You mean like taking bribes?"

"Yes, but no one would ever admit that; let's just say people got gifts over the holidays."

"There must be some cross-over between the sheriff's territory and yours?"

"Of course, the sheriff's department is responsible for the whole county, including Biloxi and Gulfport that have their own police departments. For the most part things are pretty professional; we collaborate on some cases where they have an interest. We trade information on what's going on in the city. Keep in mind their mandate is a little broader. They're responsible for the local jail, which houses prisoners from throughout the state. They also provide security for the courthouse, and they're the ones that deliver the subpoenas and summons. Speaking of things not being what they seem, let's have a look at this scrapbook." he said, polishing off his third beer.

I reached for the scrapbook I'd found yesterday and passed it to him. He took his time reading the three stories and then flipped back and forth between pictures of the three girls. Pulling out a notebook from his suit jacket, he scribbled a few notes with a stubby pencil. After about five minutes he looked at me and closed the scrapbook.

"First off, I put out an all-points bulletin on Rebecca Glaswell. Second, you're right; there is a similarity between these three girls. All three are Caucasian, young, pretty and blonde.

Third, there is the fact that the first two disappeared during Mardi Gras, and then the last one in the spring. Have you looked for any other cases?"

"No, I came across the first one by accident at the Herald. It was the last story that Alex Dermody published. The girl in the photo could be Rebecca's sister. I found the third story from New Orleans, when I found the scrapbook hidden under her bed."

"Why would Rebecca be keeping this?"

"I don't know the answer to that, and neither does the mother. Mrs. Glaswell did say something interesting though. Apparently Rebecca did an internship at the Sheriff's office and has an interest in becoming a detective when she graduates."

He looked at me appraisingly, as if to say I had confirmed his faith in me as a gumshoe. He put away his notebook and said he was going to run an inquiry at the state level about missing blonde girls disappearing around Mardi Gras time.

"I couldn't help think of that girl that was murdered back in 1973. There was an article in yesterday's Herald. Rose Marie Levandoski, they found her naked body under the bridge." I said, repeating the story from yesterday's Herald.

At the mention of the cold case, his demeanor changed and he looked down at the ground and shook his head. "I was thinking the same thing. Some cases you just can't get over. She was only 13, a junior in high school. I was the one that found her."

"What? That must have been terrible."

He took a deep breath; this was obviously difficult for him. "I had the day off and was fishing in the Tchoutacabouffa River just east of Corso's Bridge in Biloxi. She was lying in some bushes; someone had stabbed her in the back. Rose Marie wasn't even supposed to be in school that day, she was going to stay home sick except they were having a test. She complained of a headache, and the teacher gave her permission to use the washroom to take an aspirin. She had to leave the school to use the washroom because they were using portables. When she didn't return, the teacher didn't alert anyone and marked her present. She didn't want her to get in trouble. Had we known sooner…?"

"Was she the type of student to run off?" I asked.

"Not at all. Straight "A", and never in trouble. I know what you're thinking. Keep in mind all of this might just be a coincidence."

"Do you believe in coincidences? I asked.

"Funny, I was just about to ask you the same question."

"There's no such thing as a coincidence. Some things that happen can give the illusion of a coincidence. For example, there are 24 bottles of beer in a case and 24 hours in the day. What happened here is not a coincidence." I said.

He pondered my logic for a minute as I finished off my beer.

"Did you ever get close?" I followed up.

"To finding who did it? Yes and no, I think the best lead we got was a phone call. I was staying late by myself one night about a month after I found her. I picked up a call, and there was someone on the line, I could tell from the breathing. It's funny. I get dozens of calls each day, but I could have told you that this was the guy. Somehow I just knew. I could sense there was something evil on the line. The voice finally said he had done Rose Marie and that he would kill again. Then he hung up."

"That's creepy! Do you think it could be the same guy?"

"Anything is possible. The one aspect of the Levandoski case and these missing girls is they took place around Mardi Gras. Roughly a half a million people visit the area around that time. There's bound to be a few wackos."

I asked if he could get me the Levandoski file, just to see if anything jumped out at me.

"Sure, can't hurt getting another set of eyes on this." Then, looking to change the topic, "What's on for the agenda for you tomorrow?"

"Probably more surveillance, Jacqueline is anxious to find out if he is cheating on her, and I foolishly promised her results by Friday."

"That wasn't smart." he said with a grin, understanding.

"Did you get a chance to interview Rebecca's teachers?"

"I haven't had a chance; this new chief Ricketts is making me chase my tail with paperwork."

"Maybe I will run by tomorrow, and see what I can find out." I held Rebecca's picture in my hands, and for a moment or two there was silence. "She's a pretty girl; hard to believe there wasn't someone…"

Ben ignored the comment. "What do you know about her father?" he asked.

I referred to my notes, "His name is Michael Glaswell, and the mother hasn't seen him in a couple of years. She claims he's a low life, and that he lives in California."

"Just because she hasn't seen him doesn't mean he isn't here. I'll do some checking on that. It wouldn't be the first time a long-lost parent came back into the picture. The girl might not tell the mother if there were bad feelings." Ben got up to leave.

"So, getting back to the Sheriff, what's your take? I asked.

"I don't have one. Like I said to you, watch your step on this one. There are whispers out there about his ties to some known felons. Nothing concrete that can get proven."

"And what about the case at hand… is he cheating on his wife?"

With that Ben cracked a smile, drained the last of his beer, and said that cheating on Jacqueline Cooper should be grounds for being committed to Gulf Oaks. Before opening the door, he turned back to face me and said, "I almost forgot, there was speculation about the Rose Marie case that it might have been a cop."

"Why's that?"

"Ask yourself what would make a girl like Rose Marie get in a car with a stranger?"

Chapter 13

Gabriel – Wednesday Morning, Day 3

This time I was better prepared. I stopped by the hardware store on my way to the surveillance and picked up a cooler and a bag of ice. Along with all the other equipment, I was set for a day of exciting stalking. I arrived shortly after 10 and to my surprise; I saw both cars still in the driveway.

The weather forecast was for another hot day with a light breeze and temperatures hitting 85 degrees. After about an hour, I decided to get out and stretch my legs. Grabbing a soft drink, I climbed up a small hill which afforded a view of most of the Cooper's backyard. The old surveillance rule was to remember that if you could see someone, then they could see you. There was a small pine tree at the top of the hill that promised a little cover. Looking at their backyard it was clear that the Coopers had spent a pile of dough on landscaping around their kidney-shaped pool. Using the telephoto, I was able to zero in on everything. I panned the camera from right to left looking for movement. It was already getting hot, making the pool water look as inviting as a rainstorm in hell. My panning froze and I adjusted the lens to reveal Jacqueline Cooper lying on a lounge chair, wearing the tiniest of bikinis. The sight of her reconfirmed that she was clearly the most beautiful woman in the universe. She was rubbing oil on her long, long exquisite legs. Up and down, then back up her smooth, now buttery legs. Beads of sweat from the heat dripped down the cleavage of her pouting breasts. I snapped a few pictures, maybe twenty. I eventually came to my senses, scolding myself for being such a pervert.

Jacqueline was alone, no sign of the Sheriff. She rolled over onto her front and reached behind her to unhook her bikini top. Oh my god, she needed me to rub oil onto her back! I decided to test out the camera some more.

The crack of a twig came from somewhere behind me. Turning, I saw a young boy staring up at me. He couldn't have been more than 10, with red curly hair and a mischievous look on his freckled face.

"What are you doing there?" I called out to him with my most authoritative voice.

"I own this place, and you're on my land." The kid replied imperiously.

"That's clearly a lie," I replied moving closer. "What's your name, kid?"

"What's yours, trespasser?" he said "trespasser" harshly and as if it was all one syllable.

"My name is ...Tab," I replied, looking down at the soft drink bottle in my hand.

"Well then, my name's Jimmy Carter," he replied, pronouncing it with a southern drawl, like Kahhrtur, and giving no indication that he was making it up. Clearly I was dealing with a pathological liar.

"Shouldn't you be in school.....JIMMY?" I was wondering how fast he was, and whether I could out run him.

"No, I have more important things to attend to TAB," in a dismissive tone, accentuating TAB to show he didn't believe I was telling the truth.

"Like what Mr. PRESIDENT?"

"How 'bout kicking your ass off my property?"

"Yeah, you and what army?" I replied childishly.

"I could probably whip your skinny little ass in less than a minute."

I couldn't believe I was having this conversation with someone who was less than 4 feet tall. The idea of a physical confrontation was too ridiculous to consider, so I decided on a different tactic. "See the camera. I was taking pictures of birds."

"Who said you could do that?" Before I could answer, he waved me off saying, "Besides, I don't believe you. I think you were taking pictures of that house over there."

"No, and for your information MISTER PRESIDENT you've scared all of the birds away," I said indignantly. "I'm going to have to leave, and find a new spot." I turned to go back to my car. I saw that the Sheriff's cruiser was no longer in the driveway. Cursing the kid under my breath, I made my way down the hill.

"You're a short little bull fart." Jimmy called out behind me. I resisted the childish temptation to yell back, I know you are, but what am I?

"I'm going over to that house over there to tell them you were spying on them."

Turning to face the little delinquent, "Ok, kid, what do you want? I don't want you to harass and upset people."

"I want to know what you're doing here." My car caught his attention, "Hey neat car! Is this one of those Bugs?"

"It's called a Volkswagen Beatle, and yes, it's a neat car."

"Say, what's in that cooler on the front seat?" he asked, looking in the window.

"Nothing, just a couple of sandwiches and some soft drinks."

"Tell you what, you give me a ride in your bug car and a soft drink, and maybe I won't tell those people you were spying on them."

I felt like slapping him into next week, but it would be unseemly to have a grown man do that in front of the Sheriff's house. I popped the lid on the cooler, opening up a Tab for him. Putting the cooler up front in the trunk, I said. "Ok, get in MISTER President."

"Thank you ….TAB," he said holding up the soft drink with a look of satisfaction on his face.

"Okay, a short drive only. I'll drive you home, where do you live?"

"The White House," he replied, putting his hands out and flashing the victory sign, a la Richard Nixon.

I ended up leaving the little twerp at the McDonald's with a buck for a sundae. I was still not sure he would keep his promise. For effect, I told him "If I hear about you bothering the people in that big house, I'll be back, and I'll clean your clock."

"In your dreams, TAB."

Chapter 14

Gabriel – Wednesday Morning, Day 3

I headed downtown hopeful that I could pick up the trail. I decided not to park in the drugstore parking lot again, and opted instead for parking at Realty Depot further down the street. While the view of the entrance to the Sheriff's office wasn't as direct, I could still see the building well enough. As the minutes crawled along, there was a steady flow of people coming, and going through the building's front doors. Cruisers arrived, and left the parking lot, but I had yet to see any sign of Cooper.

It was past noon when the little voice in my head said, *"Why don't you take a walk-through the office, and see if he's there."* Thankfully, before I could put this wildly stupid idea into action, the front door opened with Cooper and a deputy coming out and walking in my direction. I recognized the deputy as the guy from Rebecca's picture. The one with the pumpkin hair. I wondered if he even knew his protégé was missing. An idea started to form in my mind, and I grabbed some of Mrs. Glaswell's flyers off the back seat. I watched them amble down the sidewalk towards me. The Sheriff didn't seem to be in a hurry, stopping and having a friendly conversation with different shopkeepers and passersby.

Before they got to me, I quickly exited the car and, turning my back to them, went into the real estate office. Once inside, a middle-aged woman wearing a yellow and black business suit, and a beehive hairdo greeted me. She gave me the standard, "How y'all doin today," greeting, her voice as sweet as the maple syrup on your pancakes. I looked at her and smiled, wondering, what's with all of the beehives? I looked back and observed the Sheriff and deputy walk past.

"Y'all looking for a new house today honey?" asked the Beehive.

"Sure. How expensive are the houses down here?" I said, my eyes shifting between Cooper and Beehive like balls in a pinball machine.

"We have a full range of prices and homes in our inventory. Why don't I ask Mr. Benjamin to come out, he's the owner?"

I was about to beg off, when a tall gentleman wearing a plaid shirt with a yellow bow tie came from the back room. I was about a dozen feet away, and he crossed over to me with his hand outstretched, in record time. He grabbed my hand and pumped, like he was expecting my fingertips to start squirting milk.

"Welcome, welcome, welcome!" he said much too enthusiastically. "I'm Pat Benjamin, the owner of Realty Depot. At the mention of the business name, he pointed his gun finger at me and added "Call Pat… for your Real Estate Chat."

There was an awkward pause, as if he was expecting more than my smile in reaction to his slogan. I looked back out the window, and Cooper was nowhere in sight.

"I overheard you were in the market for a dream home. And your name is...."

"Oh, sorry it's …Tab."

"Well, I don't rightly remember ever meeting someone with the name Tab. What's it short for, if you don't mind me asking?"

"Oh. It's just Tab. You see, my Mom was a secretary and when she found out she was pregnant, she was typing a memo and looking down she saw "Tab." I was amazed at how easily I could bullshit. Pat looked at me funny, not knowing if I was joking with him. He looked over at Beehive before the two of them broke out laughing.

"It was either that or Shifty." I added, clearly on a roll. That brought out a whole new round of laughter that lasted at least a minute. When it stopped there was an awkward moment where Pat was clearly expecting me to clarify my real name. I just smiled.

"Okay Tab, why don't we go into my office, we'll be more comfortable?" Noticing that I was still periodically looking behind me..."Is there someone with you? Would you like to invite them in?"

"I was supposed to meet someone. Maybe I should find them first, and we can both come back."

"That would be fine Tab; we have a number of hot, hot, hot properties that are going fast."

"I'll be back shortly," I replied, running back out the door, desperately trying to catch sight of Cooper and the deputy. I saw them a couple of blocks ahead going into the "Friendship House Restaurant." Walking calmly, I entered the restaurant on the heels of a couple accompanied by their two toddlers. The kids must have wanted a Happy Meal because they were putting up a hurricane of objections. I picked up a real estate magazine and put it up covering my face, just in case the Sheriff looked back at the commotion.

The waitress showed Cooper and his deputy to a private booth, at the far end of the restaurant. The waitress eventually came to greet me. The name on her uniform said her name was Tweedy, and she was my height and four times as wide. She would be what my Mom called big boned.

I flashed a ten spot at her and asked, "Do you want to earn some easy money?"

She eyed me suspiciously reaching out for the sawbuck, "I don't go for any weird shit."

"No, it's nothing like that. I want to sit in a booth over there," nodding to the back of the restaurant. "Also, I want you to slip a copy of these flyers in the menu you give to the Sheriff and his deputy. If they ask you about the flyer, I want you to say some lady dropped it off and asked you to pass them out."

"That's it?" she asked, disappointedly reading the flyer. I nodded, and she said, "I'll put one of these flyers in every menu if y'all want."

"That would be great; I'm trying to help the family."

She seated me in a booth, which was about 10 feet away and directly across from Cooper. They were speaking in hushed tones so I couldn't make out what they were saying. Peering over the top of my real estate book I watched them. Their conversation seemed relaxed and easy going. Tweedy handed each of them a menu and took their drink order. They opened up the menu to the flyer, and all of sudden their conversation became more animated. Pumpkin Hair was gesturing at the flyer and looking back over his shoulder signaling for Tweedy. She arrived back to the table, and Cooper talked to her. The discussion was short and seemed to calm things down. As Tweedy retreated to the kitchen, she turned and gave me a wink. I would have loved to have heard what the Sheriff and his Deputy were saying. Were they upset about their protégé going missing, or was it because someone put a flyer in their menu?

Tweedy came back to my table to take my order, and I quietly asked what the Sheriff said. "He just wanted to know how come the flyer was in their menu. I told them like you said, a lady stopped by with flyers, and I wanted to help her by putting them in the menus. I think the Sheriff bought it, but as I walked away I heard the other guy say bullshit."

I thanked her for her help and ordered a Tab along with a cheeseburger. I continued to observe them behind the real estate book. They now had their food and were talking quietly.

My thoughts were interrupted by a loud voice calling out, "Well, Tab is that you, or should I say Shifty?" It was Pat from the real estate office. "Oh my heavens, heavens, heavens, you're not looking at any other real estate listings are you?" And with that he yanked the book from in front of my face. Looking up at Pat, I noticed that both Cooper and Pumpkin Hair were looking over at me.

"Oh, the book. They had a stand out front, and I wanted something to look at while having my lunch."

"Did your friend stand you up?" Pat inquired.

"No, she's just running a little late. Don't worry Pat, when she gets here, we'll be over to see you to have that… chat."

That must have appeased him as he left smiling, saying "Enjoy your lunch." Once he was gone, I looked over at Cooper, who was busy eating. Pumpkin Hair, however was staring at me.

Chapter 15

Gabriel –Wednesday Afternoon, Day 3

I tailed Cooper back to the office and settled in the VW for another uncomfortable sweltering afternoon. By 3:00 pm, I couldn't take it anymore. There was no sign that Cooper was going to leave. I kept on thinking about that newspaper article this morning and the connection between the missing teens. Could I have stumbled onto something that explained all of the girls' disappearances as well as the girl who disappeared in 1973? I didn't know for sure, but Pumpkin Hair's reaction to the flyer told me that he knew something about her disappearance.

The thought fluttered back at me like a persistent moth. I put the VW in gear and headed back to Biloxi. Rebecca's high school, St. Patrick's, was on Highway 67 in the north end of Biloxi. Mrs. Glaswell had given me the names of Rebecca's friends from school, as well as the kids she hung out with in the neighborhood. The verdict from everyone I interviewed was the same. Rebecca left school around 3:30 last Friday and never made it home. The teen was not a party animal, had no boyfriend and was liked by everyone. While I had interviewed everyone, I didn't get a chance to question Rebecca's homeroom teacher.

As I pulled the Bug into the school parking lot, it looked like the school day was ending. Yellow school buses, like giant caterpillars, lined up in front of the school. Kids were milling about; the girls all wearing white blouses and plaid skirts. The boys were dressed in white shirts, blue ties and gray pants. Getting out of the car, I asked a kid where I might find the Grade Eleven class. It took about ten minutes to decipher the instructions and find the right classroom. The sign on the door indicated it was Mr. Jackson's territory. I opened the door and found myself with a middle-aged man who was talking to an attractive young girl. As I entered the room, I sensed I was interrupting something private. Both looked up at me, growing quiet.

"Can I help you with something?" said the person I presumed to be Jackson. Perched on the edge of his desk, he looked to be in his early fifties. He had a cheesy toupee, and wore thick heavy glasses; you know the type, someone who needed to look younger. He was one of those guys that must bathe in cologne; I could smell it as soon as I entered the room. Maybe it was the powder blue polyester pants, the white belt, the flowery shirt, or perhaps just the white shoes, but I thought he was as oily as John Travolta's hair in Grease.

"You can if you're Mr. Jackson?" I asked.

"Yes, I was finishing with Janet." Turning to the young student, he said that she should be okay and that if she still had problems he would see her again tomorrow after class for private tutoring. I looked at the girl. She might only be 16 year old, but she had a body that spelt trouble. Her parents should consider a convent.

"What can I do for you Mr. …".as he watched Janet leave the room.

"My name is Ross, Gabriel Ross. I'm a Private Detective working the Rebecca Glaswell case." I handed him one of my spiffy "Eye on You" detective agency business cards.

"Oh Rebecca. We are all very concerned about Rebecca, and pray for her safe return." When he said this, he linked his fingers together and bowed his head like he was in church.

"You can help by telling me your impressions of Rebecca."

"You don't think her running away has anything to do with school, do you?" he asked indignantly.

There was something about the way he said "running away" that sounded dismissive. Maybe it was my early impressions of the case being mirrored back to me, but the guy was starting to piss me off. I waited for a response.

"Well, she's a lovely student, worked hard in class. She did her homework and was quite popular with the kids. That is to say with most kids."

"What do you mean by that Mr. Jackson?"

"Well, she was a very attractive girl, some of the boys wanted to get to know her, if you know what I mean. But I believe she was saving herself. Some of the girls might have been a little jealous."

"Saving herself? She was only 16." I decided I had enough of this creep. "Was Rebecca getting some of your special tutoring too?" I felt like wasting him like a Popsicle on a hot Biloxi day.

"I resent the implication you're making." he said, acting as if he was offended.

I grabbed him by the collar and pushed him against the blackboard. "Answer the question Jackson, were you giving her the "special" treatment?" I yelled at him, slipping into my Bogart persona.

He started to babble like a baby with a wet diaper. For a moment, I thought about slapping him, but in the end I let him go. He was too much of a lightweight to have done anything.

As I walked out of his classroom, he yelled after me, holding my business card and saying he was going to complain to my supervisor.

While I was at the school, I decided to drop off some flyers to the principal's office. When I got there, a young dark haired lady met me at the counter. She was happy to take some of my flyers and promised to put them up around the school.

"Do you mind if I ask you if you know Rebecca?" I asked.

"Only to see her, she was not the type that got sent to the principal's office."

"Any thought about what happened to her?"

"None at all, I'm not sure how things were at home. Maybe she ran away."

The statistics from the Herald article swept across my mind. In particular the one that reported that 80% of runaway teenage girls were victims of abuse. "Are you basing the comment about her home life on anything specific you heard?"

"Not really," she lowered her voice and looked around as if someone might be listening. In the faculty lunch room I overheard some teachers say her father's a real sicko."

"Do you remember which teacher said that?"

"No, but it seemed like a statement that other people might have heard. A couple of people might have agreed or nodded their agreement."

"What about her teacher Mr. Jackson, he seems a little odd?"

"That's putting it mildly. It might have been him. It was fourth period lunch, so he was there."

"Could he be …somehow involved with Rebecca?"

"Ugh! I seriously doubt it. Not that he would be beyond trying. Rebecca's a smart girl; she wouldn't need to lower herself to his level."

I thanked the girl and gave her one of my cards in case she remembered anything else. On my way out, I met a young man, maybe in his late twenties, pushing a mop around the floor like he was swabbing the deck. I introduced myself and gave him one of my cards. He looked at the card as if it was a precious gift. He had huge eyes like a wide eyed Tarsier monkey from the Biloxi Zoo. He must have been 6 and half feet tall with hands the size of my head. He said his name was Stevie. Not Stephen, not Steve but Stevie, like a kid's name.

"Do you know Rebecca Glaswell?" I showed him the flyer.

"Seen her around," he said nodding over-enthusiastically. There was something not quite right with Stevie.

"Have you seen her since last Friday?"

"Yup." Again with the insane head nodding.

"Where was that, Stevie?"

He looked away, embarrassed, and went back to his mopping, splashing soapy water all over my shoes. I asked again before he mumbled, "In town."

"Stevie, can you look at me and concentrate, this is important. Rebecca's missing, her mother is very worried." He excitedly moved the mop about, splashing more water around. He was becoming agitated and I didn't know why. I decided to be patient and waited for him to respond. His mopping had thoroughly soaked my pant legs by the time he finally looked up at me, eyes bulging like Marty Feldman.

He blurted out all at once, "I saw her last week at the drugstore. I wasn't supposed to be there. Mother sent me to the hardware store to get some nails….. It's just that ... I like the ice cream."

"You saw Rebecca at the ice cream place?"

"Yeah, Momma says I'm not supposed to eat ice cream on account of it not being good for me." He started to mop again.

I quickly grabbed hold of the mop and suggested we give it a break for a bit. "What drug store was that, Stevie?"

"Peoples."

"Was she with someone?"

"She was there with the policeman."

Chapter 16

Gabriel – Thursday Morning, Day 4

My first thought the next morning was about Stevie and his comment about seeing Rebecca at the ice cream parlor with the policeman. The more I went over it in my head, the less certain I was that he was a reliable witness. He had no details about the policeman, only that he had a uniform that he couldn't identify, and carried a gun in a holster like they did in the westerns. That would describe a regular policeman, a sheriff's deputy or for that matter a security guard. Towards the end he said it might not have been Friday, maybe Thursday.

I still felt I had made progress. Okay well, maybe I didn't score a touchdown, but the ball was further down the field. I now had a number of avenues to explore; there was "the scumbag" father, who may have re-entered Rebecca's life; that oily teacher Mr. Jackson, and lastly a possible connection to a uniformed policeman or guard.

As I thought about the case, I suddenly panicked with a realization. I had promised Jacqueline definitive results by Friday. Damn! I felt pulled in two directions. My surveillance of Cooper didn't appear to be paying off. I had found no evidence that he was anything but a model citizen. What's more, the game had now changed. He had seen me. I felt like I was swimming at Amity Beach with a great white shark circling around me. I decided to call Ben and ask for his advice.

He answered right away. I quickly told him about what happened in the restaurant and Cooper and the deputy's reaction to the flyer. I also sheepishly told him how they'd seen my face.

Thankfully he reassured me. "I wouldn't be too concerned about that. I'm sure they see hundreds of people in a week, although I suggest you do something to change your appearance."

"You mean like dying my hair blonde and getting a fake beard?"

"That's a little drastic. I was thinking of a hat, a trench coat ...maybe rent another car for a few days."

I said alright, and then asked him if there was an update on the APB he put out for Rebecca. He took a moment to check the overnight reports. Getting back to me, he said, "Sorry, there were no reported sightings. "After a moment he added, "I went to visit Mrs. Glaswell yesterday to take a formal statement. I think she's putting up a brave front. She expressed confidence in you Gabriel. I think you impressed her by finding that scrapbook. Oh and she gave me some biscuits for you, she said you really liked them."

I ignored the comment and asked if there was any word about the father.

"Nothing yet, but I have a picture of him, and I know where he used to work. I'll work on that today."

We made plans to meet at the diner later in the evening. I needed help on what to say to Jacqueline tomorrow. I decided not to rent a car just yet. The Bug was super dependable, and well, I just didn't want to drive another car. I did pick up a baseball cap and dressed down into jeans and a t-shirt. The trench coat idea seemed a little cliché, and with a forecast of 85 degrees again for today, a little impractical.

I arrived at the Sheriff's house a little after 9 am. Once again I parked down the street. The Sheriff's cruiser was in the driveway, but the Cadillac was nowhere in sight. Probably out shopping for a new bikini, I speculated. I started reading the Herald, waiting for Cooper to come out. "Margaret Thatcher elected Prime Minister of Britain," was the main headline. I had just read the first page when all of a sudden my passenger door opened. Full of enthusiasm, happening at Jimmy Carter deposited himself with a "Good Morning Tab! You doing more bird watching behind your paper?"

"I have already taken lots of photographs. I'm taking a break."

"Yeah, I'd love to see those pictures."

"You should be in school, how will you ever grow up to be PRESIDENT?"

Tab changed the subject and looked over at the house, "She left real early this morning in case you're wondering."

"Who are you talking about?"

"The fox that lives in that big house, the one with the rack you've been peeping at."

I would have to be on my toes with this kid. I had half a mind to slap him into next week, but instead I decided to ignore him.

"So you're some kind of perv, aren't you?"

"I tell you what, you tell me why you're not in school, and I might not drive you down to the sheriff's office and report you for truancy."

"That doesn't scare me, but if you must know, I am on a break from school. The teacher and half the class have chicken pox, and my folks told me not to go. They don't want me catching it."

"Are you telling me the truth?"

"Does Dolly Parton sleep on her back?"

"Funny guy, you're too young to be talking like that."

"What do you think of her coconuts?" He held his hands out in front of him, holding imaginary breasts.

All of sudden the door to the house opened, and Cooper came out. I held up the newspaper in front of my face again, taking occasional glances as he got into his car. I looked over at Jimmy. He too was holding up a section of the paper peeking over the top. We must have made a great sight.

"Geez Tab, do you want me to help you tail that guy?"

"No. I don't know what you're talking about, but you have to leave now, I have to go somewhere."

"I don't think so. I think I'll sit right here. So you better get moving Tab, or you're going to lose him."

Shaking my head in frustration, I reluctantly put the car in gear, following the cruiser down the street. "First chance I get, I'm going to ditch you MR PRESIDENT."

"He's turning onto Highway 15 heading north. You better hang back a bit, or he might pick up our tail. So what do you have on this guy?"

I make the turn onto Highway 15 and kept Cooper in my sights. "I don't know if he's done anything yet, I've just been asked to find out."

"So TAB, you're some private eye aren't you?" I ignored the question and concentrated on not losing Cooper.

"Look, he's crossing the bridge to D'Iberville." We followed him for a good ten minutes, always keeping our distance. We passed Highway 10 going east, and tailed him as the Highway merged into Route 67. At one point, he was a half mile ahead and seemed to be speeding up. Jimmy suggested I give the Bug a little more gas. Ironically we were getting close to where Jacqueline said her car originally broke down seven years ago.

"You're pretty good at this MR. PRESIDENT. How did you figure out I was a P.I.?"

"Well, you're way too puny to be a police detective, and you were clearly watching that house so I figured it made the most sense."

I sped the car up and followed the Sheriff as the road curved to the west. Could he be leading me to the big break in the case? Maybe he was going to meet his girlfriend. I was careful to stay a couple of hundred yards back, keeping a car or two in between us. After about fifteen minutes the city was left behind, and we found ourselves driving in a rural area. On one side of the road there was a pine forest, on the other there was grazing land. There were fewer cars out this way, and Cooper had sped up. I coaxed my straining VW to keep up, putting the pedal to the metal. Instead of pulling into his mistress' house, we saw him turn right onto a dirt road leading into the forest. Decision time. There was no mailbox by the road, so it was unlikely that he was visiting someone. We proceeded past the turnoff and pulled over onto the shoulder a couple of hundred yards from the turn off. I told Jimmy to stay in the car and I grabbed my camera.

"What are you going to do?" asked Jimmy.

"Sneak through the forest and see if I can see what he's doing."

"And if they catch you, are you going to give him that bullshit bird watching story?"

"You leave that up to me." I got out of the car and started to make my way to the forest. I had gotten maybe 10 yards when I heard the car door open with Jimmy Carter running after me.

"I said stay in the car."

"Do you know the difference between a cottonmouth and a ribbon snake?" I shook my head. "Well I'd better come with you. These forests are full of them."

Taking a deep breath of resignation, I realized I didn't have time to debate the issue. "Okay, but stay behind me. If your folks ever found out I brought you all the way out here, I'd be in deep trouble." We made our way through the prickly pine forest and the tall grass toward the dirt road. It was slow going, and my nerves were on edge like a cat taking his first swimming lesson. It's amazing how many twigs and branches look like venomous snakes. We slowed at the sound of voices. Taking a knee and staying in the shadow of the trees, I could just make out Cooper's cruiser and another car. It was dark in color and looked like a Caprice. They had parked the cars in opposite directions, and the conversation was taking place as the occupants sat in their driver's seat.

"You sure like this spot, don't you Cooper?" The voice had an Italian accent. Not like Marlon Brando in the Godfather, more like De Niro in Taxi Driver.

"Nice place here Frankie, out of the way place, no one to bother us."

I couldn't get a clear view of the driver of the Caprice, but I could see Cooper well enough. I made a note of the Caprice's license plate, figuring Ben could run it down. I moved slightly, stepping on a twig which sounded as loud as a tree falling. I heard Cooper tell the other guy to be quiet, and he opened the door to get out. I was trying my best to fit behind the tree, holding Jimmy to me my hand covering his mouth. I had put on a few pounds recently and regretted not starting that diet …or maybe just finding a bigger tree. The Sheriff approached. I was close enough to hear the leather on his belt as he drew his gun. Holding our breath, we stayed as still as possible as we heard the unmistakable cocking of a hammer. All of a sudden, I felt something on my foot and looked down. A thin, striped snake slithered its way across my foot. The snake had to be four feet long. It was all I could do to not kick it away and run screaming like a lunatic out of the forest. Jimmy sensed my fear and looked down. He shook his head at me as the snake made its way back into the brush. I was just starting to exhale when a shot rang out. A twig not four feet from us flew up in the air. I was just about to come out with my hands up waving my bird watching camera when I heard the Sheriff.

"Must have been a critter, maybe a snake, these woods are full of them."

I didn't breathe for the next thirty seconds. Finally, I heard footsteps heading away from us. Taking a quick peak, I saw the two men standing next to their cars. I could make out some of what they were saying.

"You still drilling that Angela from the club?" Asked Robert De Niro.

"Yeah, Jacqueline's tenses up every time I go near her. Something's up with that broad. Maybe we need a little time away."

"Why don't you bring her down to Orleans, Nick will show you both a great time. Or if you aren't having such a great time maybe we can arrange a little accident."

I took a chance and looked over at Cooper who smiled at De Niro and said, "I'll do that."

"In the meantime make sure that Angela doesn't know anything about our business." De Niro got back into the Caprice. "Remember Tuesday's delivery. It's happening at two at the usual spot."

I wanted to take a picture of the other guy, but I was frozen solid behind that tree. We waited there spot until both cars drove away. When it was safe, we both let out a gasp.

"Wow, that was cool, who were those guys? What's coming in at two on Tuesday?" asked Jimmy.

"I don't know, but I'll take you to McDonalds if you promise to go home and never say a word about any of this."

"Okay, but no more of that Tab crap, I want a chocolate shake!"

Chapter 17

Gabriel – Thursday Afternoon Day 4

Jimmy was a little quiet at McDonalds, at least for him. There wasn't anything wrong with his appetite as he devoured a Big Mac and fries and washed it down with his chocolate shake. In the absence of his normal chatter, I tried to make sense of what I overheard in the woods. Clearly Cooper was cheating on Jacqueline. I even had a name, Angela. Jacqueline should be satisfied for now. At least until I could get her some pictures.

In addition to the affair, from the sound of the conversation out in the woods, Cooper was involved in something illegal. If the delivery on Tuesday at 2 was for anything legitimate, they wouldn't be meeting out in the woods. What to do about this information was a different story. I thought about my meeting that evening with Ben. I felt anxious about finally making some progress. I was helping Jacqueline while helping to gather evidence on what now appeared to be a crooked Sheriff.

Jimmy was still unusually quiet. The morning adventure must have been terrifying for him. I realized that I had so far avoided telling Ben about meeting Jimmy. I knew he wouldn't approve of me involving Jimmy and possibly putting his life in danger.

After lunch, I drove Jimmy back to Cooper's street. Once again he refused to tell me where he lived, what his parents did for a living, or whether he had any brothers or sisters. All he said was what I already knew. He was lord of the manor, and this was all his land. As we neared Cooper's street Jimmy finally opened up.

"So what's your next step?"

"I don't know. I have another case I need to work on."

"Can I help you chase down clues or something?"

"You've had enough excitement for one day. Besides my next appointment will be pretty boring. "I pulled over down the street from Cooper's house.

"What are you going to do about Tuesday?"

"I have a contact with the police, I'll ask him tonight."

He started to say something then stopped. I waited for the inevitable blackmail I had come to expect from Jimmy, but it didn't come. Getting out of the car, he thanked me for lunch. Before shutting the door, he leaned in and said, "My last day off from school is tomorrow. If you decide that you need some help or just want to hang out, then you know where to find me."

I thanked him for his great detective work today and said I would catch up with him later.

Driving around, I tried to assemble the various pieces of what I had uncovered. Cooper, in what had to be proof of his craziness, was cheating on his gorgeous wife. Second, I would be willing to bet that when Cooper was talking to the Italian guy out in the middle of a forest about Tuesday's delivery, he was not talking about ordering a pizza.

I decided to head over to Debuys Rd and the Gulf Oaks Psychiatric Center. This was where Alex Dermody, the Herald's former reporter, now resided. The hospital was a sprawling, three-story building surrounded by parking lots and a park. Before entering the hospital, I concocted a story about how I was Dermody's long lost step-brother, and wanted a chance to visit with him.

The nurse was pretty, and I guessed mid-twenties. She had long, dark curly hair and bright eyes. Her name tag identified her as Rachel. She seemed to accept my story about the step-brother and asked to see my identification.

"You know, Mr. Ross, your brother is in a vegetative state. The accident did a tremendous amount of damage. Most days he just sits and stares out the window," she said as she recorded my ID on a log sheet.

"Is he paralyzed?"

"His spine was severed in the accident. He's paralyzed from the waist down. As for the rest of his body, no one knows for sure."

"Does he get many visitors?

"No, not many, his wife visits maybe once a week. That's about it. I didn't know he had other family until you showed up."

"We weren't that close and I'm just passing through. Does he understand anything you say to him?"

"The doctor says no, but sometimes I wonder ….because of his eyes."

"What about his eyes?

"Well.... They're more alive than I would expect for someone in his condition. Sometimes I'll make a joke while looking after him, and well, this is going to sound weird, but it's almost as if I can see the laughter in his eyes."

112

"Thank you for taking such good care of him. It sounds like you like him."

"You can't help but get attached to people." She escorted me to Dermody's room. He was sitting in a wheelchair facing a window looking out at the park. The room was antiseptic, with six beds arranged in rows along the yellow walls. Small tables were placed beside the bed, most containing picture frames of loved ones.

"I usually talk to him when I'm here. He probably doesn't understand, but you never know. Alex, look who's here. Your step-brother Gabriel has come for a visit. Isn't that nice!" She rolled him away from the window and positioned him in front of me.

Dermody's expression was vacant. His eyes looked empty. I suspected Rachel saw something that wasn't there. He was wearing a standard blue hospital gown. His hands were at his side; his salt and pepper hair was cut short. Looking at him sitting in that wheelchair, I guessed he couldn't have weighed more than 100 pounds.

"I'll go now and give you two some privacy. I'm down the hall if you need anything." Rachel said.

We were alone; I decided to try my hand at communicating with him. "Alex, I told your nurse I was your half-brother; you obviously know that was a lie. I'm not here to hurt you. I'm a private investigator looking into a case that you might be familiar with." There was still no change in his look. His eyes seemed unconnected. No doubt I was wasting my time. Before leaving, I decided to give it another try. "There's a girl missing, Mr. Dermody. Her mother misses her very much. You wrote about another girl who looked a lot like her. It was your last story before your accident. Do you remember?" His eyes continued to be vacant. Getting up to

113

leave, I reached into my briefcase; I pulled out the picture of Anne Mullens and held it up to his face. At first there was no response ... then something. It wasn't recognition. It was something else; a shiver ran down my spine as I realized that what I saw was fear.

"You know this girl, don't you?" The fear I read in his eyes was gone, replaced by the same dim look as before.

Going back down the hall, I thanked Rachel again for her kindness.

"Was there ... anything?" she asked.

"At one point, maybe. I'm not sure. Listen Rachel, you said Mrs. Dermody still visits him. Do you know how I can get in touch with her?"

"That would be against hospital policy". Then she looked at me, winked and whispered, "She lives in D'Iberville, and she's in the book I believe."

"You've been a big help Rachel." I scrawled my name and my number at the agency on the back of a doctor's card. "Will you call me if there's a change in my brother's condition?"

"Of course," she said putting the card in her pocket.

On my way to D'Iberville, I stopped for gas and used a pay phone to look up the number for Mrs. Alex Dermody. The only listing was for a Trixie Dermody on Welch Street. I decided to give her a call rather than show up unannounced. She answered on the fifth ring.

"Hello, Mrs. Dermody, my name is Gabriel Ross. I'm up visiting with your husband at Gulf Oaks."

There was a pause on the line followed by the sucking sound of someone taking a drag on a cigarette. "Do you know my husband?" Her voice contained a hint of boredom.

"No, never had the pleasure. I'm working with the police on some cold cases and thought …well I just thought maybe," I said, not really knowing whether calling her husband a vegetable was politically correct.

Another pause letting the words sink in. Her tone suddenly became suspicious…"Did you say you were with the police?"

"I'm not with the police. I'm working in connection with them on a cold case that your husband covered."

All of a sudden her tone became angry, "I told you people from the Sheriff's Department to leave me the fuck alone."

Anticipating that she was going to hang up, I quickly responded that I meant the Biloxi Police Department. This seemed to relax her a little, and I heard the tinkle of a drink, ice cubes rubbing up against glass.

"So Gabriel, whatcha want with me?" The mention of the Biloxi Police Department seemed to calm her.

"If you are up for a visit, I'm in the area. I would just like to ask a few questions. Are you okay with that?" I asked hopefully.

Once again a long drag on the cigarette followed by an exhale that I could almost feel through the phone. I stifled a cough. "You're wasting your time. I don't know anything about some whatchamacallit frozen case?" She started to laugh. I must have missed the punch line. She had a throaty laugh that ended with what sounded like her retching.

"It's about some missing girls Mrs. Dermody. There's a lady whose young daughter's missing. It won't take but a few minutes."

There was a pause on the line before she said, "Alright, Mr. Ross you can stop by."

Meanwhile the Texaco attendant, an older gentleman, was waiting patiently for me. He was all decked out in his uniform with the star and a bowtie. I was starting to think that Biloxi was the land of Bowties and Beehives. "Your car's all gassed up; windows and headlights cleaned, I checked your oil level and filters too. That's quite the car you have Mister, not many foreign cars around these parts. I had to look around before I found the engine where the trunk should be." He seemed like a friendly guy with a down-home twang to his voice.

"Listen, have you lived around here long?"

"All my life. Grew up right here in D'Iberville"

"Do you remember a big car accident involving a newspaper reporter a couple of years back?"

The question stumped him for a minute then his eyes lit up, and he said. "You talking about Dermody?"

"Yes that's the name."

"That was a shame what happened to him. I used to read his articles."

"I read somewhere that impaired driving was the cause of the accident."

"People round here were sure surprised when we heard about that. No one ever remembered a time when they saw him with a drink. I don't want to tell tales out of school but Mrs. Dermody? She's the drinker."

He sold me a Texaco street map and showed me how to get to Mrs. Dermody's house. I thanked him for the information and gave him a couple of sawbucks for the gas, and told him to keep the change.

Mrs. Dermody lived in a bungalow that had seen better days. The house had fallen into disrepair. A rusty, push lawn mower was abandoned in the front yard, surrounded by grass that had to be 12 inches tall. It was early afternoon, and the sun had shifted in the sky making it a little less sweltering. I climbed the creaky wooden steps wondering whether Mrs. Dermody was in any way like the drunk I imagined her to be from the phone call. After the 4th knock on the door, a voice echoed from the back of the house. "Okay, Okay I hear ya!"

The door finally opened and before me was a middle-aged woman about 5 feet 2, wearing a low cut top and tight fitting jeans. In her hand she balanced both a cigarette and a whisky glass. She looked as though she had been poured into her clothes, her jeans hugging her body like shrink-wrap on a rump roast. Her hair was dirty blond and had come out of a bottle as did her personality. "I was busy putting on my makeup and making myself presentable. You're Gabriel, right?"

Coming into the entry way, I introduced myself. She looked at me appraisingly. "I rarely meet men who are shorter than me."

I smiled and ignored the comment. I asked her if we could sit in the living room while we talked.

"Sure, unless you want me to give you the grand tour." she slurred.

Entering the living room, I picked up a pile of clothes off a chair, putting them on the floor as I sat down.

"Want something?" She pointed at her glass.

"I'm fine, thanks Mrs. Dermody. I know you're probably busy so why don't I get right down to it?"

"It's Trixie, and I'm not busy," she lit up another cigarette that she'd taken from a metal box on the coffee table. As she bent over, hers breasts loomed like boulders poised to start a landslide.

She caught me looking, and smiled. "You're not from around here are you little guy?"

I ignored the question. "The Sheriff's report indicated that your husband was inebriated and lost control of his car. He sustained his injuries by smashing into a tree. Was your husband a big drinker?"

Sitting on the couch across from me, she let out a deep sigh and took another drag of her cigarette. "My husband didn't drink. He drank a lot when he went to Ole Miss. He couldn't handle his booze like me. It was starting to get the best of him, so he quit and joined AA."

I wanted to ask her how he felt about her drinking like a fish, but couldn't find the words. "So how do you explain the sheriff's report?"

"Bullshit! That's what I told them...all bullshit", she said taking a long swallow. "Alex wouldn't have been drunk. He was very proud of being sober. I called those bastards at the sheriff's office every day for a month, but they told me to accept the fact that he fell off the wagon. They even showed me a Coroner's report that supposedly said he had booze in his system. I kept calling, and calling, and calling. I tell ya there's something wotten in the city of Denmark," she mumbled.

I decided not to correct the quote, and asked if there were other reasons that prompted her to feel that way.

"As soon as Alex was in that hospital, that deputy busted in here and demanded to look through my husband's papers. He said some bullshit thing about evidence. I called the editor of the Herald where Alex worked and he told me that they had no right to come in here and take stuff. But by that time it was too late, they walked out of here with two big boxes that belonged to Alex."

"Was Sheriff Cooper one of those people that took away the boxes?"

"No, he would never have done that. He and Alex were good friends. They graduated college together. I think the Sheriff was the one who got him his job." She pointed to an end table containing a veritable zoo of porcelain animal figurines and a snow globe. Pointing to the snow globe - "That was a gift from the Sheriff to Alex."

"Do you remember very much about the cases he might have worked on?"

"No, but you can march your cute little butt down to the Herald and read about them in the papers." With that, she let out a howl, and swung her arms back and forth like a soldier.

I looked at my watch and smiled with relief, realizing that I wouldn't need to listen to much more. "I did go to the Herald and I came across a story about an Anne Mullens, a young blonde haired teen who disappeared just before your husband's accident. Do you remember anything about that?"

"I remember there was something about a missing girl. He was upset. I don't recall very much from back then, except he went to Orleans. He came back and started talking crazy; he wanted to pull up stakes and move up north."

"Did he say why he went to New Orleans?"

"No, I figured it had to do with Mardi Gras and some story he was covering."

"Would you have moved up north?"

"Of course, if that's what Alex wanted. I'm a good wife. I do my duty." I was waiting for her to start the arm swinging again. She added, "I even called up a real estate agent that his buddy the Sheriff recommended."

"I understand you go up to the hospital to see Alex every week. Does he communicate to you?"

"No, he's a vegetable. Not much good for anything," she looked at me as if I was a moron.

"It must be difficult for you." I asked, not really caring.

For the first time, her expression softened, and her eyes moistened. "I miss him very much. I never used to drink like this you know. I feel so lost without him." She started to cry, not just a whimper, but a full blown downpour. I knew I was supposed to go to the couch and put my arm around her, but I couldn't summon the sympathy. Finally she collected herself and looked at me with her puffy, watery eyes. The rainfall had washed away the makeup making her look like a circus clown.

I got up to leave, "Thank you for all of your help, Mrs. Dermody."

She got up from the couch and followed me to the door. I felt awkward and put my hand on her shoulder. This little human gesture seemed to perk her up. Before leaving I asked her one last question.

"Do you remember the deputy that came and took away the boxes?"

"Yeah, it was that creepy one with the orange hair."

Chapter 18

Gabriel – Thursday Afternoon, Day 4

It was agonizing waiting at the diner for Ben, who was thirty minutes late. I was on my 3rd coffee refill and was wired like Western Union. I was about to burst with all the news I'd discovered today.

He finally arrived wearing a blue sports jacket and a peach shirt and green bowtie. He was full of apologies; chaos had apparently erupted in the office. When I asked him what happened, he dismissed my question with a simple "cop stuff." As soon as the waitress left with our orders he pulled out his notebook and told me that he had an update on a couple of things.

"There are still no hits on Rebecca's APB. The girl seems to have vanished into thin air. Her picture went out on the front page of the afternoon's edition of the Sun Herald. We set up a tip line. You never know, we might get lucky."

"Has the tip line ever paid off?"

"No, at least not very often. You get a lot of weirdoes, a few would-be psychics, and people calling up and asking if there's a reward. Once in a blue moon the perp might call just to brag, like in the Levandoski case." He pulled a file folder out of his bag and passed it across to me. "You said you wanted to review that case."

"Thanks. Do you have anything else?"

"We retraced your steps and interviewed friends and neighbors, but struck out. Then I took the photo of the father over to McKittrick's hardware. The owner remembered Glaswell as an 'okay' worker. He only fired him because one of the secretaries in the office complained that he was pestering her. Last he heard Glaswell went out west." Looking back down at his notepad, "The Sacramento police called and said that the picture looked like someone they busted about six months ago for a B&E. I guess he made bail. They said they would check him out and get back to me by end of day tomorrow. That's pretty well it partner. How did you make out?" He put the notebook away.

Since we were talking about Rebecca, I brought him up to date on my visit to the hospital and with Mrs. Dermody.

"That's good work. I'm not sure a deputy collecting a couple of boxes of evidence from a reporter's home is very damaging. The fact that Dermody all of a sudden comes back from New Orleans and wants to get out of town is suspicious though. Did Mrs. Dermody have any idea who he went to meet in New Orleans?"

"No, she just figured he was covering Mardi Gras. What about him all of a sudden becoming an alcoholic?"

"Added all together, it smells like rotting cottage cheese. We should remember that he might have been reporting on the Mardi Gras, and while there he might have fallen off the wagon."

"Maybe. When I was in Rebecca's house, I saw a photograph of her with Mr. Pumpkin Head. Apparently she did the "take your kid to school day" at the Sheriff's office." Before he could tell me that this was just a coincidence, I told him about the stunt I played at the restaurant.

"They might not have realized that she was missing so they could have innocently been surprised. Listen, I think you're making great progress, but taking unnecessary chances. Now they can recognize you. Tell you what, I'll run a background check on the deputy. Someone at the station will know his name."

I went on to tell him about Jimmy, and he reacted as I predicted. "If this kid gets hurt, then you, we, the agency are done."

"I can appreciate that, but listen to the rest of it." I told him about what happened in the forest.

"Whoa, do you know who this other guy is?"

"No. I heard Cooper call him Frankie. I couldn't get a clear picture of him, but I did copy down the license of his Capri." Ben made copious notes and was clearly excited about the development. "He also told the other guy that he was still drilling Angela from the club. It's pretty clear to me that he's playing around on Jacqueline."

The waitress interrupted, delivering our plates. I had chosen the meatloaf while he was poised to devour an order of southern fried steak. After she left, we resumed our conversation.

"Great, you still meeting up with her tomorrow?"

"I was going to ask her to have lunch with me."

"Do yourself a favor and go out of town. Having a lunch date with her in Biloxi is going to get back to him."

"The guy in the Caprice said something about the Sheriff going to New Orleans and that someone named Nick would show him a good time. Any idea who that might be?"

"The guy in the Caprice might be Frankie Galliano. He's high up in what is being called the Dixie Mafia. The other guy might be Nick Castelanno a local New Orleans wise guy."

"What's the Dixie Mafia?"

"It's kind of like the Italian Mafia, except not based on family connections or all of them coming from the same part of Sicily. These guys are more informal, but just as deadly. There's a loose hierarchy, and this Frankie G. is one of the higher ups. These guys are involved in all kinds of illegal activities ranging from influence peddling, protection, bribery, drugs, prostitution and of course illegal gambling. There are also investigations going on by the FBI into their involvement in a couple of murders."

"It all started back in the sixties; they were into residential burglary, bank robbery and contract killings. Their motto was "Get R' Done." Most of their contract killings are against former members. These former members were quite often accused of being snitches or to have cooperated with the police. Ever heard of "Blue Eyes" Miller?"

I shook my head and then he continued, "Blue Eyes" was what they call a button man. He was thought to have carried out most of the killings. Of course, any witnesses conveniently disappeared before they could testify. This strip in Biloxi is home base for the Dixie Mafia. Galliano owns a lot of those nightclubs that double as strip joints and gambling dens."

"But Bud Carson owns the Rockaway?"

"He does, at least he does now. I think there may be some pressure on him to join Galliano's little empire. It's a very profitable business that includes gambling, drinking, prostitution, drugs, you name it….."

"Do you think this delivery on Tuesday might be drugs?"

"Probably a good bet, but without knowing where the drop is, I'm not sure what we can do. He could have been referring to a ship coming to any number of piers, a truck on the highway, a plane landing or dropping something in a field… you name it. Any way you can drop a wire, so that we can hear what's being said?"

"My case was to prove the adultery remember? This whole corruption investigation and the Dixie Mafia are well over my head. Besides, can't you just get a wiretap on his phone?"

"Doesn't work like that Gabriel. For me to get permission to tap his phone, I would have to go to a judge with a little something called evidence."

"I could sign a statement to what I overheard in the woods."

Ben smiled and shook his head. "As soon as I ask the judge for a wiretap on the County Sheriff everyone's going to know. You would be dead meat and so would that kid."

Chapter 19

Gabriel – Friday Morning, Day 5

I thought about the conversation with Ben for the rest of the evening. One of the reasons he set me up in business was that as a private detective, it would be easier for me to operate without all the red tape that sometimes limits the effectiveness of the police. It's true that my case with Jacqueline was winding up, but I suspected she was going to want more evidence than a conversation I overheard. Further, Mrs. Glaswell was also my client, and I wanted to know what happened to her daughter. I suspected part of the answer rested with either Cooper or Pumpkin Hair.

I came up with a plan of sorts and loaded the Bug one more time with my surveillance equipment. I drove by Cooper's house and noted that both the Cadillac and the cruiser were in the driveway. I parked down the street and unfolded the morning paper and settled in to wait. I didn't have to wait long. There was a rap on the passenger window, followed by Jimmy opening the door and joining me in the front seat.

"Morning Tab, what are the dynamic duo going to do today?"

"I appreciate your help yesterday Jimmy. You'd make a pretty good private detective."

"So send me in, Coach. How can I help?"

"Were you scared yesterday, Jimmy? The reason I asked was you got really quiet after we came back from the woods."

"No, I was just thinking about stuff."

I waited for him to elaborate but he eventually broke the silence with, "Are we going to tail that guy again?"

"Listen, I have a job for you, but if you think it's too much then I want you to say so and we won't do it."

"Don't be silly, what's the mission Tab?"

I pulled the item out of a leather case. It was approximately the size of a thick dime and had a wire attached that was maybe 5 inches long. I showed it to Jimmy and asked him if he knew what it was. When he shook his head, I said, "It's a listening device. Once planted, this receiver will pick up the sound as long as it's no more than a football field away."

"Did you want me to bug the big house for you so you can hear what they're saying?"

"No, I think it would be better if you could plant the device right on the guy we followed yesterday. That way, if he says anything more about Tuesday's delivery then we'll know."

"Where do I put it?" As soon as he asked that question, Cooper's front door opened and out came the Sheriff. "You see that hat he's wearing? I've been watching him, and he is either wearing it or carrying it wherever he goes." We watched Cooper take the hat off and put it in the car as he got in. "I bet he takes it off when he gets to the office too. That hat has a star in front and along the base of the crown, it has a ribbon that goes around the top of the hat. Do you understand what I am talking about?"

"Sure - you want me to plant the bug under the ribbon of his hat, right?"

"That's it exactly Jimmy."

"How do I do that without him seeing me?"

"Well, the Sheriff likes to start the day with a large coffee and I'd be willing to bet that he doesn't bring that big hat with him when he goes to the bathroom. All you have to do is go in and do your normal chatter until he goes to the bathroom. When he gets up to leave stay at his desk and when the coast is clear, plant the bug."

"What happens if someone sees me?"

"Then grab the bug and run. I'll be waiting outside." He didn't say anything for a minute. "Look, don't do it if you are scared. I can see if I can plant it some other way."

"Do I get to sit in the car and listen to the bug?"

"Yes, well for a little while."

"Ok, I'll do it.

"You're not nervous?"

"This is a piece of cake. Let's go, before you lose him."

Once again I parked across from the Sheriff's office in the drug store parking lot. We watched from our vantage point and saw a deputy walking down the street carrying coffee. As soon as the deputy went in, Jimmy opened the door, the listening device in his pocket. "Listen Jimmy - if you can't plant it within twenty minutes or if you think you can't do it safely, then get out of there, ok?"

He shut the door, and I watched the kid jaywalk across the street and enter the Sheriff's office.

The minute hand on my Timex seemed to be moving in slow motion. At the five-minute mark, I got out of the car and walked around the parking lot, hoping to quell my nerves. I felt as powerless as a man sinking in quicksand. After ten minutes, I got back in the car and tried reading yesterday's paper. It was hopeless; I couldn't focus. At the fifteen-minute mark, I got out again and walked up and down the street, keeping my eyes trained on the front door. After twenty minutes, fear for Jimmy tore through me. I put my hands on the hood of the VW, and noticed perspiration handprints when I lifted them. Why doesn't he get out of there! Guilt washed over me. This was clearly the worst idea I'd ever had. I figured the Sheriff had caught Jimmy and right now they were berating him under bright lights. Shit, shit, shit!

Just when I was going to say the fourth shit, the front door opened and Jimmy came strolling down the stairs. He turned left and walked down to the corner. Crossing at the light, he casually strolled down the street, making a show of looking in store windows. I put the car in gear and pulled out. Two blocks down I pulled up beside him, and he got in with a big grin.

"Are you ok? Did you get it planted? What happened?"

"Went pretty much as expected. Most of the deputies were on patrol. There was just the Sheriff and a couple of others in the back. I went into the Sheriff's office and told him that I needed his help on a school project. I told him I was interested in his viewpoint as a police officer, about who he thought assassinated President Kennedy. He went on and on and just like you said until he told me he had to hit the bathroom. His hat was sitting on his desk. I looked around, and there was no one watching, so I slipped the bug in the back part of the ribbon. The hardest part was waiting while he was in the can ... guy took forever. He came back and kept going on about some guy named Oswald. I stood up and said I had enough for the project."

I gave him a high five and drove in search of a phone booth. "I have to make a call, but I'll be right back." I said, leaving Jimmy in the car.

I had memorized her number and hoped that she was at home and able to talk. She answered on the 2nd ring. "Hi Jacqueline, it's Gabriel Ross."

"Yes Gabriel, I was wondering when you would call."

"I have some information I would like to share with you. I was wondering if you are free for lunch."

She started to object, but I cut her off and mentioned a quiet place up in D'Iberville where we could review the information together.

"Can't you just....."

I cut her off again and gave her the name and address of the restaurant I found yesterday. I ended the call by saying I would see her at noon. Getting back in the car, I told Jimmy that we could listen to the bug for an hour and then I would have to take him back as I have a lunch meeting. Once again, there was no objection from Jimmy.

Parking down the street from the Sheriff's office I hooked up the receiver. The signal came in pretty clear. At first we heard general background noises. We listened for ten minutes before the microphone picked up anything useful.

"Kin ah bother yo' Sheriff?"

"What can I do for you, Mr.....?

"Mah name is Luke Timmins an' I've come t'see about mah boy. He was taken late last night on his way home fum a party."

"That so?" said the Sheriff, his voice disinterested. "Let me look up the reports from last night." There was some shuffling of paper and then the Sheriff's voice." Looks like a pretty minor affair Mr. Timmins."

"He's a fine boy Sheriff, fine raised an' church gwine. Maybe yo'd jest let him come home wif me. Ah promise he will behave. Ah voted fo' yo' in th' last eleckshun."

There was a rustle of leather signaling the Sheriff moving in his chair. "I do thank you for that Mr. Timmins. Now there's the matter of paying for the overnight here at the jail, all of the paperwork, the deputy's time, etc."

"How much is yo' gwine charge?" Mr. Timmins' voice had a cautious tone.

"I figure $500 will cover it, but seeing as you voted for me let's make it $400."

"Thet's a pile of money, sir."

"You can always take your chance with the circuit judge; he'll be here sometime next week. Meanwhile, your son stays where he is. Keep in mind Mr. Timmins that the judge might fine your son more, plus he'll get a record."

"Y'all suggest I get a lawyer?"

"Jackson get in here," yelled Cooper.

"Yes Sheriff," a new voice.

"Didn't you say that colored boy resisted arrest last night?"

"Yes, he was right uppi…trouble. I had a mind to charge him with an assault."

"Listen Mr. Timmins, you mosey on home and talk to your wife. While you're gone, we'll take good care of your son."

"Please Sheriff. I'll be right back, the boy's mother, she got some savings."

We watched the front door as a tall black man with graying hair came out and hustled down the street. The microphone picked up Cooper's voice again laughing along with the deputy. "Good work Deputy, I'll split the fine with you when the old guy comes back. Go back there and get the boy cleaned up and tell him that if he opens his mouth about the licking we gave him, then I'll be taking my belt to his daddy."

Chapter 20

Gabriel – Friday Morning, Day 5

I hightailed it back to drop Jimmy off. I knew I needed to call Ben to bring him up to date on the listening device. Jimmy was geared up about the covert planting of the listening device, and about what we heard from the Sheriff's office.

"That Sheriff wasn't very nice to that old man," Jimmy said resolutely. "I also don't believe all that bullshit about Lee Harvey Oswald being a spy for Russia."

"From what we could hear, it looks like he took advantage of that old man and might have done harm to his son."

"I feel like going in there and beating his sorry ass!" said Jimmy with a little too much bravado. "Is anyone going to believe us about what he said?"

"I believe they will, because the microphone comes with a little mini recorder." I showed him the Memorex tape. "Everything we just listened to is recorded and we can play it back for the police. The Biloxi Police Department is going to be very interested. They'll probably want to set up a listening station so that they don't miss anything important."

Arriving across from Cooper's house, Jimmy quipped, "That was pretty cool, a bug in a bug," performing a drum solo on my dashboard.

"Listen Jimmy, you did great work this morning, thank you. I want you to remember that this isn't a game. You can tell from the small part we overheard. The Sheriff's not someone to take lightly. Make sure you keep everything to yourself."

"No problem. When do we get to listen to more of it?"

"I'm not sure Jimmy, I'm going to turn this over to the professionals and let them run with it." He looked disappointed. "If you're not busy, maybe I can use you for another mission."

His face lit up like a Star Wars pinball machine. As he got out of the car, "It's Travis."

"What?" I asked, looking around the neighborhood.

"Travis, that's my name."

I was speechless for a moment. "Great to work with you Travis, you're a brave man. My name's not really Tab either."

"I know that Gabriel."

"How did you...."

"When you ran into the woods, I opened up the glove box and saw the ownership. You should get the address changed."

"Well, I'll be a monkey's uncle. Brave and sneaky too!"

"I like Tab better. There's a girl in my class named Gabriella. I hate her because she's always making fun of my red hair. Gabriel's a wussy name. If it's alright with you, I'll keep calling you Tab."

"Okay, Mister President."

I thanked him again and put the car in gear. Driving in the neighborhood, I looked for a phone booth. I contemplated whether Jimmy's actions this morning were brave or the result of youthful foolishness. My plan to plant a listening device couldn't have gone better thanks to him. Other than washroom breaks and shower time, the hat probably wouldn't leave Cooper's side. I ended up driving aimlessly, distracted with the thought of whether he wore his hat when he and Jacqueline had sex. I finally snapped out of it and found a phone booth in a small plaza.

I dialed Ben's number. As it rang, I thought of the recording and Mr. Timmins. I made up my mind that this was no longer about a cheating spouse. It was about exposing Cooper for the corrupt and cruel person I believed he was. Ben answered on the fifth ring. I quickly brought him up to date. His reaction went from disbelief, amazement and appreciation all within thirty seconds. I deliberately left Jimmy out of the story, because I knew what his reaction would be, and I didn't want to burst the bubble.

"So tell me how you planted the bug?" he asked with a new measure of respect in his voice.

"Thankfully, there were only a few people in the office. I hung around the entrance looking at wanted posters until Cooper went to the washroom. When he did, I snuck into his office. He left the hat right there on his desk."

"You put the bug in his hat?"

"Yeah, he takes it just about everywhere. There's a ribbon around the crown, that's where I hid the bug and the antenna.

"You sure no one saw you?" Doubt was creeping into his voice.

"I must have timed it just right." Jimmy's aptitude for lying was rubbing off on me.

"On behalf of the Biloxi PD, I salute you sir for your bravery. I'll start rolling on setting up a listening post right away. There are a couple of guys I can trust to not say anything about this. How long before he notices it?"

"It's anyone's guess, but I hope it's long enough for you to get what you need."

"Well done Gabriel. There is something that I should explain to you though; we won't be able to use the tapes made from the listening device as evidence. We didn't get a court order to plant the bug so the judge would rule that any information obtained would inadmissible."

"What if he happens to mention details about a drug operation? Can you raid the place and maybe catch him in the act?"

"Of course, and depending on what he says it might make it easier to get the court order."

"There's something else Ben. I tested the microphone and recorded a conversation that clearly shows Cooper extorting money. There's a young guy in his jail named Luke Timmins. I'm worried about him. Cooper made what I thought was a threat against the kid if his father doesn't come up with four hundred dollars."

"I'll find a way to make sure he gets out of there even if I have to bail him out myself."

I felt on a high ending the call and heading off to my lunch date with Jacqueline, and wondered when the other shoe was going to fall. I didn't have to wait long.

Chapter 21

Gabriel – Friday Afternoon, Day 5

I arrived at the restaurant a few minutes late and made my way to the booth at the back where Jacqueline was sitting. She gave me a cautious hello. Her beautiful brown hair was tied in a ponytail and she was wearing a plaid top and jeans. We remained silent as the waitress stopped by to take our order. Jacqueline's brown eyes were ablaze with anticipation, awaiting the news. She ordered a chef's salad, and I asked for a BLT with fries.

When the waitress left she asked, "So is my husband having an affair?"

I must have rehearsed the next part a hundred times on the way over to the restaurant. "Jacqueline your husband must be crazy, but yes, he is spending time with someone else."

She paused for a moment, trying to maintain her composure. "What do you mean spending time with someone else?"

"I was trying to be delicate. He is, you know being intimate with someone else."

"You mean fucking?"

"Okay, we'll use your words; he is fucking someone named Angela."

"I knew it. There are just too many signs, late nights, not wanting sex, strange calls. I could almost smell her on him. She must be a little French whore because her perfume smells like Yves St Laurent." Her voice started to raise a few levels. I looked around for anyone listening. "Where can I find this An-Ge-La?"

"I don't know yet. Hearing this must be very hard for you Jacqueline, and I'm sorry to have brought you such bad news. I suggest we speak quietly, people might recognize a beautiful woman raising her voice."

She slapped the compliment away like a John McEnroe backhand. "Show me the proof," she commanded.

I told her about tailing him out to the woods and the conversation about Angela.

"That bastard, let's see the pictures."

"I took some pictures, but I haven't had a chance to have them developed yet. Regardless you probably want pictures of him....you know."

"Fucking?"

I nodded my head and said, "There's more, Jacqueline."

"What, is he fucking someone else too?" I was sure the kitchen staff must have heard that one. I started to laugh, and to my relief she did too. "No, the conversation out in the woods kind of implicates him in some illegal activities. I don't know what, but the Biloxi police are looking into his activities. "

"I'm not surprised. I've long thought he was looking the other way when it came to crime."

The waitress brought our food. Once she was safely away from the table, Jacqueline said, "So when are you going to get me proof that I can wave in his face?"

"I'm going to stay on the case at least for another week. But.....I think you should be careful about confronting him and waving things in his face."

"Worried that he'll trace it back to you?"

"No, it's not that at all; let's just say I overheard another conversation that makes me wonder if he actually enjoys hurting people."

Her eyes softened a little. "I can take care of myself, just get me the proof."

"There's one last thing Jacqueline. I overheard him and the other man in the woods talking about taking a trip to New Orleans. If he suggests it, make an excuse and get away."

She looked at me, searching for what was behind those words. For the first time, I saw fear in her eyes.

"You told me how you met him, but you never shared how things developed to the point that you decided to marry him. Can you tell me about that?"

She paused for a minute looking at me. I think she was deciding whether I was worth it. "I left off the story with my car being repaired and my friends going on to New Orleans. The Sheriff put us up at the Trade Winds apartments down on the beach. He and his deputies were there the next morning to take us for breakfast. After a great meal and to the disappointment of the deputies, Chevon and Catherine decided to continue on to our hotel reservation in New Orleans, and I'd join them later when my car was repaired. The Trade Winds was a beautiful building, and the beach and weather were wonderful after living through the northern winter. That day Will took me sightseeing. We saw the beach, the pier, and the lighthouse. We had ice cream on the beach strip and later we had lunch at the Cabana Beach Motel. He seemed to know everyone, and people lined up to get their pictures taken with him. I guess I got swept up in his popularity. I was twenty-three and up to that point I'd lived a pretty sheltered life. He looked so handsome in his uniform. After lunch, he drove me in his cruiser up to Keesler field where they have all of the air force planes. We had a tour and he introduced me to the base commander a Colonel …something.

When we got back to the apartment we went for a swim in the pool and then had cocktails on the beach. Under the moonlight, we shared stories about college and growing up. I was fascinated by the culture and charm of the old south. There are so many beautiful homes and such a rich history here. A wedding reception was going on with dancing in one of the big ballrooms. Of course, he happened to know the family and before you knew it, we were dancing beside the bride and groom. No one seemed to care that we didn't have an invitation. They were just happy to have Sheriff William Cooper at their event.

Sometimes he could get a little sappy. We were dancing to Crystal Gale's "Don't it Make My Brown Eyes Blue", and he said he would always think of me and my brown eyes when he heard that song. It was so late by the time either of us thought of dinner that we ended up at a special table setup by the owner in the kitchen. I remember it was well past midnight, and I was famished. My Mom used to say, she was so hungry she could eat a horse…. And then chase the jockey down."

We both laughed at the saying. Jacqueline seemed to relax for the first time since I met her.

"It was a perfect night, and when it was over, he was a perfect gentleman. The following morning he showed up with a bouquet of roses. He had cleared his schedule to spend another day with me. The second day we toured the Jefferson Davis home and ate shrimp outside on the patio at the Edgewater hotel. He introduced me to Bobby Vinton, who was appearing at the hotel that night.

Later we strolled along the beach and drank champagne under the sunset. We ended up back in my room and well, you can use your imagination from there. The next morning my car was waiting for me as good as new, courtesy of Will. It was hard to leave such a perfect vacation, but I knew I needed to connect with Catherine and Chevon in New Orleans. We agreed to write each other and that I would come down as soon as the school year was over."

"Did your parents approve of Cooper?"

"Well, I never told them about my car breaking down and being left in Biloxi while my two friends went on to Mardi Gras. My Dad would have called for the National Guard. As I got to know Will better, they came down with me and met him. He knew how to turn on the charm with my Mom. My Dad liked him right away; I think it's a cultural respect for authority."

"So love is blind or did Cooper change over the years?"

"I don't know, maybe a little of both. I might have missed some things, but I saw a change in him once we got married."

"What things did you miss?"

"Little things, like we would be out for dinner, somewhere like the Edgewater, and a man come by and whisper something in his ear and pass him an envelope. When I asked about it, he would say just police business. If I persisted he'd get real quiet, like he was angry."

"Do you remember a friend of Will's named Dermody?"

"Alex Dermody, the reporter?"

"Yes that's him. Were they friends?"

"They were best buddies from school, at least initially. Will got him his job at the paper. He and his wife Trixie were always coming over. Alex and Will loved to play snooker and hang out near the pool."

"So did they have a falling out?"

"I don't know. I never connected with Trixie; I always thought she had eyes for Will. One day they just fell off the William Cooper invite list."

"What do you know about what happened to Dermody?"

"That was pretty sad. By that time Alex was on the outs with Will. I was told about the booze and what had happened, which seemed strange because all the times he came over he never had anything other than a Coke. When I brought it up to Will he said that Alex had fallen off the wagon on a trip to New Orleans and that caused a rift between them."

"Looking back Jacqueline, were there any other times you felt he wasn't everything he made himself out to be?"

"There was one more time where I felt uneasy about him. It was Thanksgiving, and I agreed to come down so that Will and I could announce our engagement. I hadn't yet met the Coopers, so I was a little nervous. We walked into the family home, and his mother and father were there along with both his brother and sister. They treated me well and congratulated us on our engagement. There were a couple of items I soon learned not to discuss. One was politics. They didn't have anything good to say about Jimmy Carter and the Democrats. The second was religion. My parents raised me as a Roman Catholic, and Cooper's family were staunch Southern Baptists. They insisted on the wedding taking place in Biloxi and that everything happen in the First Baptist Church. My Mom wasn't happy about that, but in the end, I don't have that big a family up in Chicago, so we had the wedding down here. "

"That's sounds difficult, but what was it that made you nervous?"

"Well, when I was there he introduced me to his brother Boone. He's like night and day compared to Will. There's definitely something off about him. While Will went off to college, Boone dropped out of school and started working at a service center. Over dinner Boone said to me that he was the one that fixed my car. So no big deal right? It wasn't just that Will said a friend was fixing the car, when Boone spoke up, Will shot him a look that would frighten a statue."

"So what do you make of that."

"I was almost positive that he told his brother to take his time fixing my car."

"Once you got married how did things change?"

"He was very controlling. He didn't want me to work. I had to stay home and take care of the house and cook his meals. He even got upset when I said I was going to take a college course. I graduated from Oberlin in Art History. I wanted to look into working at the historical society. But no way! It would conflict with what he wanted. He had to know where I was at all times. On the other hand, it was quite alright for him to come home late, or disappear on weekends because he had an important job."

"The real problem was when the subject of children came up. At first we tried, but I couldn't get pregnant. When I suggested he get tested, he told me that I was the problem. He would get very impatient with me sometimes, and he has a terrible temper. It got to the point that I didn't want to have children with him, so secretly I started to take birth control pills. I made the mistake one time of leaving the bottle out on the counter. He found it and confronted me in a rage. He punched me so hard in the stomach I hurt for over two weeks. He said if I ever lied to him again, I wouldn't be able to walk for a week. After that, I tried to stay away from him. If we had sex, I would just lay there waiting for him to finish. He eventually stopped wanting to. I guess I know why now."

"Why didn't you just leave?"

"I tried once and one of his deputies stopped me on the highway. He took me back in handcuffs like I was a criminal. My asshole husband kept them on me for the rest of the day. He said I needed a lesson in loyalty."

There you go, another lesson about loyalty, I thought. "What an asshole. If I could get you out of town would you go?"

I saw a tear fall on her cheek. The first time she had cried on me, I thought she was trying to manipulate me into taking her case. This time I was convinced that she was sincere. I also was convinced she should not be confronting William Cooper alone.

Chapter 22

Gabriel – Friday Afternoon, Day 5

We talked for almost 2 hours. Our lunch ended with her telling me she needed to get home. Cooper often called in the afternoon and got upset if she wasn't there. We made plans to meet again in a few days to review the photos of Cooper and Angela. Photos that I hopefully would have by then.

I made it back to the office by 4 and found Ben waiting for me. He had Bourbon on his lap and his big feet on the desk. "We were thinking you were having a pretty long lunch. How did it go?"

"Excellent." Ben must have clocked out early as he was wearing blue jeans and a T-shirt that said "Cops love a Big Bust." I brought him up to date with the Sheriff's anger issues. "I don't think it's a good idea to let Jacqueline confront him about the affair, he's hit her before."

"What are you planning to do to protect her? Keep in mind this guy has the power of the law on his side. The whole reason she didn't report him when he hit her the first time was because she was smart enough to know she can't be protected."

"I don't know what I'm planning; I just know that I won't let her go through that alone."

"Bourbon and I think you're either a nut job or getting a little too close to your client." Ben said, giving Bourbon a much appreciated chin rub.

"Is that right? You both should know I would never take advantage of a helpless client." I heard my mouth say this, but the rest of my body was ready to jump ship and go rogue.

"Let me bring you up to speed on the listening device. I'm dying to brag to everyone at the station about the bug being planted in his hat, but I'm worried this would get back to him. We've made arrangements for a listening station out in front of his office starting Monday. We're using a city road repair truck. Everything they say will be captured and recorded. We'll have a guy in a city road uniform changing the tape every day."

"So Chief Ricketts authorized the manpower?"

"Yes and no, I convinced him that the manpower was for a Columbian drug gang that's come into the area. So far I'm keeping all the details to myself. I'm not sure how long I can keep a lid on all of this. I hope something good comes from the listening device."

"The listening station is only going to pick up what is said at the Sheriff's office. The best stuff might come when he's on the road meeting people like yesterday."

"Are you still ok to stick with him? You're probably our best bet."

"Absolutely, I still need to get Jacqueline some photo evidence."

"Ok, so will you be on him tomorrow?"

"Tomorrow's Saturday. Maybe I'll sleep in a bit and then head out. He'll likely be either at the office or at home." I stifled a yawn; it had been a long day. We agreed to get together nightly to listen to the tapes. "Hopefully something will come from this by Tuesday and we can nail him. On another note, any news on the APB?"

"Sorry Gabriel. I would love to have brought you something, anything about where Rebecca might be. It's been almost a week so it doesn't look good," he said with a dour expression on his face. "Sacramento called earlier. They're sure that their break and enter is Michael Glaswell, except he's now going by the name Marty Glassford. The unfortunate part is they paid him a visit and it looks like he jumped bail shortly after he was released. The timing works. He made bail and then skipped, coming east to meet up with his long lost daughter."

"I guess I should stop by and update Mrs. Glaswell. What about that deputy, you were going to see if there is anything on him?"

"Yes, some interesting stuff came up." he pulled out his note book. "He graduated from Ole Miss on June 3rd 1968. Care to guess who else was in the graduating class?"

"William Cooper?

"Bingo - and Alex Dermody. According to the people up at the college the three of them were pretty tight. The deputy, whose name is Franklin, spent 5 months working with the Jackson Police before he left abruptly. A couple of months later he was hired by Cooper as a deputy."

"Any idea of why he only lasted 5 months?"

"No, but I have someone checking into that. Also I'm still waiting to hear if there are any other cases of missing girls. Nothing has come back yet."

"Ben, do you remember when we first started; we took a statement from a young high school girl. She said she thought she was almost abducted by someone in a white van."

"I remember the statement, but not the girl's name." He looked in his notebook, flipping back a bunch of pages.... "Janice McVeigh."

"That's it. I know it's a long shot but what about coming up with a list of residents who own a white van?"

"There are a ton of white vans on the road. Remember we talked about the number of visitors that descend on this area around Mardi Gras?"

I ignored him and continued, "She said she thought it was a Ford, so it's probably an Econoline."

"Do you really think a 16 year girl would know the difference between a Ford and a Dodge?"

"Good point. But we know it didn't have any business signage, so you only need to search individuals."

"Gabriel, I think you're going crazy. Sure, we can get a list from the Department of Public Safety and then starting looking for Biloxi addresses. But how do you know the guy doesn't live in Gulfport or one of the other towns? How do you know the van wasn't stolen? As for manpower to help check out lists, I know Chief Ricketts won't authorize it. I already got him to give me manpower for the listening station, also known as the Columbian operation."

"It hadn't occurred to me that the van might have been stolen. What about starting out by seeing how many white vans were reported stolen last fall. If you can get the list, I'll start running it down myself."

He nodded and made a note. He got up to leave saying it had been a full day. On his way out he turned to me and said, "Are you having any fun yet?"

I didn't know it then, but the craziness was just starting.

Chapter 23

Gabriel – Saturday Morning, Day 6

I was running in a field of corn that was almost six feet high. I jumped up every so often, to see if there was anything on the horizon. Sweat, from the oppressive heat, was dripping from my face. My legs were caught in the undergrowth, trapping me. I pulled free and continued to run frantically. A sound was coming from behind me…a large engine or something chasing me. I needed to get away, run faster; the thing was gaining on me. I turned around and jumped as high as I could; there was something ten yards or so behind me chewing down the tall grasses. Whatever it was, it was big and loud… RRRRROARRRRR. The sound was getting louder, getting closer. I stumbled. My mind was telling me just to lie down, it'll be over soon. But no, I fought on and renewed my struggles to get away. I came to a little rise. Surely this corn field must be almost finished. I crested a small hill, the RRRROARRR, louder still; I looked back and saw the Weasel from Ford, driving a Pinto. He was bearing down on me, turning the steering wheel to catch my every move. He was wearing a sheriff's uniform. As he got closer, I saw the manic look on his face. I scrambled further away. I heard him yelling something about teaching me a fucking lesson. "No, no, no," I screamed.

I woke up tangled in my sheets and blankets; everything damp from my sweat. There was a loud noise coming from the hall. I scrambled out of bed and opened the door to the inner hallway. I saw a woman wearing a hijab maneuvering a huge industrial vacuum, just down the hall. When she saw me standing there in my boxers, she turned off the machine and apologized for the noise. I rubbed the sleep from my eyes and waved to her, mumbling that I needed to get up. The Timex showed that it was 11 am… I had not slept this late in years.

Grabbing a quick coffee at the snack bar next to the Trade Winds, I raced out to the car. The hot spell was over; the temperature now unseasonably cool. Huge gray clouds crowded the sky and threatened foul weather. I decided to stop by Mrs. Glaswell's house to bring her up to date.

Climbing up the stairs to the house on stilts, I heard Gracie sounding the alarm again. I knocked gently on the front door. When she opened the door, Mrs. Glaswell looked like she had aged ten years in the past week. She invited me in and asked if I wanted more ice tea. "No thank you, I can't stay. I wanted to update you on a few things." I bent down and petted Gracie, who brought me her ball. Mrs. Glaswell patiently awaited my news, her hands wringing nervously. "We have some information concerning your husband. He's known to the Sacramento Police Department out in California. As of a couple of weeks ago, he was living there. It seems that he got into some trouble, and the police arrested him. The police out there think he jumped bail and took off. They're looking for him, and although it's unlikely he would head back here we can't rule it out."

"I told you he was a scum sucker."

I ignored her comment, "Also, we have a lead on a vehicle that we might be able to connect to Rebecca's disappearance." It occurred to me that this was the first time we discussed Rebecca's disappearance being anything but a runaway.

"You mean someone took Rebecca, and they were driving this vehicle?" She looked like she was going to break down.

"We still don't know what happened. We have to accept that it's been over a week since she disappeared. If she were at a party, chances are she would have come home by now. We have to consider that someone might have taken her. As for the vehicle, I interviewed a girl who reported a possible abduction attempt by a man driving a white van. The two situations may be unrelated, but it is something to go on."

"I have to believe that Rebecca is alive. You see Mr. Ross, Rebecca is all I have. God would never take her from me." She put on a brave face to hide the pain, then stood up and went to the front window and said, "You mean like that white van parked down the street?"

I joined her at the window and sure enough; there was a plain white van parked about five houses down the street. Could this be just a coincidence? "Do you know if it belongs to a neighbor?"

"I don't think so. Come to think of it though I think I have seen it in the neighborhood. Something about it looks familiar."

"Okay Mrs. Glaswell I'm going to take a closer look. I'll copy down the plate number and ask Ben to look up the registration. It's probably a coincidence." I left promising her that I would be in touch as soon as I got more information. Walking towards the van I copied down the Mississippi license plates. It was a Ford Econoline. I looked back at the house and saw that Mrs. Glaswell was watching from the front window.

I approached the driver's door with caution. Looking in the window, I saw that the van was empty. A toolbox lay sitting on the passenger seat. It had no windows in the back, just like the van Janice had described. I decided to take a closer look at the front of the van. Sure enough both fenders had a little bit of rust. This was odd for a vehicle in Mississippi. In Detroit it was nothing to see a rusty Ford where the city regularly salted the roads. As I made my way around the van, I noticed that while the driver's side of the van was plain white, the passenger side had a picture of a uniformed man steam cleaning a carpet. I could have kicked myself. Janice only saw the driver's side of the van. We hadn't thought about the passenger side. The van could have been a commercial vehicle.

"Lookin' to get your rugs cleaned?" Came a voice from behind. I turned and found an older gentleman carrying a couple of containers of cleaning fluid." He was middle-aged and heavy set. A bald patch on the top of his head made him look like Friar Tuck.

"Is it expensive?" I asked

"Not at all, but if you have to ask, then you're not ready for the Rug Doctor."

"Really, how so?" The guy had my curiosity up. At that point, a middle-aged woman came out of the nearest house, wearing a print dress and apron. She was a member of the beehive clan.

"This guy's asking about how much the Rug Doctor costs, Mabel. Whatcha think, is he ready?"

"No, he's not ready," she said frowning. "If he was, he would know that the Rug Doctor is worth every penny no matter what the price."

She continued on, truly a disciple. "Just like with any doctor you pay what it takes Mister. You need to know how sick your carpets are. You go home, get on your knees, look down at your carpet, look real close, and you'll get steaming mad at the dirt."

I needed to change the subject before they asked to hold hands. Both of them looked at me anxiously waiting for me to catch their religion. "I tell you what, let me think about it and get back to you."

"My name's Clete Mumford, and here's my business card. That's our slogan. 'Steaming Mad at Dirt', and the company has been around since 1972."

"Thank you Mr. Mumford, my name is Gabriel Ross." We shook hands all around, and I said, "I'll get back to you on that steam cleaning."

"If you live around here I can drop by and give you an estimate...." offered Mr. Mumford.

"That's alright, but I do have a question for you. How long have you been working this neighborhood?"

"I've been working this area for a few weeks. Just about finished I expect."

"Have you seen many other white vans in the area?"

"I can't say that I have. No wait; there was this white panel truck a week ago or so. I always notice things like that on account of I don't want any competitors working my area."

"And do you remember if this was a competitor?"

"No, it was one of those vans that deliver parts to auto dealers. It had a name on the side of the van…something like "Artie's Auto and Parts."

I made a note of the company on the back of Mumford's card. "Do you remember anything else about the van?"

"I think it was a Ford, and I remember wondering whether all Ford vans are prone to rust."

"Thank you for the information," I said, turning to leave.

"I also remember the van because of the driver."

"Why is that Mr. Mumford?"

"He had freaky orange hair."

Chapter 24

Gabriel – Saturday Morning, Day 6

Over coffee I tried to make sense of everything. A white van used in a possible abduction being seen in the vicinity of a second possible abduction. Both vans had rust on the fenders. Both girls involved are roughly the same age with blonde hair. One of the girls, Rebecca, may have been investigating another girl's abduction before she disappeared. There was also a tie-in to the deputy in the picture with Rebecca that was possibly spotted driving the white van.

I made my way to Cooper's house, making a stop along the way to a phone booth. I checked the listings for Artie's Auto Parts but found nothing. In the Yellow Pages under Auto Parts and Supplies, I found Artie's Garage on Hanover Road. I decided to check out the garage, which was not too far out of my way. The garage was at the dead end of an industrial part of town. Like most of the nearby businesses, Artie's had fallen on hard times. The gas pumps had long since been closed off, and the business existed mainly as a service center. A few abandoned cars were parked sporadically around the side of the building. There was no sign of a white van. Old oil drums lay scattered like headstones in a cemetery of rust. I looked up and down the street. Not a soul anywhere. The place had a creepy feel to it.

Getting out of the car, I heard clanging at the back of the service bay. A 1972 Chevrolet Vega was being worked on; its hood raised. As I approached, the smell of oil and motor vehicle lubricants reminded me that I distrusted mechanics. Someone with dirty dark-blue coveralls was bent over the Vega, impervious to my presence. I was about to clear my voice, signaling my presence, when a voice came from under the hood.

"You driving one of those VW bugs, ain't you?"

"Yes," I replied, wondering if the guy had snuck a peek, recognized the engine sound, or was he just a good guesser?

With his head still under the hood, "Don't see too many around these parts; from behind it looks like they're about to take a dump."

"That's funny," I replied, except it wasn't. "My name's Gabriel Ross, can we chat for a minute?"

"Not big on chattin', fixin' cars is what I do." I decided to wait the guy out. Looking around the shop, the place looked like something out of the Fifties. A pin-up calendar displaying Miss May looked over a wooden table smeared with grease and old, rusty tools. A neon sign advertising Coke Cola as the real thing hung on another wall. From the ceiling dangled hundreds of strips of flypaper all containing flies long since dead. After a long, uncomfortable two minutes, he stood up. The guy must have carried 300 pounds on a 6ft 5 inch frame. He peered down at me with teeth that looked like tic tacs you might find in the dirt. His body odor wafting in my direction almost made me gag.

"Whacha' want to CHAT about?"

"Are you Artie?"

"Nope." His eyes looked like dark raisins pressed in dough.

"Is Artie around?"

"He's dead. But his body is probably still around here someplace."

I laughed at what I hoped was a joke. "What happened to Artie?"

"He asked too many friggin' questions."

Talking to this guy was painful. "So are you the new owner?"

"Nope." His face was expressionless, like a statue. A statue of a big idiot.

I decided to go to the heart of things. "So buddy, does this business own a white van?"

"Nope." I thought I saw a flicker of uncertainty in his eyes.

"That's funny, someone said they saw a white Ford van with this business' name on it."

"Listen, I got work to do. You want a white van, go to a car dealer." He accentuated this by putting his head back under the hood. I waited a few moments, contemplating smashing the hood on him.

I was feeling like a lighthouse in the middle of a sea of stupidity and decided to leave. As I turned and went back to the car, goose bumps ran up and down my spine. Driving away, I looked back in the rearview mirror and saw him staring at me. Okay, so he was a huge creep, but that didn't mean he was a kidnapper.

I drove by the Cooper's house and saw the driveway was empty. My stomach let out a growl and I decided to grab lunch, then head over to the sheriff's office. I went back to the Friendship House Restaurant and once again Tweedy looked after me. She gave me a big hello, which I suspected meant "I remember you as a big tipper." She showed me to a table and told me someone had complained about the flyer being put in their menu. Her manager, who she described as a toad, had given her a warning. "I don't care though; taking a little crap was worth it if it brings you closer to finding that poor girl."

I ordered the southern fried steak and told her to hold the grits. It occurred to me I never had gotten back to Pat, the bow tie guy, and I started to eat faster, thinking he might just walk in any minute. Finishing the largely forgettable meal, I gave Tweedy another nice tip and hurried back to my car. As I left the building, a sign caught my eye. Leaving the Bug in the restaurant parking lot I headed down the block. Hertz Rent-A-Car had a huge poster of O.J. Simpson sitting behind the wheel of a car with the slogan "Go O.J. Go!" The tag line below said Hertz was the Superstar in Rent-a-Car. I opened the office door and approached a young blonde girl at the counter. Pulling out my driver's license, I asked if I could rent a car for a week. She gave my license a thorough going-over and said "You live in Detroit?"

"Yes," I lied, realizing I had not done anything about the address. "I'm here on a business trip, and my car died." I made a mental note to do something about all the lying.

"I guess you want a compact car?" she said, looking down at me. I gave her a tired smile, and then she added, "Since you said it was just you."

"You're right. Something good on gas would be great."

The rental was $5 a day, which I paid in advance. Picking up my rental agreement, she handed me my keys and told me where I could pick up my car. When I got to the lot, I found my brand new fucking Pinto. It was gold-colored and sounded like the vacuum from my dream. Still, it would be less noticeable than the Bug. A quick drive got me back to where I left the Bug. I transferred my equipment to the Pinto and moved the Bug to the back of the rental lot, where it would be out of sight from the street. I put a note on the dash saying it was dead, and that a tow truck was on its way.

Parking the Pinto about forty feet from the Sheriff's office, I could see a city truck sitting in the drugstore parking lot. Strolling over, I casually looked in the window and found it empty. Back at the car, I set up the microphone and recorder and settled in for an afternoon of eavesdropping. At first there was nothing but white noise and the clackety-clack of a typewriter. The noise continued on; whoever was typing used the hunt-and-peck method. I heard a ripping noise and then someone cursing. I heard the sound of another sheet being rolled into the typewriter, followed by more clackety-clack. A minute later, the sound of a ringing phone and then, "Harrison County Sheriff's Department, Sheriff William Cooper speaking."

"Yeah, had to fill in some reports," Cooper said in response to something the caller said. "That right? Driving a blue VW? What's his name?"

"What do you mean, Gay, Gus, Gomer which is it?"

"No, I don't remember Goober from the Mayberry Show," said the Sheriff, letting his voice go higher. I guessed the Neanderthal from the service center must be the caller.

"Well, what did he look like? "

"What's this? A joke? Some midget with a faggy hair style named Goober was driving a Bug? You been drinking, Boone?" asked the Sheriff with a touch of suspicion. "So what did this midget-like person want?"

"Artie? What would he want with Artie? Don't suppose you happened to notice the plate number?"

"Let me know if you see him again."

Cooper no sooner hung up when I heard his voice again, "Jessie, I'm going out for a sandwich and then out on patrol. I won't be back for the rest of the day." I saw him coming out the front door ten seconds later. Good timing on renting the Pinto.

Chapter 25

Gabriel – Saturday Afternoon, Day 6

I tailed the Sheriff heading north on Highway 15. The microphone was picking up his radio chatter. He was talking to Car Number 14, and telling them that they should meet him at the Waffle House on Cedar Lake Rd. A few minutes later I watched as Cooper's cruiser pulled into the parking lot and parked near the entrance. I followed and found a parking space at the back of the lot in the shade under a magnolia tree in full bloom. I watched as Cooper went into the restaurant, and decided to call Ben from the phone booth outside it. This time, a different voice answered on the third ring and introduced himself as Detective Greenlaw. I asked for Ben and was told that he was currently unavailable. Greenlaw added that he was not aware of where he was or when he would be back. While I was on the phone, another cruiser pulled into the parking lot and Pumpkin Hair got out. I quickly turned my back to him, hiding my face.

I decided rather than risk being recognized, I'd go back and sit in the car and try to pick up the conversation through the listening device. Once I got settled, the microphone picked up a lot of background noises. They must have been sitting near the kitchen. I listened to the bits and pieces I could make out, and I realized that the Sheriff was telling him about a midget named Gay driving a Bug, asking about Artie and a white van. I heard a lot of laughter. I heard the waitress taking their orders for eggs, sausage and grits. Once the waitress had finished taking their order, I heard Cooper say, "So cool it and keep an eye out for gay midgets riding bugs," sparking another fit of laughter.

I mimicked their laughter silently, wishing they would move on and say something more interesting. The rest of their conversation was about sports. The Saints were playing the Lions on

Sunday, and the odds were long on the team from my hometown. They rambled on about their beloved Saints, Archie Manning this; Archie Manning that…I was about to get out and walk around the car when the Sheriff said, "A little birdie from Biloxi told me that someone's asking questions."

"That so? What were they asking?" responded a voice that I presumed belonged to the deputy.

"Initially it was about that girl, the one that interned with us a couple of months ago. The one we saw in the flyer the other day. Then, they wanted to find her daddy in California. Now I understand someone's asking about our time with Alex up at Ole Miss, and about what happened in Jackson."

The Sheriff's tone was relaxed and unconcerned. The reaction he received from the deputy was in sharp contrast. "Who the fuck is doing the asking?" the deputy said, his voice rising.

"Keep your voice down. There's a detective named O'Shea. He's the guy from up north. Not sure why he was asking, but I bet it ties in with someone asking about the white van."

"O'Shea? That's the guy who was in our office a few months back asking about the fire at Bud's club."

"Seems like he's been asking a lot of questions lately. I wonder what the connection is to the gay midget."

"I'm not gay. I'm not a midget, and I'm driving a Pinto you shits." I said aloud.

The noise in the restaurant all of sudden got loud and I only caught the odd phrase. It sounded like the deputy was asking what they should do about the old guy. Then the Sheriff's reply was muffled by someone in the kitchen calling out to the cook to hold the grits. All I picked up was the word accident.

The next voice I heard clearly was the deputy's, "So how much do you think they know about Artie?"

"I don't know. It's been 3 years and no one has come asking until now. Might be nothing," said the Sheriff.

"Tell your bro' there's nothing to fear about the van. I took care of it and there's nothing to connect anyone to anything."

A few minutes later I saw the door of the restaurant open and the two piled out. The deputy lit up a cigarette. With a newspaper up covering my face, I heard the Sheriff," I have a meeting tonight with Frank at the club. We're going to talk about that thing on Tuesday; and what to do about our friend Bud. I guess I'll ask him about the nosy detective too."

After they left, I hightailed it to the phone booth and tried Ben. Once again Detective Greenlaw answered and said he had left for the day, he didn't know where he'd gone or when he'd be back. I was about to leave a message when it occurred to me that I didn't know who the Sheriff was referring to when he said the birdie.

Chapter 26

Gabriel – Saturday Evening Day 6

By the time I hung up from Greenlaw, both the Sheriff and his deputy were gone. Cooper had said he wouldn't return for the day, so I decided to go back to his place and see if I could pick up his trail.

I slipped the Pinto into a parking spot along the curb about a block from their home. Sure enough, the cruiser was in the driveway, but Jacqueline's Cadillac was nowhere in sight. I tried the receiver to see if I could pick up anything. All I got was someone singing in a high voice coupled with the sound of the shower. "Well, you can tell, by the way, I use my walk, I'm a woman's man, no time to talk." I'd never been a big Bee Gees fan, but from now on, every time I hear the song I'll envision a naked William Cooper singing in the shower.

I settled in to wait for him to leave for his meeting with Frank. As night fell, I spied Cooper without his usual uniform and hat, at his front door in the glow of the house light. I gave him a head start to the end of the street before putting the Pinto in gear. With no receiver to listen to, I idly wondered where Jacqueline was.

Out on the main road heading into town, Cooper sped-up. The Pinto's automatic transmission responded sluggishly, feeling as full of elephants going uphill. Cooper started taking corners recklessly…as if he suspected a tail. I tried my best to stay with him, verbally whipping the Pinto. He turned onto Beach Boulevard, headed in the direction of the bars and restaurants. I saw him pull along the curb a few yards from the Rockaway Bar. This was the same place that Ben and I visited about three months ago because of the arson case. I remembered the owner, a guy named Carson, was less than forthcoming. As I drove by, I saw the Sheriff make his way to the main entrance. His choice of discarding the uniform started to make sense. As the Sheriff, you probably wouldn't want to be seen in a place like this. Ben said there was illegal gambling happening most nights. Judging by the cars in the parking lot the place must be full. Without the benefit of the listening device, it would be stupid to just sit here and wait. I decided to park on a side street. Donning my baseball cap and jacket, I put the camera in my coat pocket.

I heard the Rolling Stones' "Brown Sugar "even before I got to the door. As I entered the bar a kaleidoscope of flashing lights illuminated the room. To my left, couples were dancing; the lighting made them look like they were moving in slow motion. Cigarette smoke filled the room like a grey cloud. To my right, a buxom black woman was onstage dancing and swinging around a metal pole like Hulk Hogan in the wrestling ring. Once my eyes became accustomed to the dark I picked out the Sheriff sitting off at the far end of the stage. Beside him was Frank, the guy I'd seen in the woods; along with a huge creature that looked like the Incredible Hulk, except he wasn't green and didn't have red eyes. Cooper and Frank were deep in conversation. I spotted the only vacant table directly in front of the stage. I sat down and was immediately approached by a young lady with short hair, numerous tattoos and a skimpy outfit.

"What'll ya have buddy?" she asked, giving my table a wipe.

"Rye and Coke would be great," I replied, slouching and using the cap to shield my face from Cooper.

"I'm Amber. I'll look after you. Table dances are only a buck tonight!"

"Just the drink, please."

Cooper was about three tables over. I wished I wasn't sitting in the front. The stripper was now lying on her back pushing her pelvis up suggestively at me. The eyes of the crowd watched her gyrations. I thought about how I could possibly take a picture of Cooper sitting with Frank, without putting my life on the line.

Amber was back with my drink. Putting her hand on my thigh, she bent over and gave me a view of her cleavage. Her breasts were threatening to break out and make a run for it. "So would you like a little company?" I felt like telling her to take a hike, but instead I said maybe later.

I had an idea of how to take a picture of Cooper and his pals. I took my hat off and put it on my lap. I casually looked around and saw that Amber had caught the move with the hat and winked at me, making a disgusting motion with her hand. In my most casual move, I took the camera out of my pocket and placed it in my cap, putting it on the table with my coat covering everything. I took a few minutes to nonchalantly reach under my coat and position the camera so it pointed at Cooper through the opening at the back of the baseball cap. My timing was perfect as the audience was distracted by the stripper. A wild cheer erupted from the crowd. I looked up at the stage and saw that the stripper had donned propellers on her huge hooters. The crowd was clapping in rhythm as she made the propellers rotate clockwise. They gathered speed. The crowd really got rowdy when she heaved her enormous bosoms and made the propellers reverse direction. I took the opportunity while everyone else was riveted, to snap a few pictures of Cooper and his buddies.

I was congratulating myself on my ingenuity when Amber came by and tried to sit on my lap. "Want another drink lover?"

"Sure," I said, to get her off of me.

Standing she gave me a wink and said, "Let's make the next one a double?" I nodded in agreement. All of a sudden, the music stopped.

"Let's hear it for one of our home-town sweethearts…Brown Sugarrrrr!!!" I started clapping only because of the propeller thing. "In a minute, we'll be in for a real treat. The lovely and sexy Angela Foxxx will be taking the stage."

At the mention of the name, I looked over at Cooper, who was staring at the stage. I saw the bar owner Carson was now sitting at their table. Frank was doing the talking and waving his hands for effect. Across from Carson, the Incredible Hulk was glaring and cracking his enormous knuckles.

Returning with my drink, Amber purred, "Is there anything I can do to make your time at the Rockaway more memorable?"

Taking a sip of my drink, I tried not to gag at how strong it was. "I'll think about it."

The music of Chic singing Le Freak blasted over the loud speaker and a small Latino girl wearing a leopard-skin outfit came out dancing from behind the stage. She was a sultry, curvy girl in her early twenties with a chest that would make her plastic surgeon proud.

Brimming with confidence, I turned my camera to take a couple of pictures of Jacqueline's rival. I snuck a quick look at Cooper and saw his eyes were glued to the stage. I was sure she had to be the one. I was taking a few pictures of her acting like a snake writhing around the pole, when suddenly all hell broke loose. Two huge hands grabbed my shoulders and lifted me right out of my seat. "That's him. He's a pervert" yelled Amber, pulling my coat away to reveal the camera. The Incredible Hulk threw me to the ground. "What kind of sicko would come to a strip club and take pictures?" yelled Amber. "I saw him jerking off inside his hat too."

The music ended and was replaced by a deafening silence. Everyone was looking down at me. Hulk had my camera, turning it in his hands like a blind man trying to solve a Rubik's Cube. I slowly got to my feet and saw that Carson had joined the fray. He was looking at me trying to figure out where he'd seen me. Turning to the Hulk, he said "Give the perv back his camera. He turned to address me, "And you get the fuck out of here and don't ever come back."

The Hulk picked me up and threw me like a Frisbee towards the entrance. I scrambled to hold onto the camera. As I fell through the door, I once again heard the melodious sounds of the Bee Gees singing, "Stayin Alive."

Chapter 27

Gabriel – Sunday Morning, Day 7

I woke up Sunday morning with sore shoulders and the song "Stayin Alive" bouncing around in my head. When I'd gotten back to the room last night, I had taken a cab back to the Friendship Restaurant to retrieve my car. I parked it in the Trade Winds parking lot, once again thankful I had decided to rent another car.

I showered, changed, and headed to the office hoping to get a head start on the day and my meeting with Ben. On my way, I picked up a bag of a cop's favorite breakfast…jelly donuts. I jumped on the elevator at nine am sharp, humming "At the Copa."

Getting off on seven, I saw Ben must have beaten me in, as the office door was ajar. I started to say "So where have you…" except it wasn't Ben.

Sitting in my chair was a tall, wiry man with slicked-back, black hair. He was dressed in a black pinstripe and his cologne was peeling the paint off the walls. It was Frank from last night. A bunch of files were open on the desk. Standing next to him was the Incredible Hulk, holding Bourbon in his big mitts. I contemplated making a run for it, but I knew with that elevator, I would end up waiting like an idiot for five minutes.

"So Mr. Ross, you're a nosy little man," said Mr. Brylcreem.

"That a question?" I replied

"You shouldn't leave your door unlocked Mr. Ross," he said, closing the file.

"Why? You would have just slithered under the door."

"Tsk, tsk Mr. Ross, let's be friends. We're just looking for a little information. If you were to cooperate, then we would leave you and your little pussy alone."

"What do you want?" I asked, noticing Bourbon struggling to get away from Hulk. "You have poor tastes in associates; even the cat knows better."

"You might not want to antagonize Mr. Green."

"Seriously?" I said incredulously. "His name is Green?"

"Yes, Mr. Ross I believe you met Mr. Green at the club last night. Oh, and my name is Frank Galliano." He extended a hand which I ignored as if he were a leper. "First there's the little matter of last night. We may have made a mistake letting you maintain possession of your camera. I see you brought it to us this morning. Very considerate of you."

Frank gave the Hulk a nod, and my green friend abandoned Bourbon, taking my camera off my shoulder. He made a show of ripping the back open and pulling out the film canister. He squeezed the canister and the casing collapsed, exposing the film.

"I'm so sorry," said Mr. Green, the sound of his voice not at all suiting his physical attributes. He had a prepubescent Michael Jackson-like voice. "I'm sorry, I can be a little clumsy." He made a little sulky face and then broke out laughing like a moron.

"Nice voice, shit-head."

"Now Mr. Ross, what kind of vehicle do you drive?" Frank interjected.

"I ignored the question and nodded to the Hulk, "So, grease ball, if I throw a stick can he fetch?"

"It's not wise to antagonize Mr. Green. I believe you drive a VW bug, is that correct?"

"Only a dummy asks questions he already knows the answers to."

"Mr. Ross, I don't want to have Mr. Green throw you out the window." Mr. Brylcreem tried to pick up Bourbon, who hissed his lack of affection. "Maybe you would you like him to demonstrate with your kitty cat? Do you realize what a seven story drop does to a body?"

"Leave the cat alone." My right hand gripped the bag of jelly donuts. I could feel my blood start to boil.

"Okay, Mr. Ross," Frank said, getting up from the chair. I saw he was freakishly tall. "Your files don't have much in them; you should probably be more organized. What if someone wants to know about one of your cases?"

"Well then he can go fuck himself."

Frank gave me a disappointed look before nodding to the Hulk. I learned in public school there was only one effective way to deal with bullies, and that was to hit first. So when Hulk got in striking range, I slapped his fat face with my bag of jelly donuts. He responded with a right cross.

When my head cleared, I was looking up at him. I realized now, the bully rule only applied to grade school. He was circling for another blow when I saw with pride that the jelly donuts had stained his shirt.

"That was unfortunate. You shouldn't have provoked Mr. Green. I think you can avoid future unpleasantness by focusing your investigations in other areas. Would you like to expand on why you went to the garage asking about Artie and a white van?"

"I was looking for a good mechanic, but the monkey at the garage was as dumb as a stump." That crack earned me a kick to the ribs, making me curl up in pain.

"Are you sure you wouldn't prefer a more civilized conversation, Mr. Ross?"

I was ready to fight these assholes to the death. There was no way I would reveal anything to them. Mr. Green pulled back his leg as if he was going to drop kick me. I blurted out, "I went to the shop because one of my clients is worried about a missing girl, and someone thought they remembered seeing a white van belonging to the garage in the neighborhood."

"That's very interesting Mr. Ross. I am sure you realize now that you made a mistake as that business doesn't own a white van. There was also some talk about you following a certain Sheriff. I would like to tell you that he is a very important man in this town and doesn't like snoopy detectives."

Brylcreem tried to grab Bourbon, who had sought refuge under the desk and was now making an ungodly growling noise. "I advise you to focus your business on finding lost pets. I love most animals, except maybe your cat. I would hate to see anything happen to them."

With that, he walked over me and told the Hulk that I needed a reminder. Hulk proceeded to give me a ferocious kick in the head with his black loafer. After that I saw black loafer, black loafer, black loafer as he continued to hammer away at me. Finally, for good measure, the loafer found my kidneys. From the fetal position, I wondered which hurt more my back, my ribs or my head. My last thought before passing out was that I was pretty smart to change the film in the camera before coming to work.

Chapter 28

Gabriel – Sunday Morning, Day 7

Eventually, I crawled my way to my desk and pulled myself up onto my chair. Sitting at my desk, I put my head down and passed out. I stayed that way until Ben arrived at noon and shook me awake. "My God, you look like shit," he said as I sat back in the chair. "What happened to you?"

I mumbled "Just some comic book hero complaining about the service."

"You're getting quite a shiner. Where else does it hurt?"

"My ribs and my back." I said, as my head fell with a clunk back onto the desk.

"That must have hurt. I tell you what. Let me help you out to my car and you can bring me up to date on the way to the hospital."

I have no memory of how we got to the car or the ride to the hospital. I woke up in a hospital bed to find a doctor who looked like Colonel Sanders shining a pencil light in my eye. When he saw that I was conscious, he moved my head back and forth with his fingers, causing a wave of nausea. He followed this by poking me in the ribs like I was a piece of chicken.

"You're a lucky man Mr. Ross. Would you like to hear the diagnosis? "I nodded my head which made the room tilt sideways. "You have a concussion. Whoever hit you really did a number on you. Of course, you have a black eye which will go away in a couple of weeks. If you keep ice on it, it won't go away any faster but it won't hurt as much. Your friend here, Detective O'Shea said you were kicked in the kidneys as well as the ribs. We X-rayed and you have inflamed kidneys and a broken rib. Both situations are painful but will heal in time. We would like to keep you around for the rest of the day, but you should be able to go home with some bandages tomorrow afternoon."

I was waiting for an explanation about why I was lucky. Finally I asked.

"The kind of man who would do this to you, could have just as easily killed you." I nodded and closed my eyes. "I've given you a tranquilizer to help with the pain," Colonel Sanders said before leaving.

The next time I woke again it was dark outside. Ben was asleep in the chair next to the bed. I made a coughing noise which woke him from his nap.

'Hey, Partner. From what the Doc said it sounded like a truck hit you."

"It wasn't the truck it was the green guy, you know, the Incredible Hulk. He decided he needed field goal practice."

"The Incredible Hulk? Did you get a NAME?

"Green." I said in between grunts of pain.

"Well, nice to see you haven't lost your sense of humor. The Green Incredible Hulk, that's funny. Now, what's his real name?" he said, laughing.

My sore ribs were warning me not to laugh. I paused for a minute or two, to gather my energy. What eventually came out was practically a scream. "It was Frank, the fuckhead Galliano and his pet gorilla Mr. Green. They wanted to send a message about the way I do my job."

"Okay, I got it. Frank and his bodyguard paid you a visit and did a number on you. What set them off?"

"I hit him with a bag of jelly donuts."

Ben looked at me, and took a step back, like he thought whatever craziness I had might be contagious.

"It's a long story. If you promise to not make me laugh then I'll tell you."

I started by telling him about the white van seen in Rebecca's neighborhood "Just like with the other girl; I couldn't remember her name. I figured that the truck belonged to Artie, who they said was dead but still hanging around somewhere. There was a real creepy guy who told me that they don't have a white van, but it turns out that the creep is the Sheriff's brother. I overheard that at Waffle House, I wasn't in the Waffle house but inside my Pinto. But inside the Waffle House Cooper was meeting with Pumpkin man. I have the conversation on tape for you. Oh and he said there was a birdie in your department and he knows you did background checks on Pumpkie."

Ben's mouth was agape as he listened and tried to make sense of everything I said. He turned to leave, saying he was going to find the doctor.

"No - wait. So I followed Cooper to a titty bar, the one we went to a while back. I had to go in on account of him not wearing his hat. He met with that guy Frank and the Incredible Hulk. I took some photos for you. There was a stripper there with huge coconuts with propellers. I tried to take more pictures, but they caught me and thought I was a pervert. I went into the office today expecting to meet you, and there were these jelly donuts and well, things went dark from there. "

"Tell you what Gabriel, why don't you rest some more and I'll come back a little later and we can go over it again."

"You have to check on Jacqueline, she wasn't there!" I blurted out in a panic.

Chapter 29

Gabriel – Sometime Monday Morning –Day 8

Ben returned on Monday, the following morning. I was feeling a little better but all my damaged parts still hurt. Getting up to pee in the middle of the night was an adventure. I was dizzy from either the concussion or the painkillers. Like a dog, I think I may have left my mark on just about everything.

"Feeling better?" he asked putting a bag of jelly donuts in front of me.

I looked at his green sports jacket with a blue tie on a red shirt. "Did you wear that outfit for me? It's giving me a headache."

"Are they still releasing you today?"

"I'm not sure. The Doc said he would check me out this morning and then decide."

He pulled out his notebook. "I need to go over a few details of what happened yesterday. Are you up for that?"

I said yes and recapped what had happened on Saturday and Sunday morning. He followed along, making notes in his book and asking the occasional clarifying question. When I was done I asked about Jacqueline.

"She's fine; we took the listening post truck by their house last night and both cars were in the lane. The listening device you set up worked like a charm and we got pretty well a whole episode of Columbo."

"You heard her voice?"

"Yeah," he said tiredly "they got into an argument about the show and whether Peter Falk was realistic as a detective."

"So what's the verdict?"

"The Sheriff said it was all crap and not at all realistic. Jacqueline said she thought the rumpled raincoat and the dumb act was a smart way to get people to underestimate him. Interestingly, she also said that in real life no one is really who they make themselves out to be.

"Is that why you wear all the goofy outfits? So people will think you're a doofis?"

"Ha, Ha, Did you know that the producers originally approached Bing Crosby to play the part?"

"Interesting, so where does that leave us?"

"We can pick up Frank Galliano and this Mr. Green and charge them with assault as long as you're willing to press charges." With a smile he added, "It might, I repeat might, force them to make a mistake, and we can arrest them for murder once they finish you."

"I said don't make me laugh. I meant about the cases…first the missing teens."

"Well there's still nothing from the APB or all of the posters and the tip line. Mrs. Glaswell is willing to mortgage her house to raise the money for a reward. I haven't decided whether to let her do that. You have a witness who can tie Artie's van to the neighborhood, but that's pretty circumstantial. Besides, I checked and Artie, the owner, disappeared a few years ago. He had a partner who eventually took over the business. And there is no white van registered."

"A partner? Let me guess....the Sheriff's brother?"

"Forget Columbo - you should be on TV. There has been one other case involving a missing blonde teenager in the first half of this year, but that happened up in Abbeville. The folks up in Jackson are not talking about why Franklin, or as you refer to him, Pumpkin Hair," he added for my benefit "left the force. I have to go up to meet a colleague in Jackson tomorrow, so maybe I can go in and see if anyone is willing to talk off the record. We could always bring the deputy in on a fishing expedition, but that might backfire on us."

"What about the case against the Sheriff for all the shit he lets happen in Biloxi?"?

"I think without any real evidence you're back to square one and the word of a popular, elected official against a detective talking about green men, jelly donuts, and ladies with coconuts and propellers." He started to laugh again.

"I have the recording of the two of them in the Waffle house."

"I want to hear it when you get a chance, but keep in mind what I said. That wiretap wasn't under the order of the court, so it's not admissible. As a matter of fact, it is technically illegal since Cooper never gave you permission to record his voice."

"That's just stupid...so we have nothing." I said in desperation.

Like the good friend he was, Ben understood how I felt. "Not at all Gabriel. Because of you, we have an ear inside the Sheriff's office, we know there's something big about to go down, and you confirmed that he was cheating on his wife." He took a breath. "Say, did the stripper really have propellers or were you delirious?"

I gave a laugh and said "Yeah and don't forget I have the pictures, I hope. It will show the Sheriff consorting with a known Mafia bad guy."

"I thought you said something yesterday about the green guy destroying the film?"

"Hulk ruined what he thought was the film but I had already taken that roll out. I just need to take it somewhere to get it developed."

"Great, there's a Fotomat right by the Trade Winds. The department uses them for rush jobs. They've never let us down. The outfit specializes in overnight processing."

"Ben, before you leave, where have you been the last little while? I called in to update you a couple of times and got a guy named Greenlaw. He wouldn't tell me anything."

"I left early on Saturday, caught a 24 hour bug or something. I went home, unplugged the phone and slept the whole day."

"What about the little birdie in your office that Cooper was referring to?"

"I don't know. They know about us looking at Rebecca's Dad, and our investigations up in Jackson, but they don't seem to know about the listening device. That narrows it down. I suppose someone could have overheard something."

"I didn't hear everything but they were talking about what to do about you. The next thing I heard was the word accident."

"I'll watch my back and be extra careful about people hanging around and eavesdropping."

I felt very tired and dozed off while Ben sat in the chair. Around eleven I woke up when the Doc came in to do his exam. According to him, I was making progress, although I didn't quite feel like I was. He asked me if I felt well enough to go home to bed.

Surprisingly this was a big decision for me. Bigger than it should have been. Physically I still felt and looked like crap. But something else was bothering me. I couldn't help feeling outmatched in almost every way. Despite knowing more about crime in Biloxi, we were no closer to arresting anyone, or telling Mrs. Glaswell what had happened to her daughter. I knew taking on a private detective job would be a stretch for an accountant from Michigan. I hadn't figured on taking on the Mafia and some crooked cops... Had the job been about checking out job references, doing background searches and yes, looking for stray dogs, then I would have been fine. "Let me think about it, and see how I feel this afternoon."

Once the Doc left, a nurse came in and said my friend Detective O'Shea went for coffee but he left a message in case you woke up. She pulled out a piece of paper from her uniform and read, "Tell Gabriel that we heard on the recording that Cooper and Jacqueline are planning to go to New Orleans this weekend."

I looked at the nurse and said, "Can you help me on with my clothes? There's something I have to do."

Chapter 30

Gabriel – Monday Afternoon, Day 8

As the nurse was tying my shoes, Ben came back with coffee. He helped me out to his car and I caught a glimpse of my reflection in his side mirror. My face looked like a baboon's butt, all yellow, red and purple. The Doc had given me some painkillers but I was trying to wean myself off them. We drove in silence for a few minutes.

"You know Gabriel, when the nurse was setting up the IV in your arm she had to roll your sleeve up, we saw a tattoo that said, "No Guts, No Glory." Does that have a special significance to you?"

"I have a friend named Phil. We've been friends for as long as I can remember. All my life I've had to struggle with my height and the bullies at school. Phil was the one that taught me how to stand up for myself. I still remember it was our first day of high school." I recalled it as clearly as if it happened yesterday instead of over ten years ago. "That summer we had gone to see some war flicks like the Guns of Navarone and the Dirty Dozen. We were constantly quoting famous lines from the war movies. Like 'I came, I saw, I conquered' or 'I have not yet begun to fight.' The first day of high school we went to the cafeteria for lunch. I remember we were excited about eating in a real cafeteria; you know the ones that sold burgers, dogs and fries. Phil and I split an order of fries and were sitting at a table minding our own business when a big kid named George Lamont came over. Lamont was a pure bully. The school was full of stories about how a kid had to be taken by ambulance with a broken arm because of him. He walked up to our table along with a bunch of his groupies and started in with us."

"Hello wimps," he said, looking down at us. We just nodded, hoping that he would go away. "How are the fries?" He reached down and took one off the plate.

"Get your own," Phil said in a cold, detached voice. The tone in Phil's voice suggested trouble was brewing.

"What's your name shrimp?" he said to me, ignoring Phil's comment.

"My name's Gabriel."

"Sounds kind of faggoty, are you a fag Gabriella?" He snickered with his groupies as if he was the funniest comedian around. I didn't want to make eye contact so I looked down, hoping he would get bored of us.

When I didn't respond, George reached over and took another one of my fries, making a show of dipping it in Phil's ketchup before popping it in his mouth. His groupies burst out laughing. At that point, things seem to happen pretty quickly. I turned to Phil and said "No Guts, No Glory", and then standing up, I hit George in the face as hard as I could.

Phil jumped up to help, but the battle ended almost as quickly as it started. George was looking up at me, ketchup all over his face, saying he would get me. "I'll see you after school, kid." A teacher with supervision duty jumped in and separated everyone.

"Phil and I both got suspended, despite the fact that we received a round of applause from the other kids in the cafeteria."

"Did George ever follow up on his threat?"

"He would have but Phil beat the crap out of him before he had a chance. I learned an important lesson that day about standing up for myself. When we graduated high school Phil bought me a graduation present. It was the tattoo."

"Phil sounds like a great friend, is he the one who suggested you come down here?"

"Yes, we stay in pretty close contact. I know if I ever needed him than he'd be down here in a flash." We had arrived at the Fotomat, and I struggled to move my body out of the car.

"Did you want me to wait and drive you over to the apartment?"

The Trade Winds was across the parking lot, so I told him I was fine and that I really appreciated all that he had done for me.

"Listen, once you drop off the pictures off you might want to get to bed, no guts no glory today, ok?"

"Sure thing." I said, closing the car door and hobbling to the store.

The kid behind the counter asked "What truck ran into you, little man?" scrunching his face together as if this would make him more empathetic. I responded by asking if he could have the film ready by this time tomorrow.

"Sure no problem, all I need is your name and contact number." Passing over the film I gave him my personal information. "There's a store a couple of doors to the left that sells sunglasses. You might want to get a pair; you know, cover that up," pointing at my face.

It wasn't a bad suggestion, so I went over and bought a pair of Ray-Bans. The sign advertised that having four eyes has never been this cool. Of course, I did my best to ruin my coolness by my unusual walk across the parking lot. The only way I could walk without pain in my kidneys was to stand straight up, stiff as a board. A couple of feet of this and my ribs would start to hurt, and I would curl over. There I went across the parking lot straighten, curl over, straighten, and curl over, like a human centipede.

I finally made it to the elevator and decided that I needed pain relief. I popped and dry swallowed a couple of capsules as I stumbled down the hall to my apartment. The pain relievers hadn't quite kicked in by the time I opened the door to see my apartment had been torn to shreds. Some crazed cushion ripper had gone nuts looking for something. I hobbled and stumbled around the apartment looking at the devastation. When I got to the bedroom, I was overjoyed that the only pillow not gutted was the one on my bed. That's when I passed out.

Chapter 31

Gabriel – Monday Evening, Day 8

I awoke with an awful headache around eight o'clock that evening. Getting out of bed, I hoped the trashing of the apartment had been just another dream. It wasn't. Whoever had done this was looking for something or had a huge hate on for pillows. I made a call down to the manager Mr. Ahmed, and left him a message about the break-in and vandalism. The apartment came furnished, so whoever broke in destroyed a lot of crappy apartment furniture. Ten minutes later there was a knock on the door. It was Arnie Sims, the caretaker who had saved me that day at the beach. I let him in and he turned and examined the door. "There are no scratches on the lock" he pronounced.

"So the guy didn't use a pick?" I asked.

"No, just a credit card." He demonstrated how easy it was to open the locked door by using a plastic card. "I've been after Mr. Ahmed for years to equip each suite with a deadbolt, but he's too cheap." Arnie made his way into the living room and whistled at the destruction. He looked at me and said, "You pissed in someone's cornflakes?"

"I don't think so. I think they were looking for something that I don't even know I have. The break-in didn't make a lot of sense to me; I didn't have anything worth stealing. The bad guys thought they had destroyed the film so it couldn't be about that. My equipment was in the trunk of the Pinto, and the film was with me. Taking a knife to my couch was unnecessary.

"Maybe so, but I don't think so," he said as he made his way around the apartment.

I watched him as he looked out the window. The apartment was on the sixth floor and the window faced north and overlooked the parking lot. "If they weren't looking for something than maybe it was someone with a pillow fetish."

"Not hard to figure out who it was," he replied.

"Really? Who?"

"The same guy that trashed your VW. You can see it from the window. Even from here I can see that the driver's window's been smashed."

I went to the window and sure enough the car had been vandalized. "You said you knew who did it…?"

"Not exactly. I said it wouldn't be hard to figure out who it was. There's a difference." I think Arnie could tell from my puzzled look that I wasn't keeping up. "Listen, if they were lookin' for somethin' then there would be drawers pulled out, things yanked out of the fridge …not just a bunch of cushions ripped up. No, this is about sendin' you a message."

"Ok maybe…but whom?"

He looked at me and shook his head. "I thought you were the detective. If you can't think about whose cornflakes you might have pissed in, then ask yourself who knows that you drive a blue VW?"

We were interrupted by the ringing of the phone. I picked up and was assaulted by Mr. Ahmed's voice. I'd met him when I first signed the lease and it was his wife who had cleaned the carpets last week. The family was from Pakistan and it didn't take long to realize that he was very upset. "Golly, golly, golly, this is a very, very, very bad thing. Ve have had noooo problems until this. Who is going to pay?" he added, "You have some very, very bad friends Mr. Ross."

"Mr. Sims is here with me and whoever did this, were not friends." I gave Mr. Ahmed Ben's number and suggested that he coordinate with him. The prospect of getting the police involved seemed to make him a little happier. He said he was going to call Mr. Ben right away.

As Arnie was leaving he told me that there would be some insurance papers to sign and that in the meantime I might want to put something heavy against the door. "Oh, and I'll speak to Ahmed again about a deadbolt."

I thought back to the conversation in the car. I'd been overcome with self-pity because of the lack of progress and the ass whopping, and questioning whether or not I was wasting my time trying to be Columbo. Looking at my tattoo and thinking back to the story I told Ben gave me a weird kind of resolve. The thought of Jacqueline going off to New Orleans with Cooper at the end of the week was my deadline. I needed to get things resolved before then.

I called Ben at home and told him about my apartment. He said he'd send people over to check it out. "So what do you think they were looking for?"

"I don't have a clue, but they trashed the VW so this tells me that it's got something to do with the sheriff." I shared Arnie's thoughts with him.

"That's a good theory. If they were looking for something, they could have just beaten it out of you. Oh and by the way, we should get together tomorrow and listen to Monday's tape recordings."

"Have you listened to any of it?"

"I listened to some of it today and heard Cooper telling his wife about going to New Orleans."

"I got the message you left with the nurse. Did he say when they were planning on going?"

"I don't remember the whole conversation but I had the impression that it was this coming weekend."

I reminded Ben of the conversation in the woods and that one way or another Jacqueline wouldn't be going to New Orleans. "Was there anything about the delivery on Tuesday night?"

"Nothing. Oh, there was one cryptic call that might interest you. Other than that, I didn't hear anything about Tuesday's delivery."

"What was the cryptic call?"

"The caller was a woman with a bit of an accent. Maybe Mexican. She didn't identify herself, but Cooper was familiar with the voice. She asked if they were still on for tonight and he said 10 p.m. She said something about propellers, so until I heard about your stripper I thought it was code for a drug delivery coming in by airplane."

"Did she say Tuesday? What about the location?"

"No, she just said 10 p.m. She didn't give a location, just that propellers would be flying."

"Did she sound like a girlfriend?"

"Hard to tell, there was nothing obvious. To me it sounded like she was his boss telling him what she expected him to do." We made plans to get together at eleven the next morning.

Before he hung up, he added, "Have a good night Gabriel, tomorrow's another day."

I grabbed the telephone book off the kitchen counter. There was no listing in Biloxi for Angela Fox. I tried Gulfport but struck out. I struck gold when I found an Angela Foxxx living on Aladdin Drive in Long Beach.

The cool night air felt good on my skin as I walked out to where I had parked the car. When I got to the lot I noticed that the creep with the cushion fetish had cut the VW's seat cushions and pulled the stuffing out. Thank goodness for Hertz!

I made a mental note to call my insurance agent in Detroit as I walked over to the Pinto. They obviously didn't know about the rental yet as it was sitting there untouched beside the VW. Putting the Pinto in gear, I made my way to Long Beach and the lovely and sexy Angela Foxxx.

It wasn't hard to find the address using my Texaco map. She lived along a long road heading north away from the beach. The house was a cute bungalow with a well-manicured yard with a small fountain out front. I opted to turn around and park on the opposite side of the street. I had an excellent view of the property. It was now 9:30 pm and I figured my imitation centipede walk back along the side of the road would take me a few minutes. There was a large picture window out front and a lane leading to the backyard.

The spring air smelled of honeysuckle and freshly cut grass. In the distance, I heard the short, vibrant trill sound of horny cicadas. I'd read somewhere that there was a species of cicada that only resurfaced every seventeen years and this was the year. Sure enough, they had planned their 17-year convention here in Biloxi. As I waited for the Sheriff, my back started to stiffen. I was trying to lay off the pain killers so that I could stay alert.

Adrenaline kicked in when I saw pair of headlights coming down the street. My Timex read two minutes to ten. I waited as the car turned into Angela's lane. The sky was clear, and the crescent moon gave me just enough moonlight to see it was the sheriff's cruiser. I waited and watched as Cooper got out of the cruiser and headed for the side door. I could make him out clearly from the porch light as he opened the door and went into the house. He was wearing his uniform, so I turned on the microphone and set the unit to record. I listened for a few minutes to ensure the signal was coming through.

"Hey Babe, you looked pretty hot the other night," came a voice I recognized as the sheriff's.

"What did you tell Jacqueline about tonight?" asked a female voice that must have belonged to Miss Foxxx.

"I told her I was running a stakeout."

"Well let's not disappoint her, come here… It's time to take that steak out, big fella." Angela said, imitating Mae West.

Ugh!!! I couldn't believe she said that! The cicadas' weren't the only horny creatures tonight. The recording would be great for the guys back at the department. I would have loved to listen to more of this, but Jacqueline was paying me to get photographs. I gathered up my camera and started making my way to the rear of the house where I hoped to find a window to the bedroom. Hoping that she didn't have a dog, I hobbled my way to the backyard. I was happy to see that they'd left the curtains open. I could hear Marvin Gaye's "Let's Get it On" coming through the open window.

Once again I heard Cooper singing, this time with a deep, creepy voice. "I've been really tryin', baby, tryin' to hold back these feeling for so long and if you feel like I feel baby, come on, oh come on, let's get it on." I had to exercise self-control and suppress my giggles. The window to the bedroom was too high for me. I imagined Cooper dancing around singing while Angela twirled her propellers.

I jumped up and down, hoping to catch a glimpse of them but the pain in my legs was too much. Finally I found an aluminum garbage can by the side door. That would get me up to eye level. Quietly dumping the garbage, I turned the can upside down and placed it below the bedroom window. It took a few minutes to painfully climb onto the wobbly can, while grabbing hold of the window. When I stood up, I saw a good size bedroom with a double bed pushed up against the far wall. On the bed, I saw Angela sitting astride Cooper, who was wearing his hat. Angela was bouncing up and down like she was riding a pogo stick. She was screaming "Yes baby, yes baby". Every couple of minutes her voice would go deeper, and she would say "Faster, harder." I had a pretty good view of the up and downs, which I captured on film. Changing into the missionary position, Angela cried, "Give it to me!"

Cooper responded with, 'I'm gonna plough you like a cornfield!" I couldn't help but let out a small laugh. Angela must have heard me as she looked over at me and let out a scream.

Cooper continued ploughing the cornfield, totally impervious. Angela finally got his attention and pointed to the window. Her scream was so loud it caused me to skitter off balance. I fell with a thud, flat on my face. The garbage can made a loud clanging noise alerting the neighbor's dogs and setting off a chorus of barking. With Angela continuing to scream, porch lights coming on, the clanging of the garbage can and now the barking dogs, it was time for me to get out of there. As I tried to catch my wind, I heard Cooper yell, "What was that?"

"There was a peeping Tom taking pictures of us …; he looked like a….baboon."

I knew that Cooper would come running out of the yard as fast as he could get dressed. I finally made it to my feet and hobbled quickly to the other side of the house. I heard the sheriff yell out, "Who's out here? You degenerate!"

I made my way down the side of the hedge crossing over to the neighbor's yard and the cover of their hedges. I lay there in the dark trying to muffle my pain while Cooper circled the house looking for baboons. He walked right by me, his foot a mere six inches from my hand. Eventually he gave up the search, probably hoping to rekindle the Marvin Gaye act. Sure enough, "Let's Get it on" started up again as I hobbled back to the car. Along with the pictures I'd taken, I now had a pretty good story to tell.

Chapter 32

Gabriel – Tuesday Morning, Day 9

I woke up Tuesday feeling sore all over from the previous night's fun and games. My mental state was improving now that I had conclusive evidence of Cooper's affair. A shower and shave further revitalized me, energizing me for my appointment with Ben. He'd said he wanted to go to the police station beforehand and check on his outstanding inquiries. The landlord had been in and removed most of the trashed furniture, leaving the apartment next to empty. He left a note to say this type of vandalism was most unusual and maybe I had taken up with the wrong crowd. He sure had that right.

I decided to call Jacqueline, hoping that Cooper had already left for the day. She picked up after a few rings, prompting me to say," Jacqueline, it's me Gabriel. Are you free to talk?"

"Ok, thanks for the reminder; I'll pick them up on Wednesday," she replied. "It's just the cleaners about the dress I sent for cleaning," she said, presumably speaking to Cooper, who must have been in earshot.

"I have the pictures for you; can we get together for lunch tomorrow at the same place?"

"That would be fine; I need the dress for Friday because I'm going to New Orleans with my husband."

"I'll see you at noon ok? And you're not going to New Orleans."

"Okay, I can pick it up tomorrow, thanks for calling."

I sensed the anxiety in her voice when she spoke about New Orleans. My hope was that Cooper was not as sensitive as me.

Grabbing a coffee at Dunkin Donuts, I picked up the local paper along with another bag of jelly donuts. I was hoping that I wasn't going to have to teach someone another lesson. I pulled into the Fotomat and inquired about yesterday's pictures. The same kid told me that I had beaten the truck, and that the delivery would be in a couple of hours. I had left last night's roll of film and asked that he put a rush on it as it was police business.

I headed into the office, parking the Pinto in the lot. I took my Ray Bans off once I got in the elevator and was momentarily startled at the baboon staring back at me in the reflection of the elevator door. The yellow and purple around my eyes seemed to be spreading. As I got off on the 7th floor I looked over at my closed office door. I slowly made my way down the corridor, my back and ribs reminding me of the beating. I held the bag of jelly donuts ready to strike.

"Hiya Mr. Ross," came a voice from behind, startling me. I turned around and saw the beaming face of Larry the superintendent. He was an aging black man, who never missed a greeting and loved to share a joke. I returned the greeting. "Say Mr. Ross, what happened to your face? It sure looks painful."

"Oh it's nothing, comes with the job."

"Well, you let me know if you need me to whup somebody," with that he did a little shuffle with his feet, raising his fists, juking back and forth like a boxer. I laughed and thanked him for looking out for me. A sense of relief came over me when I unlocked the door and found that they hadn't ransacked my office. I turned on the light and the fan and opened the window in case Bourbon eventually decided to show up.

I sat down and spread the Herald out on the desk. The major headline was about the escalating price of gas caused by the revolution in Iran. The revolutionaries had seized the means of oil production, creating instability in the markets. When I'd stopped at the Texaco station earlier to fill up, the price was a ridiculous 90 cents a gallon costing almost $10 to fill the tank. A secondary article was a report on the cleanup taking place in Pennsylvania due to the partial nuclear meltdown of the reactor on 3 Mile Island. I wasn't the only one in the midst of an energy crisis. I almost missed reading a small story buried at the bottom of page two. It was an update on the ongoing search for Rebecca Glaswell. The reporter quoted Biloxi Detective Ben O'Shea, saying the department was following up on a number of promising leads. He went on to say that the department was looking into the teen's disappearance in connection to other disappearances that had happened in the past. I wondered if Edith Glaswell was reading the story. Mrs. Glaswell bravely hung onto the belief her daughter would one day return and walk through her door.

My thoughts were interrupted by the ringing of the phone. I responded, "Eye on You Detective Agency – when you really need to know, Gabriel Ross speaking."

"Mr. Ross, it's Rachel Henderson from the Gulf Oaks mental hospital. Do you remember you wrote your number of the back of a card for me? You said you wanted to know if there was a change in Mr. Dermody's condition."

"Of course I remember. You were very nice and helpful when I came to visit…my stepbrother."

"I have something, but I'm not sure it means anything. I don't want to waste your time."

"That's alright Rachel, why don't you let me be the judge of that."

"I didn't know you're a private detective," she sounded impressed.

"Yes my partner and I opened the business about 6 months ago. Tell me about the change in Alex' condition," I said, taking a sip of my coffee.

"You know, for a man who hardly has any visitors, to have two new ones in just a couple of days might have been overwhelming for him. Especially since he hasn't seen his step brother for so long."

"Wait, did you just say that he had two visitors?"

"There was another gentleman here the next day from the local sheriff's department. He was here for maybe two minutes, not enough time really to have a proper visit."

"Did he leave his name or card?"

"He said his name was Franklin. He was about average height and build but had orange hair slicked back into a ducktail like Elvis Presley." I got the sense that she was trying to impress me with her powers of observation. She then added, "I thought Alex looked agitated after he left."

"Agitated? I thought you said his brain was disconnected from his body?"

"His eyes looked different, like they were frightened. I think seeing Deputy Franklin upset him. I had to sit with him and calm him. That's when I noticed his right hand moving ever so slightly. At first I thought it was a nervous twitch, but then another nurse said he might be trying to write something. I put a pencil in his hand. I had to hold it for him but he scratched out something on a piece of paper. It probably doesn't mean anything, but it might make sense to you, seeing you're a…gumshoe…you know, a private dick."

I laughed, thinking she was being a little flirty and remembering how attractive I'd thought she was. "Thank you Rachel, I can stop by on Wednesday afternoon. Will you be there to show me what you have?" Two people can play that game.

I hung up to the sound of Bourbon meowing on the window sill. I picked him up and put him on my desk. He proceeded to sniff my baboon face in a show of kitty concern. I tore off a piece of my jelly donut and gave it to him.

The next interruption was from Ben, who gave me a smile on arrival and said he was happy to see that my face wasn't resting on the desk. I laughed and invited him to sit down and share coffee and donuts with us.

"I have to ask Ben, I don't mean to offend but …what's with the outfit?" Today Ben had a striped sports jacket over a New Orleans Saints football jersey with khaki pants.

He held the jacket open and said "What do you mean? All my dress shirts are at the cleaners."

Bringing him up to date on the events last night in Long Beach earned me a scolding for taking unnecessary risks. He told me that on his way to the office the local radio station said the sheriff's department was looking into a peeping tom reported in Long Beach.

"That was me." I told him proudly, passing the recording to him.

"Did you get anything that we can use?"

"Not really but let's just say, this should be nominated for an award."

He pulled out his notepad. "I have a report on the break-in at your apartment. We talked to your neighbors and the apartment manager. He was quite upset over the company you keep. No one heard, or saw anything. Have you thought anymore about whether they were sending you a message or looking for something?"

"If they were looking then I mustn't even know I have it. Anything further on the tapes from the weekend?" I asked, finishing my coffee.

"Not really, pretty routine stuff. There was a conversation between Cooper and an unidentified male that made reference to Artie. We could hear both voices so whoever the other person was, they were in his office." Ben pulled out his notepad and continued, "The unidentified male asked Cooper if there was any way the Artie thing could come back on them. Cooper replied no at least as long as no one starts building a subdivision in the woods."

"So, the sheriff's brother Boone and Artie are partners and for whatever reason Boone knocks off Artie. Then Cooper, Boone and maybe the deputy cover it up by burying the body in the woods."

"Pretty close Gabriel. There are just a couple of other tidbits. One, the service center isn't worth much, but it is sitting on prime industrial land that has to be worth half a million. Two, we did a search on Artie's garage and found that the registered owner is Jacqueline Cooper."

I looked at him with a quizzical look spreading across my face. "I don't know, maybe you can ask her how she happened to own the service center."

As I sat there trying to make sense of things he continued, "We still don't know where the delivery is supposed to take place tonight. Greenlaw is going to pull overtime to watch the waterfront tonight. It's a waste of time given how much area there is to cover. I thought I would hang around the airfield north of town. Maybe you can tail Cooper and see if he leads you anywhere."

I nodded and asked if the inquiry on Deputy Franklin had come back.

"Officially the department is still saying no comment, but I have a friend in the FBI who did a little unofficial snooping. There was a case involving a missing girl up in Oxford. Somehow there is a connection between that case and Franklin. The contact said it had to do with evidence going missing. Anyway Franklin was asked to leave, either because he was incompetent, or somehow involved."

"You mean Oxford as in Ole Miss?"

"Yeah, that's when it gets real interesting," he reached for my pad and pencil and wrote down March 13th, 1968. "That's the year Dermody, Franklin and Cooper all graduated. It was also the year a young teenage girl named Jessica St. Paul disappeared. Guess what? She's blond and fits the age group. So we already know on February 23rd, 1973 Shannon O'Shays disappeared. On March 15th 1974, Anne Mullens goes missing and then one year later on February 11th 1975, Lynda Morrison goes AWOL. I had the FBI look into other parts of the state. There are girls missing up North in either February or March in 76, 77 and 78. We have

Rebecca Glaswell in 79. All of the girls are blonde, attractive and approximately 16 years old. Did you get a chance to look into that file I gave you?"

"Yes and you covered all the bases. I don't think Rose Marie's murder is connected to the other cases though. The victimology is different. She was younger at thirteen, and a brunette. Our guy likes blondes. Also the MO is different. Rebecca and the others just disappeared; you found Rose Marie's body in the river with a knife in her back."

"So where does that leave us?" Ben's expression showed that I had properly diagnosed the case.

"I think there's a serial killer. He has a preference for white, pretty blonde girls around 16 years old. What's more he visits the area every year for Mardi Gras."

"How do the sheriff and his deputy figure into this theory?"

"I don't know, but I bet they're involved somehow. They could be working with the killer or helping him get the girls with the white van."

"It wouldn't be the first time we had a serial killer in Mississippi. The FBI believes there's at least one active serial killer operating in each state of the union. That is except for Mississippi, where we probably have more than our share. Next to Louisiana, which is just a stone's throw from here, Mississippi has more murders per capita than any other state in the U.S. There are few things that don't fit the pattern though. First, the attempted abduction of Janice McVeigh by the guy in the white van took place in November. And the Rebecca Glaswell disappearance didn't happen until May."

"I think it might be worthwhile taking a picture of the sheriff's brother over to Janice McVeigh and see if she recognizes him."

"What makes you think he's the guy? I thought you liked the deputy for this?"

"Somehow I think the sheriff, his brother and the deputy are all involved. There's something about what the deputy said to the sheriff at the Waffle House. He told the sheriff, "Tell your brother not to worry." If his brother wasn't involved why would he worry? I don't know how this all fits together but I would stake my 6 month reputation as a private investigator, that they're all involved. As for Rebecca she might have been snatched to shut her up. Remember the scrapbook?"

We both looked at each other in silence. Ben got up to leave, closing his notebook. "I've made a note to get a picture of Boone Cooper over to Janice McVeigh."

Like they say in detective novels, the pieces of the puzzle were falling into place.

Chapter 33

Gabriel – Tuesday Afternoon, Day 9

After making a call to Mrs. Glaswell and assuring her that I was still on the case, I decided to check out something I'd been thinking about. Had Carson recognized me on Saturday night? If the answer to that was yes, then was that the reason he let me leave with the camera? Could he be ready to talk about the arson a few months ago, and his relationship with Cooper and Frank?

When I stepped outside, the heat hit me like a blast from an oven. It was hotter than the hinges of hell. Getting into the Pinto, I drove the half mile to the Rockaway. It was 3:30 in the afternoon when I pulled into the parking lot. My legs felt rubbery as I made my way to the front door. I had no desire to relive Saturday night's experience. My eyes took a moment to adjust to the darkness after I entered. I made my way to the bar where Amber was washing glasses with her back towards me. I caught her eye in the mirror behind the bar.

"Well, lookie here. If it's none other than Mr. Pervert himself. Looks like someone taught you a lesson or two," she said, working on a mouthful of gum like a cow chomping on fresh grass.

A dozen or so customers were seated at tables. "Is Carson around?" I asked, ignoring her comment.

"I think he told you to stay the fuck away."

"I think I'll take a chance that he'll talk to me for a few minutes. Why don't you make my visit more memorable by calling him for me?"

Amber rolled her eyes and yelled out, "Bud, you'll never guess who slinked in the door. The deviant from Saturday night says you'll want to talk to him."

Sitting down at my usual table, memories of propellers and being tossed around came back to me.

"Thought I told you to take a hike," a voice came from the entrance of the kitchen. He walked over to my table and started to laugh when he looked down at me. He pulled a chair over and sat down...it was my turn to laugh. The right side of his face was every bit as purple, yellow and red as mine. We were like twin cans of Budweiser. "Amber, bring us a bottle and two glasses," he commanded. His black eye was on the right side of his face, like mine.

"I don't suppose you know Mr. Green?" I said.

"Good guess. YOU must have made him really angry," he said, obviously feeling my bruise was uglier.

"He came to visit me on Saturday morning along with Frankie. I'm still not sure what I did to annoy him." I replied.

"Probably not much, they're just sending you a message to stay out of their business."

Amber put a bottle of Seagram's on the table and poured us each a couple of fingers. When she left I asked, "What makes you think I was in their business?"

"You were taking pictures of them under your coat. Mafia types and knuckleheads can be a little sensitive about that."

I held my glass up, making a toast "Death to Mafia types and knuckleheads." We clinked our glasses and took a healthy swig.

"Do you mind me asking why you let me leave with my camera on Saturday?"

"I remembered you from when you came in with that Biloxi cop trying to investigate the arson. I figured you were just trying to do your job."

"So that fire a few months ago, that was arson?"

He looked at me for a few moments, weighing how much he should say. When he shook his head, I tried to coax him, "Come on Carson, we're almost related," I pointed to the black eye. He smiled and said nothing good would come from talking about this. I felt he was about to say something else, and decided not to push.

After a few moments of silence, "My first warning was the arson, the second warning was the black eye, and there won't be a third."

"Because you decided to do whatever it is they want or because the next time there won't be a tomorrow?"

He didn't reply. I was making progress, so I sat there quietly with him. "Do you want some advice?" he finally asked.

I nodded.

"These are serious people, and this is their town. The best advice I can give you is either get out or find a new job. That's what I'm going to do."

I felt like I was in a bad western, the kind where they try to get the new sheriff Alan Ladd, to leave. I waited to see if he would elaborate, but he downed his drink and got up with a final chuckle after looking at my face. I finished my drink, and I thanked him for not throwing me out again. As I walked to the door, I saw my friend Amber hanging up the phone.

Chapter 34

Gabriel – Tuesday Evening, Day 9

On the way back from the bar I stopped by the Fotomat and picked up two different envelopes of pictures. Entering the lobby of the Trade Winds, I tried my best to avoid the manager's office and ducked into the elevator. I opened the door to my apartment and saw they had removed the vandalized furniture. The place was as empty as a bird's nest in December. Hopefully I still had a bed.

I gave Ben a call. He confirmed the stakeout was still on for the airfield and the pier that night. He and Greenlaw would be in position with some members from the local DEA office. I told him I planned to leave shortly to pick up the Sheriff's trail.

"Ok, but no crazy stuff, just follow him and see where he goes," he responded.

Parking the Pinto about a half block from Cooper's house, I saw that neither of their cars was in the driveway. I was debating about going downtown to see if he was still at work, when a sudden knock on the driver's window startled me. Relieved, I saw Travis' smiling face looking in at me quizzically. I rolled down my window, "Just coming home from school?"

He flashed me a grin, holding up his Star Wars lunch box, "Geez you really are a private detective, Tab!" I laughed and asked how school was, to which he rolled his eyes and said "boring."

Stepping back and looking at the Pinto, "Who gave you permission to bring this piece of crap onto my land?" he asked in that imperious tone of his. When I didn't answer right away he gave me a sad look, "Seriously, where's the cool car?"

"I thought this car would help me blend in better. Not so noticeable."

"How's our microphone? Is it still working?"

"Absolutely, and we picked up some valuable information already." My attention was drawn back to the house as the Sheriff pulled into his driveway in an unmarked car. I activated the receiver as Cooper got out of his car and stomped his way to the house.

"Hey, can I sit in with you and listen?" asked Travis.

"If he comes out he might recognize you from last week, so you'd better hold this newspaper up for cover." I felt it only fair to let him listen in for a while.

Something about the way Cooper moved made me nervous. He normally had an easy stroll, today he was walking fast with a determined look. The receiver picked up the sound of the door slamming and then Cooper's voice yelling out for Jacqueline. Some muffled noises came across, causing us to speculate who else might have been in the house. I heard Cooper talking to himself and thought I heard the word "bitch". The receiver picked up a crash in the distance like someone threw a bunch of bottles against the wall. We heard James Brown singing about feeling like a sex machine. Ugh, I prayed that Cooper didn't start to sing. The signal was weak; I figured he must have taken his hat off by the front door.

Travis and I listened for more, but the sound became even fainter. A few moments later we heard the ringing of a phone interrupted by the Sheriff's voice yelling "Where are you?" The caller must be Jacqueline. With us only being able to hear one side of the conversation, the bug was nearly useless. Travis thought he heard "Wifey". This supported my thought that the caller was Jacqueline.

After Cooper hung up, the receiver picked up nothing but white noise. Travis and I occupied our time talking about school, movies and music. It came down to: Travis hated school, but loved Star Wars. He also enjoyed listening to Bruce Springsteen; his favorite song being "Born to Run." The conversation turned interesting when I asked him about living in Biloxi.

"It's okay I guess, I don't have much to compare it to. My family is from up in the Delta but we moved here when I was a baby. Every summer my sister and I visit my grandparents on their farm. I have uncles and aunts and a whole pile of cousins up there too."

"So what brought the family down here?"

"I think it was because Dad got a new job."

"And what does your Dad do for a living?" I was slyly working up to asking him where he lived; I was also pretty sure his last name wasn't Carter.

He interrupted the interrogation by pointing at Cooper walking out to his car wearing street clothes. "Look, I think the suspect is leaving."

"Listen Travis, it's after 6 and your folks are going to be wondering where you are, so you need to bolt, otherwise I'm going to lose him."

Travis started to balk, but unlike last time, he opened the door, making me promise that there would be another adventure for us to go on together. I pulled the car from the curb as Cooper turned right at the stop sign.

As I pushed the car to keep up, I thought about Travis and his rich fantasy life. He was a great kid and I wondered whether our adventures would be something he'd treasure later in life. I hoped his father had the kind of job that allowed him to spend time with him. I don't know why, but for some reason I doubted it.

I caught up to Cooper on Atkinson Road, in the distance the sun dipped below the horizon like a candle being extinguished. The sheriff was putting the pedal to the metal, which forced the Pinto's 4 cylinder, vacuum cleaner engine to strain. He started taking corners with little warning. He took a quick left on Popps Ferry Rd. He either failed driver's education or he was trying to spot a tail. He was now heading south towards the Gulf. It was easier to spot a tail out on this road where there were fewer cars and stop signs or traffic lights. I eased up on the gas, letting a couple of cars pass me. After about ten minutes he pulled into a Texaco station which had an adjacent cafe. I pulled into the gas station and parked away from him near the restaurant. Not being sure what to do, I decided to wait in the car and observe. He was sitting in his car as the attendant refueled his car. When he was done I watched as the attendant and Cooper exchanged friendly greetings and the sheriff parked the cruiser in front of the café. As he got out and went into the café, I wondered whether this could somehow be the delivery spot. How could I confirm who he was meeting with, without leaving the car? I didn't want to risk being seen. He'd had more than a good look at me last Saturday night. Despite Ben's voice of caution playing at the back of my mind, I decided to risk going in. From the safety of the vestibule, I made like I was reading the community board. Taking a quick peek I saw him in a booth at the back, alone.

Ever since my close encounter with the Incredible Hulk, I'd had a renewed sense of self-preservation, so I went back to the car and waited. I watched to see if a dinner partner showed up. A steady flow of truckers and senior citizens entered the cafe. Not exactly the profile of a nefarious smuggler. I sat and waited the better part of an hour. In the night sky the crescent moon hung like a giant finger gesturing for me to leave before it was too late. My mind wandered to something from the early days of my partnership with Ben.

Chapter 35

Gabriel – 5 Months earlier

I arrived at the office to find that Ben had already beaten me in. Looking up from the chair behind my desk he said, "I have something special for you today Gabriel."

"Geez, I don't know, I already had a full day planned. I had a meeting scheduled with Larry the janitor about a proper sign for the door, a long overdue lunch with the pigeons in the square and some more action photos of Bourbon."

He insisted, and said it was a matter of life and death. My curiosity eventually won out and we headed out to his car. Getting in, he said it would involve a short road trip. He put the car in gear and headed north towards D'Iberville.

"So what's this special surprise Ben?"

"You'll see soon enough. How do you feel things are going?"

"Pretty good, I finished the file on the divorce case you referred and have a couple of other things to work on. I made some solid contacts for some insurance work, and I have a lunch next week with a local lawyer about doing some contract work. I still think we need to do some advertising to get things moving though."

"Money's pretty tight. Keep in mind it's still early days and neither of us are originally from Biloxi. You'll see once you have a few more cases under your belt, the agency will become better known. How are you feeling about detective work?"

"So far everything's been pretty routine. It's been fun learning from you, and I'm getting better at things like surveillance and background checks. I'm also getting satisfaction from catching dirt bags cheating their employer, or some husband cheating their spouse."

He nodded quietly as he drove past D'Iberville and continued on Highway 67. We drove in silence for a while. Ben turned into a lane leading to a gravel parking lot. A sign advertised the Gulf Coast Rifle & Pistol Club.

"Wait Ben, I don't like guns."

"If you're going to be a detective in gun country you need to be able to protect yourself."

"Jim Rockford said real private detectives don't need guns."

"Maybe on TV, where the bad guys are only actors. Here in Biloxi everyone has a gun. Mississippi has virtually no restrictions on guns. I got my hair cut the other day, and the barber had a gun."

"So is this the "special" surprise?"

"No, this is." He opened his jacket and removed a handgun. I'd seen enough detective shows to recognize a 38 snub-nosed special. The revolver had a short barrel and an imitation wood grip.

"Is this your gun?"

"No, I recovered it a few years ago. Someone filed off the serial numbers, so it's not traceable."

I got out of the car and reluctantly followed him into the clubhouse. He must have been a regular because everyone seemed to know him. He had us signed in, and out on the shooting range in no time. He gave me a quick lesson on gun safety and how to load the revolver. Demonstrating the proper technique, he showed me how to stand, how to balance myself and how best to hold and aim the gun.

"In your mind imagine that there's a magnet between the end of your revolver and the target. Remember to breathe and on the exhale, squeeze the trigger."

The target was thirty feet away. I followed his instructions, but all of a sudden the gun felt heavy and my hands started to tremble. I relaxed and took a few deep breaths and fired off a shot. Immediately the gun kicked back in my hand causing my shot to go skyward. I waited for the dead duck to fall at my feet.

"That's called recoil. The .38 has less recoil than most guns. Once you've practiced a bit then you won't notice it much."

I tried again and continued to fire at the target until I was out of ammunition. I reloaded, and Ben cracked that I should shoot first and claim whatever I hit, was the target. When we were done I thanked him for the lesson and the gun, knowing that if Jim Rockford didn't need a gun, then chances were I didn't either.

Chapter 36

Gabriel – Tuesday Evening, Day 9

My thoughts were brought pack to the present as I spied Cooper amble back to his car. There was no one else around. I was suddenly consumed with the urge to get out and confront him. I didn't like him; I didn't like his walk; I didn't like his face. It was a face that enjoyed hurting people. There was no way I was going to let him hurt Jacqueline. I'll admit that it had occurred to me in the hospital that running away had seemed attractive. Looking at him now, I knew he would be the one running. I was still imagining the beating I planned to lay on him, when his car pulled out back onto the road.

I fired up the Pinto and followed at a discreet distance. It was now almost 9:30 and I still had no clue about his final destination. I hoped Ben was doing better on his stakeout.

Cooper hung a left onto Pass Rd heading into town. It was almost 10:00 when he took another left onto Rodeo Road. We were almost at Kessler Air Force Base. He slowed down and pulled off to the side of the road and parked behind a cargo van. I slowed down and pulled off approximately 300 yards behind. I was parked too far away to hear any voices, and I didn't want to risk driving any closer. I turned off the engine and lights. The telephoto would be useless in the darkness.

To my right was a fence separating the road from the air base. To the left, a field dotted with the odd southern pine. Willing my aching body, I decided to do what Ben would call "crazy stuff". I took the bulb out of the overhead light and opened the car door as gently as I could, letting out a silent curse as the door gave a creaking noise. Hovering close to the ground, I moved quickly to the field. My plan was to commando-crawl my way parallel to the van and listen. After a few minutes, I was exhausted. Not wanting to make a sound, it took me a good ten minutes to get to where I could clearly hear the conversation. Under the light of Cooper's headlights, I saw a couple of shapes.

"Any problems getting the merchandise?" asked a voice that I recognized as Cooper.

I thought the other guy might be military. Maybe it was the way he carried himself or the way he spoke, or maybe it was because he was standing beside an army truck.

"No sweat, where are the monkeys?"

"They'll be here. When they arrive you might want to be careful what you call them. They're a little sensitive. So did you get everything on the shopping list?"

"I put in a dozen Colt 1903's that they decommissioned in 1970. There are a half dozen confiscated AK 47's that are in good condition. I got my hands on 10 Ingram Mac-10a. I threw in a couple of Mossberg's 500 shotguns, as well as some night scopes and ammunition. Enough to start a small war."

"That will make Mr. Escobar very happy."

I wondered if he was referring to Pablo Escobar, the Columbian drug lord that had been in the papers lately. I heard another vehicle coming from the opposite direction. The military guy turned and lit a cigarette. The new vehicle was another van, and it stopped kitty-corner to the other van. Stepping out were two men, each holding what looked like machine guns.

"Beuna Tardo, Senor Cooper."

"Evening Luis, this is my associate Mr. Brown," I wondered if Mr. Brown knew Mr. Green.

Luis nodded to Brown, not offering a hand. I guess those conventions don't apply to monkey drug dealers. In heavily accented Spanish, the one named Luis said, "Before we do this I suggest we both inspect the merchandise."

Brown nodded and waved Luis to the back of his van. Opening the door, he said "There you go, I was telling Cooper here, I got everything on your shopping list. Everything is in working condition, and ammo for everything is in the crates."

"Open up the crates." I heard Luis say.

"I said everything's there." Brown replied.

There was a momentary pause while I heard a body slam against the side of the truck. Then, Luis' voice sounding menacing, "Are you going to open the crates as I asked, or maybe you don't need both of your eyeballs?"

A moment later I heard crates being pried open and then Luis, "Very well Mr. Brown, my associate will move these crates to our vehicle. Sheriff, I take it that you are guaranteeing clear passage?"

"Absolutely, my friend."

Mr. Brown moved to the back of the other van where the other Columbian had opened the back door.

"There you go, pure Columbian Gold!" said Luis.

I watched as Brown and Cooper swapped merchandise with the Columbians.

"Mr. Brown, it is very nice to do business with you. Now that we understand each other, I may have need for more equipment next month."

"Sure, just let Cooper know your shopping list and I'll start putting the order together."

Luis slapped a hand on Cooper's back and handed him an envelope. The drug dealers got back in their van, driving past my location.

"That fucking scared the shit out of me. You weren't kidding about being sensitive," said Mr. Brown.

"It's never a good idea to mess with people who would prefer to kill you, than do business with you," replied Cooper

Brown closed up the van, thanked the sheriff for setting things up and got in and drove away. Cooper meanwhile sat in the front seat of his car counting what looked like an envelope of cash.

Once again I'd learned valuable information, but was no closer to giving Ben the evidence he needed to put an end to this craziness.

Chapter 37

Cooper - ....6 hours earlier

It was 4 PM; the Cadillac was gone. I slammed the unmarked cruiser into park and made my way to the house. I must have tried calling the house 20 times in a row; each successive busy signal further darkened my mood. The innocent, loving girl I'd swept off her feet had transformed into a conniving little bitch. For the first five years of marriage, dinner was always ready when I got home. Back then, her life revolved around my every need. Now she was ruining all my plans. When I discovered the birth control pills, it told me everything. She no longer saw me as someone worthy enough to start a family with. "Jacqueline," I yelled as I came into the house, but I already knew she wasn't there.

The house was as empty as a church on Monday morning. I left my hat by the front door and stripped off my uniform, leaving it in piles as I made my way to the bedroom. Our bedroom, that deceitful little whore! Turning on the shower, I wondered if Jacqueline was having an affair. The image of her having sex with another man further enraged me. Was she that stupid? With one solid motion, I swept all her beauty crap off the vanity and onto the floor.

My thoughts drifted to Angela, and I felt myself getting excited. That was a girl who appreciated me. The only problem with her was she was not the kind of girl you could bring to community events. She didn't belong. Oh, look there's Sheriff Cooper with his little Mexican stripper whore! Let's face it, Angela was fun but that was it.

I looked at my naked body in the full-length mirror. Not a pound since college; other men my age had to pull in their stomachs. What woman wouldn't want to be with the most important man in Harrison County? I turned the shower on then put my favorite eight tracks in the player and danced around the house naked. Why not, I'm here alone. Shadow boxing, I said "Come here you little bitch." I opened the fridge and popped a beer looking for something to eat. With a leftover chicken leg in hand, I moved around the kitchen like a graceful fencer, working the chicken leg like a sword.

The ring of the phone interrupted me. Probably the bitch, checking up on me. "Where are you?" I yelled into the phone.

The dead air lasted for an uncomfortable few moments. Then a slow, calm Italian voice said, "You were expecting someone else?"

"Yeah. Little wifey is not where she's supposed to be."

"You are alone then?" I recognized the voice as Frank Galliano.

"Yeah, just me."

"Have you been careful with surveillance as we discussed?"

"Franklin swept the place yesterday and I'm watching for tails." I responded, my tone impatient at the reminder.

"Maybe things will get resolved this weekend. Everything is set up, I promise you and your little "wifey" will have….an exciting time." After a pause the caller added, "The reason I asked if you had been careful was that I heard something about tonight."

"Yeah?"

"Our source told us that the locals are planning a little surprise party at the airfield."

"It sounds like they might know something."

"Yes I thought so too. It doesn't affect our plans, but you might want to be extra careful."

"Alright, so the delivery is still on?"

"Of course, William." He paused for a moment before adding, "This business in the paper with the missing girls, our source says that your deputy is being investigated. It came up in a conversation with Carmen, and he wanted to know why he had never heard about this. Perhaps you can tell us about it this weekend."

Frank hung up, ominously not bothering to say goodbye. I took a swig of my beer as I considered the conversation. I supposed letting Franklin run with the Mardi Gras scheme without giving a piece to Nick was a little foolhardy. It had gone on too long. I couldn't very well play dumb and blame it all on Franklin.

I stepped into the hot shower, remembering how this business with the girls all began. Franklin and I were in college together back in the winter of 1968. There was this guy, a real depraved psycho. He had a thing for young blonde girls. Franklin met him at a bar and they hit it off. Turned out the guy was loaded and travelled the world on his yacht, always ending up in New Orleans for Mardi Gras. Franklin had smelled an opportunity. He and the creep got wasted and on the way back to the dorm they picked up a girl. Her name was Jessica something. She was walking home alone from work. They offered her a ride home, which she stupidly accepted. They ended up somewhere on a deserted country road. Long story short, the creep called Franklin every year and paid top dollar for another 16 year old blonde. I didn't want to think about what he did to them.

Last year I had pressured Franklin into telling the creep that this was the end; there were too many missing girls. The business with the girls was supposed to be over except Boone, my dumbass brother, decided to go into business for himself and try to pick up another girl. Thankfully he was too stupid to get her in the van. Then came that intern asking questions about missing girls. The psycho agreed to pay extra for her.

Putting it out of my head, I got dressed in jeans and a sweatshirt. I pulled out my Colt M1911 from a shoe box stashed in the closet. A gift from some of the vets returning from Nam, the serial number had been filed off, making it virtually untraceable. I checked that it contained a clip and tucked it in the waistband of my jeans. Grabbing my leather jacket, I debated leaving a note for the bitch, then decided she could go to hell.

Chapter 38

Cooper – 8 years earlier

It all began for me in the fall of 1971. I was working as a new deputy in the Gulfport Police Department. One day a couple of suits walked into the station. One was tall, with dark hair and looked like Raymond Burr. The other was shorter mid 40's with a craggy face and a nose that had been broken a number of times. The Raymond Burr type did the talking, "Mr. Cooper, we represent some local interests that would like to invite you for lunch at Diamond Head."

"Who are these interests?" I replied, a little wary.

"Just some local businessmen who feel that you are underemployed."

I looked at them and asked "What businessmen?"

"I think they are happy to stay in the shadows for the time being. Let's just say they want you to listen to an offer they are prepared to present over lunch."

My job as a deputy in Gulfport was okay. The chief was telling me I was learning the ropes. In reality, I was getting everyone coffee and went to functions no one else was willing to attend. The guy with the broken nose must have sensed my reluctance, and passed over a business card that helped me make up my mind. "Here's the guy's card." It said Bert Hopewell, Mayor of Biloxi.

We piled into their car and headed north east. I remember walking into the Diamond Club with the feeling I was out of my league. I grew up the son of hard working middle-class parents, who had probably never set foot in any room this opulent. The large ballroom had high, ornate sculptured ceilings. Paintings of Civil War generals adorned the walls, and a Confederate flag was prominently displayed. We were shown to a table by the windows overlooking the golf course and the beautifully manicured greens.

Two gentlemen were already seated waiting for me. I recognized Bert Hopewell. His photo had been in the Herald on a regular basis. We shook hands, and the other man introduced himself as Hec Brady, Mr. Hopewell's personal advisor. My two escorts left us once we had taken our seats. I wondered what would have happened had I said no thanks.

Once the waiter had taken our order, the Mayor started the conversation by thanking me for agreeing to meet with them. "We have something very important to discuss with you William. Important not just to you but to all of us, and to Harrison County."

"Sounds mysterious."

"Let me ask you a question William. What's your take on the role of Sheriff in keeping the peace?"

For moment I felt like I was back in school. I relaxed and said to myself I had nothing to lose so I might as well be honest. "I think the sheriff has a crucial role to play in helping keep the peace. He has to protect the businesses that attract tourist dollars and make it safe to live here." I stopped at this point, I had made my views known down at the station and could have gone one for hours. The two of them looked at each other and smiled.

Hec Brady then asked a follow up question. "So you're a modern day crime fighter like Batman, but without a cape?"

I smiled at the reference and said, "No, the job is much more difficult. Not everything that's "technically illegal" is bad for tourism. The Sheriff and his deputies need to be able to keep things in balance. People visit the Gulf to blow off steam and have a little fun. If you arrest all the prostitutes and close down all the gambling joints than the town will die."

At this point the mayor took a sip of his drink and then looked me in the eye. "We are all busy people so I will lay my cards on the table. Your police chief has said some very nice things about your work and he believes you are the kind of guy that can get things done. Is that true William?"

"I'd like to think so, Mr. Mayor."

"I also know you come from a very good local family. Your father worked in the lumberyards I'm told."

I nodded, still wondering what this was all about.

"What we are wondering is whether you have any ambitions about running for election?"

The suggestion was totally from left field. I had always had a cocky confidence in myself, but running for election so soon after graduating was a stretch. I took a big gulp of my water. "Are we talking about sheriff?" I asked incredulously.

"I'm sure you have heard about the current sheriff having to step down because of those nasty corruption charges. We need a young, ambitious man to lead Harrison County. Someone who will introduce new ideas on fighting crime. To reassure the voters that we won't stand by and let corruption ruin our future."

"This is very flattering Mr. Mayor." I said, trying to keep my composure.

"Please call me Bert. I know you don't have a lot of experience, but the Mayor of Gulfport and I are in agreement on this, we have bold plans for Harrison County. We don't need another career policeman; we need a fresh face."

"But what makes you think I can win?"

"Believe me William that's not a concern. I have considerable influence, and I can introduce you to some business people who can provide the resources you need to win the election." said Mr. Brady.

I looked around the room still not believing that these two guys thought I could win an election. For a moment, it passed my mind that this was some elaborate school prank.

The mayor must have sensed my reluctance and added, "Listen William, I know you're surprised by my suggestion. The position would pay handsomely. Your career and influence would grow tremendously, and you'd be the most important lawman in the County. Think about it over the weekend, and Mr. Brady will check with you on Monday. If you're interested, he'll be able to guide you on the next steps. "For now let's enjoy our lunch, I understand you played some ball up at Ole Miss..."

As I left after lunch, I looked around the dining room, at the crystal chandelier, the fine china, and all of the rich people. I had already made up my mind. I confirmed with Mr. Brady on Monday that I was interested, and made arrangements to talk about next steps. We met for the next two days and talked about campaign strategies, what to say, what not to say, and that was pretty much it. Before I knew it, the Mayor was calling a press conference, and I found myself making a speech about cleaning up the city by getting rid of crime and corruption. Mr. Brady became my campaign manager and moneyman. There seemed to be an unlimited supply of cash for billboards, lawn signs, ads in the Herald, even radio spots. I ran against two other candidates who both had a ton more credentials and experience, but neither had the promotional team that I had. A week before the election, after looking at a poll, I said to Mr. Brady that I thought I might win. I bragged about my campaign program, as if I had anything to do with it. He just laughed and said that it was time to meet some of my financial backers.

The meeting went well. The man who did most of the talking introduced himself as Frank Galliano and said he represented a number of other supporters. They wanted to make sure that I had everything I needed and that I was excited about building my team. I hadn't spent a long time thinking about building a team. I had heard rumors about some deputies who planned to resign if I won the election. He said not to worry about the deputies because there were some quality people out there that he could recommend

At one point I made a suggestion about a campaign idea which Brady ignored, and Frank responded that I was in good hands with Mr. Brady. Any further discussion was cut off by Frank announcing that he had another pressing engagement. As he stood up to leave he looked down at me and said all I needed to do was look confident and carry the message to a landslide victory.

We had all kinds of people working like busy bees getting out the vote. It was no contest with both opponents throwing in the towel within an hour of polls closing and the first results being counted. At the victory party, booze and women were plentiful, and I thought that moment was the happiest so far in my young life.

All of this came screeching to a halt the day after the election. It was mid-afternoon, and I had just finished giving an interview to the Herald. The call came summoning me to a meeting with Frank.

"Congratulations Sheriff Cooper," he said, shaking my hand.

"I owe a vote of thanks to all the people who supported me."

"Well, speaking about that, I would like you to consider a few steps that we believe will ensure that you meet your promises to make Biloxi safe for its citizens while at the same time ensuring you get re-elected."

"Sounds great."

"The first thing we want you to do is hire a couple of ex-military guys that I know. These are people with experience you can count on. They know how to get things done and would make loyal deputies. You'll get a chance to meet them tomorrow."

I wasn't totally comfortable with someone else calling the shots. But after everything that they had done for me, the least I could do was meet these ex-military guys.

"Second, we spoke to a friend over at the Herald and we need a city reporter who'll give you and the department the kind of press that you need to inspire the confidence of the people. We have someone in mind for that, unless you know someone else?"

I thought about it for a moment then said, "I know a guy from Ole Miss. He majored in journalism, and he's looking for a job. His name is Alex Dermody."

"We aren't looking for someone wanting to make a name for themselves as an investigative journalist. It would be closer to writing a travel brochure. If you think he would be good at doing that and can operate with discretion, then have him call me."

"Third, there are a couple of businesses that we want you to target. We believe there are drugs being sold in those locations. Maybe once you get your new deputies on board you can organize something."

We ended up getting Alex hired as a city reporter at The Herald. After a few weeks, I had to admit I was starting to believe some of my press clippings. Every couple of weeks Frank would call, usually with something that the businessmen or the mayor wanted to have fixed. I started getting cash bonuses with instructions to share it with my team. The money always came with a thank you for doing such a good job.

Things became even clearer to me after I arrested a prostitute named Stormy Wave for soliciting in one of the hotels on the strip. The day after the arrest Frank called me up and asked me to join him and his associate Mr. Green on his yacht. As we headed out to sea, Frank explained how things worked. According to Frank, we should all be thankful for our jobs, to the businessmen who pulled the strings. In a tourist town like Biloxi, there was always going to be a certain amount of illegal activity. There are people who come to Biloxi to have a good time. That might include an innocent game of poker, a little romp in the hay with a lovely lady and maybe recreational drugs. The businessmen felt that it was very important that these things be allowed to continue in order to keep the tourist trade alive. The caution, however, was that we don't want these activities to upset people who may not be able to understand the importance of balance.

I guess there was something at the back of my mind flashing a warning sign, but the whole idea of balancing the needs of our citizens for protection along with the businessmen's desire to help the city prosper made sense to me. Mr. Green's role I suspected was to be the muscle and to throw my body overboard if I was to cause a problem.

The next day I released Stormy, with my apologies.

Chapter 39

Gabriel – Wednesday Morning, Day 10

Wednesday morning, and I woke up with the sunrise and the sound of someone banging on the apartment door. After everything that happened I was reluctant to blindly open the door.

"Gabriel it's me Ben, rise and shine sleepyhead."

I opened the door, "Don't you ever sleep in?" I rubbed the sleep from my eyes.

"Sure, I sleep eight hours a day and at least another ten at night."

"It is way too early for jokes." He was wearing a nice camel hair sports jacket, its effect ruined by the denim cowboy shirt. Ben carried another file under his arm.

"How did you make out last night?"

I looked at my watch, seeing that it was already 8:30. While making coffee, I brought him up to date on what he needed to know about last night's surveillance as well as the earlier call to Jacqueline when she had indicated they were going to New Orleans this coming weekend. "I won't let her go. Once I show her these pictures she needs to go into protective custody or something."

"If she's willing to leave, then put her up in a hotel someplace, preferably away from Biloxi where people might not recognize her."

"Alright. It sounds like the delivery they were talking about was a guns for drugs deal. Was the stakeout at the airfield a waste of time?"

'Pretty much, lots of commuter planes coming in but we checked out everything and saw no evidence of any smuggling. We do have some good news though. You know how you asked that we put Boone Cooper's photo in front of Janice McVeigh? She picked him out of a photo lineup; she's 90% sure that Boone Cooper was the guy that was driving the white van last January."

"That's a big break! What's next?"

"Police Chief Ricketts has given us the green light to pick him up as a person of interest. So we'll go out, pick him up and find a way to get him to talk."

"Good luck with that, he's a bit of an asshole."

"My specialty. What's your plan for today?"

"I need to run out to Gulf Oaks this morning, and then I'm having lunch with Jacqueline to show her the pictures."

"Give me a call after and we can compare notes."

I disconnected and headed for the shower. My black eye was gradually clearing –more yellow than full-fledged baboon. Last night's slithering across the field had aggravated my back and ribs. A hot shower relieved some of the pain. After a quick bite to eat and some black coffee, I was out the door by 9:00.

Getting off in the lobby, Ahmed was waiting for me. "Mr. Ross, I was very much hoping to see you today, I have some insurance forms for you to fill in." I begged off, telling him that I am on my way to a meeting. "Mr. Ross," he said, waggling his finger at me. "I cannot make a claim and get my property replaced until you complete these forms." I told him I was running late, and if he could just slide them under my door, I'd complete them tonight. "Mister Ross, I will do that for you but until you sign, no furniture for you."

Starting up the Pinto, the conversation with Ahmed reminded me that I needed to call my insurance agent up north to report the damage to the Bug. I headed east on Beach Boulevard, once again driving into the sunrise. The temperature today was going up to 88 degrees. With the humidity, it would be as hot as a Mexican tamale. I stopped off at a coffee shop and picked up coffees for Rachel and myself. Traffic was light, and I made it to Gulf Oaks in twenty minutes.

I walked into the psychiatric ward and found Rachel sitting at the reception desk. We chatted while drinking our coffee; she was easy to talk to. Within a few minutes, I found out that she had lived in Gulfport all her life and was saving money to go back to school to be a nurse. At the first lull in the conversation, she pulled a stub of paper from a folder and handed it to me. "I imagine you want to look at this."

"I'm not sure what this is supposed to say, Rachel." I looked down at the shaky scrawl.

"I think it's part of a word," Rachel volunteered.

"Still, what word begins with olb?"

She gave me an amused look and flipped the paper around. "Glo," she said as if she was talking to an idiot.

"Oh, glo!" Excitedly I ran through some of the options. "Could it be the first part of the word glove? There's a clue in a glove?"

"Doesn't sound very likely." Rachel shook her head.

"Could the answer be with Gloria? I wonder who Gloria is." Rachel gave me a smile before rolling her eyes.

"Was he feeling gloomy that day? Was he gloating about something?" Every attempt earned a frown from Rachel.

She let out a laugh and asked, "What kind of private eye are you?"

"I'm just learning the job, do YOU have any ideas?" I asked with a smile in my voice.

"No, I was never very good at puzzles. But my sister does the jumble in the Herald every Saturday. She suggested that we keep it simple. In his condition, he wouldn't have tried to write out a long word like glossary. She said maybe he was referring to something that glows like a glow-worm."

"A glow-worm? That's your best idea? He hid the clue in a glow-worm." I repeated sarcastically.

We had a good laugh before tossing glow worm in the trash heap of bad ideas. "Any change in his behavior since we talked on Monday?"

"No, and I even tried putting another piece of paper in his hand, but I didn't get any response. Maybe all of this was just a nervous spasm."

"Maybe. Let's keep thinking about it; call me if you come up with anything. Have you shown this to Mrs. Dermody?"

"Strange, but she hasn't been in since the last time you were here."

I considered that for a moment before asking, "Do you mind if I keep it? I might swing by and see if she's ok."

Rachel gave me her home number and suggested that I call her later... "You know, about Mrs. Dermody."

Chapter 40

Gabriel – Wednesday Morning, Day 10

It took me a good twenty minutes to get to D'Iberville and Trixie Dermody's house. I debated calling beforehand, but decided to head over without calling and deny her a chance to get dressed up for me again.

The lawn mower was still in the same position as my last visit, when I pulled to the curb in front of the house. I was in luck; Mrs. Dermody's Mustang was sitting in the driveway. I noticed the curtains move slightly as I got out of my car and headed up the path. I knocked a couple of times before she opened the door for me. This time she was dressed in a leopard skin outfit that hugged her body like a road full of speed bumps.

"Well, if it isn't our little detective man. Want to come in and party with me?"

"Good morning Mrs. Dermody, I was hoping that you could answer a few more questions for me?"

"Come right in darling and let Trixie fix you a little drinkypoo."

I made my way back to the living room, finding the same clothes were still on the floor. The leopard was going for height advantage wearing a pair of stiletto heels. She handed me a drink that looked to be brandy. She sat down on one end of the couch and patted the cushion, inviting me into the leopard's den. I looked over at the chair. It lay buried in a mountain of discarded clothes. Begrudgingly, I squeezed past her and sat on the couch as far away from her as I could.

I pulled the scrap of paper from the hospital out of my pocket. "I was at the hospital this morning checking on Alex, and the nurse said she hadn't seen you lately."

"Your visit last week upset me, those memories of that deputy and what happened to Alex. That's why I drink, you know."

Yeah right, I thought. "I'm sorry, I didn't mean to upset you. I just want to help find out what happened."

She reached across the couch covering my hand with hers. "I know that. You seem like a good man." She started tracing little circles on the back of my hand. I gently pulled my hand away which prompted her to say, "A little short mind you, but I bet you could still show a girl a good time."

I needed to move this along, so I showed her the scrap of paper, "The nurse that looks after Alex had said your husband wrote this." Her eyes widened with shock like a bird landing on a live wire. Looking at the note, she started to laugh uncontrollably. At one point, I thought she was going to fall off the couch.

"Alex can't think let alone write something on a piece of paper; that scamp is pulling your leg," she continued to laugh.

"You might be right Mrs. Dermody. The note might be nothing." I got up to leave.

"Just a minute, let me take another look at it." While she looked at the paper, I decided to humor her and take a sip of the drink. It was awful.

"Well, I supposed it could be glory. Like he's about to meet his glorious maker," she offered.

"I supposed that's possible. I was thinking on the way over did he have a globe in his office?"

"Sure, he used it in his work; it's in a box in the closet. I couldn't stand looking at it."

"Would I be able to see it? Maybe he made a mark or something."

"Like a treasure map? Finish your drinkypoo and I'll go get it." Slurring her words, she slinked her way to a room at the back. I debated pouring my brandy back into the bottle. As I reached for the bottle, I noticed the zoo of porcelain animal figurines on the end table. What was that she said about a gift from Cooper?

She was saying something from the back room about staying for lunch. I picked up the snow globe. She'd said that this had significance to Dermody. It looked like a simple snow globe, one of the dozens you might find at Wal-Mart. It had a switch on the bottom. Music was supposed to play while Santa's sleigh moved. I tried the switch, but got nothing. Mrs. Dermody must have let the battery die. I examined the globe for clues; shaking it and making it snow. I put the snow globe back on the table as I heard her coming back. She stumbled and bumped into a chair, then angled over to me carrying the globe in her hands.

"There you go big boy," she said, sitting beside me and rubbing my leg. "I'm kind of hungry, how about you?"

I decided to ignore her and concentrated on looking for clues on the globe in my hands. I checked it over closely and found nothing. Putting the globe onto the coffee table, I picked up the scrap of paper. "I'm sorry to have wasted your time. I have a lunch meeting so I'll have to take a rain check on lunch." I stood up, taking another small sip of the brandy. I went to put it back on the end table when an idea suddenly hit me. I picked up the snow globe, turning it upside down.

"When was the last time this worked? "

"I don't remember. Not sure if it ever did. What do you want with that old thing?"

"Just thought he might have been referring to the snow globe." Reaching into my pocket for a dime, I used it to loosen the two screws holding the battery compartment. When I got the cover off, I saw there was no battery. "Mrs. Dermody, what bank did your husband deal with?" I held out what looked like a safe deposit box key.

Chapter 41

Gabriel – Wednesday Afternoon, Day 10

Mrs. Dermody was anxious about what might be in her husband's safe deposit box. I told her I'd be back in touch about the key. The key was now evidence in a number of crimes being investigated by the Biloxi Police Department. Once they confirmed the right bank, she'd be invited to be there when they opened the box.

I dashed out of there, my mind reeling. Would Dermody have stashed evidence that could be used to indict the sheriff? Could the box contain cash that was paid under the table to write bogus stories or to hush up criminal activities?

I had just enough time to get to the restaurant to meet Jacqueline. When I got there, I found her once again sitting at the back. She was wearing a loose grey sweater over black slacks. As I sat down in the booth, I saw her face was wrought with worry.

"What happened to your face, Gabriel?"

"Someone told me I needed more color."

She brushed off my attempt at humor, a bad sign. "Did someone hurt you because of me?"

"Well first, there were five of them, and second, if you think this looks bad, you should see them."

She finally cracked a smile, shaking her head. "That looks so painful. Seriously, did Will do that to you?"

"No, I still don't think he's clued in about our investigation. There is another case that might involve him." I changed the subject. "Jacqueline, has anything further happened since our call yesterday?"

"No, I've tried to avoid him. I know it angers him when I am not where he wants me to be, but I can't stand to be around him."

"So where do you go during the day?"

"Anywhere, I drive, trying to find a place where I can put all this behind me."

"I understand. You've been through a lot." The waitress came to take our orders. After she left, "I have a question for you Jacqueline. Are you familiar with a service center called Arties?"

"No, Will looked after all our car maintenance. Why do you ask?"

"Well, Artie's came up during the investigation into some missing girls. I went to check it out and met Boone Cooper, who works there."

"I knew he worked at a service center. I was never interested enough to look into which one. I don't follow, what does this have to do with me?"

"As it turns out the owner, Artie mysteriously disappeared leaving his business to his business partner. We were kind of suspicious, thinking that there might have been a motive to get rid of Artie. The business isn't much but apparently the land is worth quite a bit."

Jacqueline gave a hand roll to show her growing frustration with the relevance of the story.

"Jacqueline, we did a search at the registry office and found that the service is owned by you."

"What?" I don't own a service center! I don't know anyone named Artie. There must be some mistake."

"There's no mistake. Is it possible that Cooper could have got your signature on a bunch of forms without explaining things?"

"I signed a bunch of stuff at a lawyer's office a couple of years back. The lawyer explained that it had to do with liability in case Will ever got sued for something that happened at work."

"That's probably when it happened. Do you remember the lawyer's name?"

"Not off hand, I might have his card somewhere. What's this all about?"

"I don't know, but Cooper might have had a reason to hide the true owner of the service center."

"You can't just take someone's property and give it to someone else. There are laws. He couldn't get away with that."

"I believe Artie is buried somewhere and is not in a position to prevent his partner from taking over the business."

"This is all hard to believe. I wonder how many other businesses I own."

"I don't know, but I can find out." There was a pause in the conversation, before I passed the envelope containing the photographs to her. "Here is the proof you wanted. Before you look at them, I want to warn you that they're pretty graphic. Even a little perverted."

She opened up the envelope and looked at the 8 ½ by 11 stills I had ordered from Fotomat. She looked at a couple of the pictures and then gave me a quizzical look. "These are pictures of me sunbathing in my backyard."

Oops! I should have taken those out of the envelope. I passed her the other envelope and said something stupid about testing my camera.

"You must have thirty pictures of me! What's the matter with you?" Her voice rising.

"Seriously, I know this looks bad, I got to your house intending to do surveillance on the sheriff, and, well, I got carried away."

"You're the one that's sick. These other pictures better not be of me." She grabbed the other envelope. After looking through the first few pictures, "There are some lousy shots of Will drinking beer with a bunch of guys? What does this prove?"

"Continue to look through the set." I said, knowing I was on thin ice.

"You took pictures of strippers? Oh my God, I have to get away from you." Her voice was rising as she got up to leave. I put my hand out and told her to finish looking at all of the pictures. "Why, what else do you have?"

"There are some pictures of Cooper and Angela. She's the stripper in that picture doing ....you know...."

247

"You mean fucking?"

I slap myself on the forehead and said, "That's the word. I keep forgetting it." She was now looking at the picture in question. Her expression darkened like a rain cloud. I could sense the outpouring of anger and humiliation emanating from across the table.

"I asked him if he was having an affair, and you know what he said? Do you know what he said?" she repeated, her voice almost shouting. "He said no, but that if he did, nobody would blame him. Bastard!" Her temper was rising like a Saturn rocket.

I looked around and whispered, "Ah, Jacqueline, people are starting to look at us."

She took the pictures of her in a bikini and ripped them in half. I was crestfallen. I started to mumble "I was going to keep…" She gave me a, "Don't you dare" look that would frighten a statue and handed back the ones from the strip club. She put the ones of Cooper and Angela back into the envelope and her purse.

"I know you're angry Jacqueline, but I want to make a suggestion. I think confronting him with those pictures will enrage him. He's a very violent man. I know things about him. He belongs behind bars. If you go with him to New Orleans then I suspect he might try to harm you. I overheard Cooper and the other guy in the picture talking." I pointed out Frank and said he was a known mafia boss. "They were talking about arranging an accident. You have an opportunity to get away from all of this. Give us a little more time, and we'll arrest him."

"So I'm just supposed to go back and act like the perfect wife until you can have him arrested? No. You've done your job Mr. Ross; I hired you to prove he was having an affair. Thank you very much."

"It's Gabriel." I mumbled. "I'm not nearly finished." I broke a breadstick for effect.

She was clearly not impressed. "You're not on the case anymore Mr. Ross. You're fired."

I was trying hard to figure her out. The thought that Cooper would want to be with another woman infuriated her, almost as if she was angrier at not being wanted than about the betrayal. When I first met her I'd thought she was spoiled, used to having everything handed to her. Now I thought that scornful arrogance was a defense mechanism. I wondered what she was like before he hurt her.

"Did you hear me, I said you're fired," she repeated.

It seemed to me that if I acted polite and respectful, she'd just walk all over me. So I decided to give it right back to her. "Maybe you've fired me, but I haven't fired me. I didn't start all of this, but I sure as hell am not going to quit before I finish it." I raised my voice a couple of octaves and, continued... "And this is what you're going to do. I'm going to take you to a hotel outside of Biloxi, and you're going to stay there until we get the guy. And don't doubt that we're going to get him. Now don't waste your salad!"

Chapter 42

Gabriel, Wednesday Afternoon, Day 10

I left the restaurant with Jacqueline following reluctantly in her car. I headed east on Lemoyne Road then south on Tucker to the town of Ocean Springs. I didn't have a plan. I just wanted to find something off the beaten path. Ocean Springs was an artsy beach town of about 12,000 people. It was big enough to get lost in, but not so big as to attract the wrong kind of people. Who was I kidding? I was the wrong kind of people. In one week I'd been to a strip bar, peeked in a bedroom window, called a pervert, and had my ass kicked.

Shortly after 2 pm, we turned onto a dirt road leading to the Good Night Motel. The place was a tired looking one story building, screaming for a coat of fresh paint. The rusted-out cars at the back of the lot gave new meaning to the word "dump." I knew it was the right place when I saw a sign by the road promoting the motel as a place to "Get Further Away."

Getting out of her car, Jacqueline had had time to regain her venom, "He's going to be so pissed when he finds I'm gone. He'll put out an APB on my car, and he's going to find me," she glared at me.

"No, he's not." I calmly replied. "I'm going to drive your car back into town. I know just where to leave it."

"But what about all my clothes and stuff?"

"If you leave me your key and tell me what you need, I'll go to your house and pack a bag for you."

"What if he finds you?"

I almost hope he does, I thought to myself. "Don't worry; I'll wait until he leaves before I go in."

I told her to wait in the car while I registered. I walked into the office wearing my Ray-Bans. The smell of Mr. Clean hung in the air, smothering any fresh air. A middle-aged clerk sat behind the counter doing a jumble. The sun blazed in through the window illuminating the dust motes. The place reminded of the motel in Psycho. It even had the stuffed owl on the counter. The clerk gave me a tired look as if the sight of a paying customer held no spark, everyday boredom on his job hdumpingaving poisoned his outlook. I registered under my name, paying a week in advance. "What kind of car are you driving sonny?" He asked. I was deciding between the Bug, the Pinto and the Cadillac, when he peered over his glasses and in a conspiratorial tone added, "Something small, right?" I gave him my best fake laugh and said Cadillac. I would have mentioned that a young lady would be staying in the room, but by the looks of the place, additional details were not needed.

I crossed the dusty parking lot and accompanied Jacqueline to Room number 16, strategically located beside a long-broken pop machine and a fly infested dumpster. I opened the door, revealing a standard motel room, with yellow wallpaper, threadbare orange carpet, and a queen size bed bowed in the middle from the bulk of thousands of overweight truckers. Once again, Mr. Clean was hard at work masking the aroma of dead cigars.

Jacqueline made a brave face that lasted all of ten seconds before the tears started to flow. I didn't know what to say to comfort her. I ran through the options...."I'll get that bastard," "don't worry this dump is just temporary" "the fleas don't do any real damage"...before deciding on saying nothing. She was sitting on the bed, the tears running down her cheeks like raindrops on a window pane. I sat down beside her, extending a handkerchief. I was going to put my arm around her but thought, what if she thinks I'm making a move. After the business with the photographs I should take it slow.

I need not have worried. She turned towards me and before I could react she launched herself into my arms. I held her tight to show her that I understood. In between the sobs I heard her say, "Thank you." This was one of those satisfying moments that Ben had promised. It was a once in a lifetime chance to comfort an amazing girl, who appreciated that I just rescued her from a villain. I felt myself getting caught up in the emotion of her tears.

"Don't worry Gabriel, this room is ok," sniff, "it's not for long. I know you'll get him, and put him away where he can't hurt me." I continued to hold her … well past the end of her tears. It was starting to get weird when she pushed away from my embrace, almost knocking me to the floor. "I'll write out a list of what you should collect at the house," she said.

While she was busy making a list I opened the curtains to look out in the parking lot. Other than the Cadillac the only other car was the Pinto. "I was married before," I said.

"I didn't know that, what happened?"

"I've never told this to anyone down here. Even my partner doesn't know. "I told her about my last day at Ford, the weasel, the bobble head, little balls, everything. "I went home to tell my wife I'd lost my job, and she freaked out. She said she wasn't surprised and that I wasn't worthy of the job. Then she told me about the affair she'd been having."

"Oh my god. Both things in one day? That's terrible." She approached and put her arms around me.

"Do you want to know the worst part?"

She looked up at my eyes, searching in wonder - how there could be anything worse than finding out your spouse has been cheating on you and losing your job in the same day?

"She was having an affair with the mechanic that fixed her Pinto."

She looked at me for a couple of seconds and then the two of us spontaneously started laughing at how ridiculous that was. We shared a moment, one that said things were going to be alright. I hoped.

I decided to leave on a high note, taking her list and her car and house keys while leaving the room key and the key to the Pinto. "I'll be back with your stuff before the bed bugs attack."

Chapter 43

Gabriel – Wednesday Afternoon, Day 10

I drove the Cadillac back across the causeway to Biloxi and stopped at a strip plaza to try Ben's number. He answered right away.

"So are you sweating a confession out of the sheriff's brother, Boone?" I asked.

"Nope. By the time we got the warrant, the guy had disappeared. The garage was all closed up, and there's a note on the door saying Gone Fishing."

"Sounds like someone might have tipped him off."

"That's a definite possibility. I just don't know who it might be."

"Does anyone know about the microphone?"

"No, I would have loved to tell people, but I'd get reamed out for encouraging illegal activities."

I brought him up to date on finding the safe deposit box key and that the next step was to go to Alex Dermody's bank and see what was in the box.

"That's great detective work, partner. Maybe that will confirm your theories about what this is all about." We made a plan to meet in front of the Sun Trust bank at 10:00 am the next morning. I then started to tell him where I had stashed Jacqueline, when he interrupted. "Don't tell me. I'll drop a rumor about where she is hiding once I see that she's been reported missing. You know, like Hattiesburg and Gulfport. That way I might be able to flush out the leak."

I told him it was worth a try. He asked what I planned to do next, and I decided to play my cards close to my chest and said I had some running around to do before getting back to the client. I hung up from him wondering how difficult it must be to not trust those you work beside. I wondered about that Greenlaw guy. His desk was adjacent to Ben's…easily within earshot. I got in the Cadillac and drove to Gulfport and did a drive-by of the Sheriff's office. I had left the receiver in the Pinto, so I didn't have the benefit of hearing his voice. His cruiser however was parked in the lot.

Next stop was Cooper's house, to gather up Jacqueline's things. It was 4:30 by the time I pulled the Cadillac into the drive. I figured I had at least 30 minutes to pick up her stuff and get out of there before he got home. Using the key, I unlocked the front door. The house was nicely furnished and had a number of stuffed hunting trophies prominently displayed. I quickly made my way to the bedroom and grabbed a Samsonite suitcase out of the closet. I lifted the suitcase and opened it on the bed. It was a big suitcase, one of the ones with hard-shell sides. I pulled the list out of my pocket. I had told her to figure on a week. The list had enough outfits for a month. I started to gather the items, filling up the suitcase. I noticed some nice lingerie in her dresser. It wasn't on the list, but I decided to throw them in along with that cute little bikini. I took a quick look at my watch. I had already been in the house for 15 minutes. I headed into the bathroom for her supplies. The scene in the bathroom looked like a battle zone, with most of her stuff thrown on the floor. It looked like Cooper had indulged in a temper tantrum. I hastily gathered some essentials and put them in a toiletries bag. Putting everything in the suitcase, I tried to close it and realized that there was no way. I was sitting on the suitcase fiddling with the snaps, when I heard the front door opening. Shit, shit, shit. Double shit! I wasn't sure I was ready for a confrontation.

"Jacqueline?" Cooper called from the doorway. "I'm glad you're home. We need to talk."

I frantically looked around the room for a place to hide. Behind some curtains, a pair of French doors led outside. I dumped some of the clothes out and snapped the suitcase closed. I heard footsteps coming closer as I tried hefting it. Why do they make these things so heavy! I tried the door to the pool; it wouldn't budge. I heard Cooper call out to Jacqueline again, his footsteps echoing in the hall. I saw that there was a security bar in the track stopping the patio door from opening. Shit, shit, shit. "Is that you honey?" His voice was coming nearer down the hall and sounded angry. For a moment, I considered mimicking Jacqueline's voice, when I finally got the patio door opened.

I made my way past the pool cabana to the 6 foot fence bordering their yard. I tried to lob the suitcase over the fence, but it was too heavy. Even an Olympic discus thrower couldn't have done it. Madly, I cleaned and jerked it over my head and pushed it over the top of the fence. I heard the French doors open behind me, and Cooper's voice calling out, "Who's there?" Hopefully he wouldn't see me behind the cabana. I leaped for the top of the fence, hurling my 5 foot frame as high as possible. I fell back down having missed the top of the fence by a few inches. I tried again. I was like a dog jumping for a treat. Out of breath, I resigned myself; like Custer, I would make my last stand.

That's when I noticed the gate. As I heard Cooper approach, I had just enough time to open the gate and get out of sight. I recovered the suitcase and scrambled across the street, dragging the suitcase up the little hill. I was half way up the hill in plain sight to anyone coming from the house when I heard Travis' familiar voice. "Hello, Sheriff Cooper - a great day for a swim."

I continued scrambling up the hill until I was safely out of view behind the little pine tree. I looked down and heard Cooper ask Travis whether he had seen anyone coming out of the backyard. "Nope, just you…how about letting me go for that swim?"

"Beat it kid or I'll tell your old man you've been hassling me." Cooper turned around and headed back to the front of the house. Travis gave Cooper's back the finger and went the other way. From my vantage point I watched Cooper put his hand on the hood of the Cadillac. He slammed his hand down on the hood and looked up and down the street.

Cooper had disappeared back into the house for 5 minutes when I decided I needed to get out of there. That's when I heard Travis' voice come from behind me, "Who gave you permission to trespass here?"

"Thanks, Travis. That was close. If you hadn't come along, he would have caught me."

"What were you doing in his house and what's in the suitcase?"

"Long story but right now I need to get out of here before he starts searching the area."

"No problem Gabriel, grab your suitcase and follow me." He then led me back into the pine trees away from the street. After a five minute walk, the small woods opened up onto a park bordering a major road. By the time we reached the road, I was exhausted from lugging the suitcase.

"Someone should invent one with wheels," said Travis.

We sat along the side of the road for a good 20 minutes before I saw a cab. I waved my arms desperately and the driver pulled his cab over to the side of the road. The cab had the

Confederate battle flag on its doors as the company's official logo. A middle-aged man with long grey hair tied in a ponytail and sporting the grey uniform of the Confederacy was behind the wheel. I thanked Travis again and scrambled into the back of the cab along with the suitcase.

"Where y'all headed Mr.?" The cabbie turned around and gave me a smile. He was wearing a peaked Civil War cap. All that was missing was a musket.

"Can you drop me at the Trade Winds Apartments?"

"No problem, you a Yankee?" he asked as he put the Confederate flag meter down and pulled into traffic.

"I guess so, I'm from Detroit."

"That so? Just visiting?" His Mississippi drawl was as thick as molasses.

"Sort of, more like doing business." We drove in silence for a few minutes, and I wondered whether the presence of a northerner in his cab was upsetting him. "So what's with the get-up and the battle flag on the door?"

"A group of us cab drivers were working for the Union Cab company, and we didn't like the policies that the new owners were enforcing. So the bunch of us pooled what money we had, and we left Union to start our own cab company. The name and the uniforms just kind of made sense."

"Aren't you afraid of people taking offence?"

"No, it's a free country. The battle flag is part of the state flag. We're just embracing our heritage. Most of our drivers are Civil War buffs and folks seem to enjoy the history lesson while getting a ride. Getting back to your comment about offending people, we'd never refuse a ride to colored folk as long as they paid up front."

I was tempted to ask him if he realized the South lost the war, but I'd had enough excitement for the day. The driver had a picture of himself on the back of his seat along with the standard disclosure about fees, and his name....Robert Lee. "So Mr. Lee why don't you give me a history lesson while we ride to the Trade Winds."

"Well, most of the battles were fought north of here. The Battle for Vicksburg, Coffeeville, Corinth, Tupelo....down south here they had a relatively easy time of it. I don't believe the folks down here on the coast felt they had that much in common with the rest of the southern states. They did send some men, the 3rd Mississippi Infantry to fight, but most of the people wondered why. You see, the area down near the coast is quite different from the rest of the state. We have more in common with New Orleans and Mobile. Few folks had slaves and believed in a more southern European lifestyle. Getting back to the war, there's a number of old forts that were built back around the War of 1812. The Union forces took over most of these, as well as the fortress on Ship Island, and launched their campaigns against New Orleans and Mobile from there. The war down here started with seceding from the Union in January 1861 and ended in December that same year when Biloxi surrendered to Union forces. If you look over to your left you can see the Jefferson Davis homestead, it's called Beauvoir. After the Civil War, Davis was penniless, and a widow named Sarah Dorsey took pity on him and gave him a cottage so he could write his memoirs. When she died, she left the whole property to him."

I had General Lee drop me off in the parking lot of the Trade Winds. I gave him a handsome tip, not just for being a lifesaver, but also for the history lesson. I walked over to the VW and loaded the suitcase in the trunk. It was a little uncomfortable with the seats cut open, but it would be fine for the drive out to Ocean Springs.

Chapter 44

Gabriel – Wednesday Evening, Day 10

It was after six by the time I finally arrived back to the Good Night Motel. I had stopped and picked up some food and drinks on the way. Knocking on the door, I was happy to finally wind down my day. I knocked a second, and then third time, and there was no answer. The Pinto was still the only other car in the lot. I tried the motel room door only to find it locked. Panicked, I immediately wondered if Jacqueline had gone stir crazy, and walked into town. Could she have done something stupid and called Cooper, telling him about the pictures? Could Cooper have somehow found her here? I was about to go to the office and ask for a spare key when the bathroom door opened. Jacqueline stood wrapped in a bath towel, smiling when she saw the relief flash across my face. "I'm so sorry, I didn't hear the knocking over the shower," she said.

"I was starting to get worried." I lugged her suitcase into the room and heaved it onto the bed.

"Thank you very much for getting my stuff. Were there any problems?"

"Nothing I couldn't handle. Your husband came home a little sooner than I expected, so I had to leave in a bit of a hurry. I ended up leaving the Cadillac at your house. I drove my other car out here."

"So does William know that I left?"

"If he doesn't, then he'll figure it out pretty soon."

"I thought I'd like to go home to Chicago. I'd feel safer there."

"No doubt you would be, but if there isn't an APB out on you by now, there will be shortly. If he raises the alarm he can have people watching airports, train stations and bus depots. With all of the abductions you see in the Herald, he won't have a problem getting your face on the cover of the local paper."

"So I'm stuck here watching the Beverly Hillbillies and taking five showers a day to get the filth of this room off of me?"

"I kind of like the Beverly Hillbillies, but I tell you what, I stopped and picked up some Chinese food. Why don't we have something to eat and then decide what to do?"

"Did you pick up Chinese food because I'm half Chinese?"

"I thought it would make you feel at home."

She looked around the motel room and then gave me a disbelieving look. We both broke out laughing. Grabbing clothes from her suitcase she said she would be back in a second. She went into the bathroom leaving the door slightly ajar. If I stood at the right angle, I could see her in the bathroom mirror. She had a hot figure, like beach sand on a blazing summer day. I suddenly realized that if I could see her, she could see me watching her.

Her voice came from the bathroom, "Why are you doing all of this Gabriel?"

I spread out the Chinese food on the small table, opening two beers. "You mean helping you, protecting you, hiding you and rescuing your silky lingerie?"

"Yes, I hired you to prove the affair; you've done that.....wait a minute. You were touching my lingerie?"

"I'm actually wearing a pair."

Laughing again, "You really are a pervert aren't you?"

We were both famished, and the food hit the spot. During the meal, I filled her in on the investigation into the missing girls, including Boone disappearing, the snow globe, and finding the safe deposit box key.

"Are you saying there might be evidence that could incriminate my husband in the disappearance of these girls?"

"Um! I'm hoping." I took a bite of a chicken dish with noodles. "The deputies raided Dermody's house after the accident looking for something. A few days ago a psycho pillow killer trashed my apartment. I originally thought they were sending me a message, now I'm wondering if they were looking for whatever might be in that safe deposit box. We'll know for sure tomorrow. Mmm! This chicken dish is fantastic."

"You believe you can get him Gabriel, cross your heart?"

"Yes I do, we can connect him to the mafia, I watched as he did a drugs for guns deal. He's going down; I promise." I said with a confidence I didn't quite feel.

"Cooper is a controlling, manipulative sociopath, doing something to those girls' sounds too weird even for him," she said, taking a bite of an egg roll.

"It might not have been him directly; maybe it was that orange haired freak of a deputy."

"You mean Franklin? He and my husband are best friends. He lives one block over from our house. I always thought there was something off about that guy. My mom has an expression, "he left the store without all of his groceries."

I smiled at the expression. "Let's open our fortune cookies."

"My Dad tells me that stuff is a load of bull," she replied. "Do you know that almost all of the fortune cookies eaten around the world get made in the US? The one place where they don't eat fortune cookies is China."

She cracked hers open and read it out loud, "Every exit is an entrance to new experience."

"Wow, I'm sold," I said. "It's like that saying was meant just for you and what you're going through."

She urged me to open mine. "That wasn't chicken." We both groaned. "Speaking of food, I need to go do some shopping. Can you make a list of what you might need?"

"You're seriously expecting me to wait here until you have him arrested? Ocean Springs? No one knows me here."

"There's probably a dozen Chinese women in the whole state, and none that look ...well, like you. I think it's the safest thing to do. Besides we should know more tomorrow when we go to the bank."

"I think I should call him. Tell him I have proof of his affair, and that I have a lawyer who is going to take him for everything he has."

"I know you're anxious to move through to that new experience but wait for a few days." Using my most authoritative voice I said, "Now sit down and write out your list while I clean up."

When she finished the list, I took it and headed out in the Pinto to the Winn Dixie a couple of miles east of the motel. I picked up snack foods, juice boxes, drinks, reading material and a bunch of other stuff. When I got back, she helped me unload everything. She stopped all of a sudden and said, "You never answered my question about why, and don't start about my silky lingerie."

"I don't know, I guess I like you, and I don't want to see you getting hurt."

With that, she gave me an embrace, and magically my lips found hers. The kiss was tentative at first, her bending down, me on my tippy-toes. Her lips were soft, full, moist, her scent intoxicating. My heart was racing. The passion bottled up inside me since that first meeting came out like fireworks. She moaned softly, I took that as encouragement. She pushed me back gently with her hand. "Slow down big guy."

Chapter 45

Gabriel- Thursday Morning, Day 11

I arrived at the Sun Bank shortly before ten on Thursday morning, after spending the early part of the morning completing insurance forms for Ahmed. I found Ben waiting anxiously for the doors to open. My comments yesterday must have hit home as he was nattily attired in a brown suit with a striped shirt and paisley tie. He had called the bank manager yesterday about opening the safe deposit box. I had met the manager, Mr. Grayson a couple of weeks ago when I was inquiring about the activity on Rebecca Glaswell's account. He was a thin man, in his mid-fifties and a member of the bowtie club. I remembered him as a little officious with a nervous personality. Letting us in the door, Grayson led us into his office and asked us to be seated. After taking the key from me, he left us for a few minutes.

"How was last night?" asked Ben with a sly look on his face.

"Pretty uneventful, I left her watching the Beverly Hillbillies. You know the episode where Jethro wants to become a frogman and practices his scuba diving in the "Ceeement Pond?"

"The one where Granny is convinced that Jethro has turned into a frog, after he goes swimming because he said he wanted to take frogman lessons...., yeah I remember it...a classic."

Grayson came back in with the key, carrying an index card. "You gentleman may have made a trip down here for nothing. I can positively confirm that Mr. Alex Dermody was the registered owner of box 239. I can further confirm that this key will open box 239. However, unless Mr. Dermody presents himself, or you have a court order, then I'm afraid that I will be unable to open the box for you."

"You know that Mr. Dermody is physically unable to come to the bank." said Ben.

"I am aware of Mr. Dermody's condition but that is immaterial." said Mr. Know-it-All.

"Would the Bank have a copy of the power of attorney granted by Mr. Dermody to his wife Trixie?" I asked.

"Ur...I would have to check on that ...but she would need to be present to sign the safe deposit box admittance card."

"That's okay; I talked to her and she should be along any minute," I said smugly.

Ben and I waited again while Grayson went out searching for the Power of Attorney. "Have you been practicing with that revolver I gave you?" asked Ben.

"As I told you, good detectives don't need guns. I hid it under the seat of the car."

"I think you might need it when Cooper discovers his little birdie has flown the coop."

I was about to make some brave comment about not needing no stinkin' gun, when Mr. Know-it-All came back in the room with the Power of Attorney and Mrs. Dermody in tow. The running mascara told me that she wasn't having a great day. Once again she was packed into her clothes like a polish sausage that had split apart in the pan, wearing the same makeup and clothes she'd worn yesterday. Grayson had Mrs. Dermody sign the admittance card and then he escorted us into a small, windowless room with a table and chairs. Grayson and Ben excused themselves and went to get the box. As we waited at the table, I looked over at Trixie. She was clearly hung-over. Her eyes looked like someone had made them with a two-hole punch. It struck me how this incident must have dredged up emotions in her that she had long since buried.

Ben came back in carrying a long box that was 4 inches tall and about 5 inches wide. The first thing we saw when we opened the box was Benjamin Franklin. Lots of them. Five hundred to be precise. I watched Trixie's eyes bulge like a lizard. "Where did all this money come from?" She said. She started to pull the money out of the box, looking through the bundles and checking the denomination. Once the money had been taken out she pulled out a clear plastic baggie containing a silver locket. The only other item was a letter that Trixie passed to me to read. I assumed that the long flowing script belonged to her husband.

To my Darling Trixie,

If you're reading this then, I must be dead. My guess is that my attorney, upon my death, has instructed you to retrieve the key from the globe. I have hidden a great deal from you in order to protect you from getting involved in the mess that I created. My hope is that you will sell the house and move away as we had planned. There is enough money in this box to help you start somewhere new. If anyone other than my wife is reading this note, I want to make it clear that Trixie had no knowledge or involvement in what I am about to explain.

I'd like to begin by getting a few things off my chest. I first met William Cooper at college in Oxford Mississippi. When he was elected Sheriff of Harrison County, he called me and asked me to join him in Biloxi. He said he needed someone who would have his back with the local press. He said he was working with people who could help my career as a journalist. These people, he explained, were influential businessmen who helped him get elected and would be willing to pay a fee for articles that promoted Biloxi and cast the Sheriff's department in the best possible light. As part of the post-election campaign, this was explained as something that would help citizens feel safer. The cash was small at first, and I guess I knew that what I was doing was wrong, but I allowed myself to not think too much about it. I valued the experience I was getting. Looking back at what happened, I confess that I may have been gullible in my involvement in the beginning. As time went by, the bonus money increased, as did the demands that I suppress instances of bribery and influence-peddling. With this letter, I admit my involvement in this scheme. It was with my full understanding and agreement. In addition, I believe this scheme involved my boss Roscoe Perry. As the editor, he never questioned me on the veracity of my reporting.

During my time at the Herald, I came to have a different opinion of William Cooper. I learned that he was involved in a vast, well organized, criminal network. His participation, like mine no doubt, began gradually; starting with looking the wrong way for the right people, to later being actively involved in drug smuggling and gun running. I fully regret getting involved in this scheme and should you decide to donate the funds to a worthy charity I would not blame you. I decided to write this letter because I learned through my investigations of a terrible crime. A crime, so heinous even I could not sweep under the rug. One of the Sheriff's deputies, Barry Franklin, was involved in the case of a 16 year old teenage girl named Anne Mullens. She went missing in March of 1974. I believe that there may have been other related disappearances in other parts of the state. I went to William about my concerns, and we argued. When I threatened to go to the FBI, I was threatened. If you are reading this, then chances are that something has happened to me. Don't believe anything they tell you. These people, including Sheriff Cooper and Deputy Franklin, cannot afford to have a loose end causing problems.

My darling Trixie, I suggest you accept my death as my penance for what I have done. I am not asking you to go to the police. All that would do is invite reprisals. Get as far away from Biloxi as you can.

Please forgive me

Love Alex

P.S. I have enclosed a locket that I believe belonged to Anne Mullens. When I interviewed her mother, she said Anne always wore it as it was a gift from her grandmother. While arguing with Sheriff Cooper, I went looking for a pencil and found it in Deputy Franklin's desk. I kept it in the little plastic bag just in case there are prints tying Anne Mullens to her killer.

The three of us sat in the room without speaking. The letter was a lot to take in. I couldn't imagine what Mrs. Dermody was thinking and wondered whether this latest development would drive her further into a bottle.

"OK Ben, we have an assault that sounds like it might have been staged to look like an accident. We have Dermody's confession on the collusion to mislead the citizens of Biloxi. We have the connection through the letter and the locket to either the deputy or the Sheriff or both. We have Dermody confirming what I witnessed the other night that William Cooper was involved in drug smuggling and selling illegal firearms. Now I know I'm not a genius but I can't help but think we must have enough to put this guy away."

Ben did not immediately answer; instead he turned his gaze to Mrs. Dermody.

"Alex wasn't a very smart man. I don't care about his money. As for leaving here though, I will never leave my husband. I want you to arrest the assholes that did this to him." I silently cheered, thinking maybe that I had misjudged her.

"Ok folks, we are all in agreement. Please keep in mind that the letter by itself will not be enough to convict these guys. The letter alleges crimes that he was party to. In his present condition, he won't be able to add his testimony or be cross-examined. Now if the locket does belong to the missing girl and has Franklin or Cooper's fingerprint, than I think we have him for at least one of the disappearances."

"So what's the next step?"

"I'll take the note, the cash and the locket with me and I'll have the locket dusted for prints. Depending on what we find I can speak to Chief of Police Ricketts and the District Attorney about a warrant. If there are no prints then, I am going to suggest that I bring Franklin in for questioning."

Chapter 46

Gabriel – Thursday Afternoon, Day 11

After a quick lunch, I decided to stop by and see Bud at the Rockaway. Parking the Pinto, I walked into the bar. Amber was at the bar washing glasses. She rolled her eyes when she saw me, then turned her back, saying "Why don't you make somebody happy and mind your own business?"

"Whatever it is that's eating you sweetheart, it must be suffering horribly. I came to see Bud. Is he around?"

"I haven't seen him since you were here last; you must have scared him away." She turned towards me, her hands drying a beer glass. There was something about her tone and her look that told me there was something she wasn't saying.

"Is it unusual for him not to come in every day?"

"There you go with the questions again, Perv. Ordinary people live and learn, but you, you just live."

"Is there another number I can reach him at?" I asked ignoring her jibe.

"Here's some free advice, this might be an excellent time for you to become a missing person." With that she walked back into the kitchen. That was most likely the only truthful thing she'd said.

I decided my next stop should be my office to see if any goons were looking for me. Thankfully there weren't, just Bourbon waiting patiently on the fire escape. I let the cat in and gave him his normal treat. I looked up all the Bud Carsons in the book, and found one on Magnolia Street. The phone rang until a woman with a thick Irish accent answered. "Would Bud Carson be home?" I asked.

"E's not hooome, who's this?" There was a touch of suspicion in her voice.

"My name's Gabriel Ross. I met with him a couple of days ago. I'd like to speak to him again."

"You said you met with my Bud a couple of days agoooo?"

"Yes, we had a drink together at his bar."

"Well, I'm his wife and I haven't seen him since Tuesday, when he left to go to work."

"Is it unusual for him to leave on his own without telling you Mrs. Carson?"

"Yea it is. I'm very worried about him. I called the sheriff's office, and they told me to wait a couple of days. Those gombeens… nothing but useless lie-abouts. They said he was probably checking out some new talent."

I could tell she was getting upset. I wasn't helping. "Was that true, do you think Mrs. Carson?"

"Nay, Bud always came home to me. He knows not to get involved with those slappers that work in his bar. He never goes away without checking in with me."

"Usually the cops don't do anything until a person is missing for 48 hours. Why don't you call the Biloxi Police Department? Ask to speak to Detective Ben O'Shea. He's a friend of mine. Tell him that I suggested you call. And if Bud happens to show, please ask him to call me, it's urgent." I dictated my office number, ending the call with a lame "Try not to worry."

I figured I had best place a call to Ben, and see whether anything had developed since our meeting that morning. I tried his office line but got Greenlaw again, talking in a tired, robotic voice, "Detective O'Shea has left for the day, I have no idea when he's returning, and no I don't know where he went."

I decided to check out the grocery store across the street, Bourbon's tuna supplies were getting low. I picked out Star-Kist, mainly because I thought Bourbon had good taste. As I paid for the tuna, my attention was diverted to a sedan that came to a stop and double parked in front of my building. I watched as the Incredible Hulk got out and pimp-walked his way into the building. Crossing the street, I followed him in, and watched as he got on the elevator by himself. The building janitor Larry was in the lobby changing the building directory. "Hey Larry, do you want to help me payback that guy who beat me up?"

"Sure thing Mr. Ross, where's he at?" He assumed the boxer's stance again, fists at the ready.

"Do you have a key for the elevator?"

He pulled a bunch of keys off his belt and pointed to the one that controlled the elevator. "Turn this key in that panel and the elevator will stop on a dime."

I inserted and turned the key. The elevator stopped between the 5th and 6th floors. A few moments later the elevator phone rang. I let it ring a few times, gesturing to Larry to let me handle it. After about a minute I answered.

"Hello, you have reached Larry, the Superintendent; I can't come to the phone right now. Please leave your name, phone number, short message, social security number, and credit card number, and I'll call you when I'm finished shopping."

Larry could hardly contain himself as I hung up. We shared a good laugh at Mr. Green's expense. The phone rang again a few minutes later. I answered, "Do you have that credit card number Mr. Green?"

"Who is this? You son of a bitch," he said in that Michael Jackson voice.

"We have notified the elevator company. They will be sending a technician from their service center in Jackson. It should be no more than a few hours. We do apologize for the inconvenience. For your enjoyment, please join me in singing...at the Copa, Copacabana, the hottest spot north of Havana, at the Copa." I warbled. Mr. Green slammed the phone down rudely, cutting off my rendition.

I peeled off a couple of sawbucks and handed them to Larry. "I suggest you go have a late lunch on me. When you get back, turn the key and then get the hell out of here."

I took the stairs up to my office and put Bourbon back out on the fire escape and locked the door. I decided to head out to Ocean Springs, after a quick stop at a local store. I was anxious to see Jacqueline. The lines on the highway flashed by as I counted down the minutes before I got to the motel. This time the motel room door opened as soon as I got out of the Pinto. A flurry of questions hit me as soon as I got into the room. I silenced her by drawing her close in to me and kissing her hard and passionately. When I pulled away, she said, "Whew, now can I have some answers?"

"Have you ever played Jeopardy? As long as I get a kiss for every answer." I kissed her again, a long one.

"Is William in jail?"

"Not yet," I said, moving in for another kiss. I was loving this game.

"Did you guys go to the bank?" The questions were coming more slowly now as if it was harder for her to keep focused.

"Yes," moving in for another kiss, this one even longer.

She started to laugh with a husky tone in her voice. "What was in the safe deposit box?"

"There was roughly $50,000 in cash, plus a letter to his wife confessing to writing biased stories, and implicating your husband in a drugs-for-guns scheme. There was also a locket that belonged to one of the missing girls. My partner is having it checked for prints. All of this must be worth a double kiss!" I took her in my arms. As I kissed her, my hands roamed her body looking for fun places.

"I'm getting a kink in my neck. How about we carry on the Jeopardy game from the bed?" Climbing onto the bed she asked, "So is the letter enough to arrest him?"

"No, but the locket might do it if we find a fingerprint. Otherwise, we'd need to catch him in the act or get a confession. As they say in Jeopardy that was the daily double." Now I knew why the bed was bowed in the middle. Our bodies fit together like they were meant for each other.

After a couple of rounds of Double Jeopardy, she begged for a rest. While we lay on the bed, I noticed that she had a heart-shaped birthmark on her inner thigh. I commented on it, and she told me that Cooper felt it somehow translated into a sign of her love for him. "I told you he could be sappy."

"Let me ask you…does Cooper take off his hat when he has sex?"

"Sometimes he likes to leave it on…it's kind of power thing. Why do you ask?"

"Just curious."

I turned on the TV, and ironically Jeopardy was just coming on the air. I whistled along with the Frisco Disco, the catchy theme song. As I started to get dressed, the broadcast was pre-empted by an urgent public service announcement. In a surreal moment, a picture of the woman I had just made love to flashed on the screen.

Chapter 47

Gabriel – Thursday Evening, Day 11

Turning up the sound, the reporter was saying "Her name is Jacqueline Cooper, wife of Harrison County's own Sheriff William Cooper. She was last seen this past Tuesday. The sheriff's department has placed an urgent alert with all neighboring towns and state police. There is speculation that Mrs. Cooper's disappearance may be linked to the investigation into a missing teen. The public should be on the lookout for her and report any sightings to the Harrison County Sheriff's Office. Jacqueline Cooper as shown in this wedding photo is a Chinese American approximately 5 foot 10 and weighing approximately 150 pounds. She is slim and has shoulder length dark brown hair." The screen then showed a picture of William Cooper talking at a news conference.

"Jacqueline, honey if you can hear me, don't lose hope." Then speaking as if he was looking directly at me, he said in an icy tone, "I'll find you, and when I do, the person behind this will suffer the full weight of justice."

"Oh my God, Gabriel he's going to find us. You saw that look on his face; he's going to kill us."

"Five foot 10? Are your parents tall?"

"Get serious Gabriel, what are we going to do?"

"I wouldn't worry," I said, lying down with my hands behind my head.

"What, you said yourself that there are only a handful of Chinese people here. I'll stand out like the Great Wall of China!"

"I said I wouldn't worry about it because they are looking for a Chinese woman." On seeing her blank expression, I added, "Did you know that Cassius Clay converted to Islam? Have you ever considered converting to Islam?"

"What? Gabriel, we need to figure out what to do!" She was clearly getting exasperated.

Getting up and going to the bag I'd brought with me, I pulled out a beautiful black niqab and other garments I'd picked up from a store in Biloxi. The idea had come to me after watching Mrs. Ahmed vacuum the carpets. A person could wear the outfit and as long as no one got too close or asked a question, they would just assume you were from some Islamic country.

"What am I supposed to do with this?" Jacqueline wailed.

"Just humor me and try it on." I watched as she tried on the outfit, looking at herself in the mirror from various angles. She seemed pleased. You couldn't tell she was Chinese. "Are you sure it'll work?"

"Absolutely." Watching her in her niqab prompted a suggestion that it was time for Final Jeopardy.

Chapter 48

Cooper – Thursday a few hours before

I arrived home at around 4:15 and the bitch's car was in the driveway. She's going to learn an important lesson. The Cadillac's hood was still warm; she must have just arrived home. I opened the front door and yelled, "Jacqueline." I thought I heard something in the bedroom. Good, maybe she'd do a little penance for her sins. I moved through the kitchen and picked up a bread roller. "Oh Jacqueline." I heard the sound of something being dragged coming from the bedroom, and the patio door opening. Bet she's going out to get some sun. I slapped the roller against my open palm. As I entered the bedroom, I saw the room was in disarray, drawers pulled out, closet open. What the fuck? I looked outside on the patio, but there was nothing. I sensed that someone had just been here. Walking outside, I heard a noise to the right, but once again nothing.

Crossing the pool area, I exited at the gate and looked up and down the street. That impudent little kid Travis was there wanting to go swimming in the pool. I told him to take a hike. Could that little creep have been in the house? Where the fuck was Jacqueline? I walked over to the driveway and peered into the Cadillac's window. Something was wrong. I looked around the neighborhood again. All I saw was that kid running back down the street. I suddenly realized what was wrong. Opening the driver's door, I tried to sit in the driver's seat but I couldn't. Someone had adjusted it, a much shorter person. Someone really short, almost midget-like. I realized I was still carrying the bread roller and headed back into the house, trying to figure out what was going on. I suspected that she had left me, obviously getting help from someone short. Could this be the same guy driving around in the VW? The private detective who was at the club the other night taking pictures? What was the connection between Jacqueline and that little runt? Were they having an affair? Anger was welling up inside me, a hurricane of wrath that exploded with the bread roller going into the TV.

I threw my hat on the counter and rubbed my forehead from the headache she had given me. Where could they have gone? Jacqueline had no friends. All of our friends were really my friends, and they wouldn't hesitate to call me if she showed up.

I noticed a slight bulge in the ribbon around the base of my hat as it sat on the counter. Picking it up, I pulled the ribbon back and a small metal object fell onto the table. Son of a bitch, it was a bug! Who the fuck? The FBI must be on to me, but how? I replayed the conversations I'd had recently, and wondered if I had somehow divulged something. Was it safe? How could they have planted the bug?

That kid Travis! He was in my office asking me all those stupid questions about JFK! I'd bet he planted it when I went to the washroom. He could have easily done it. But why? He's just a kid, where would he get something like this? Events and people were clicking into place like the tumblers of a lock lining up. That kid is Franklin's son! Maybe Franklin had turned and was working with the FBI. What a fucker!!! That must be it. Franklin had come to me about Boone the other day and said that the Biloxi police wanted to talk to him about the missing girls and the van. Franklin suggested we set Boone up to be the fall guy. I'd said no way, so maybe he got pissed and decided to be a rat. I was glad I'd called Boone and had him get out safely. A blind rage swept over me like a fire. Leaving the bug on the table, I angrily stomped out of the house.

Driving to the plaza down the street, I stopped at a payphone. My first call was to the sheriff's office. Deputy Jenkins answered the phone.

"Listen Jenkins, it's Sheriff Cooper. I want an all-points bulletin put out right away as a county emergency. I believe someone has abducted my wife. Probably the same sick fuck that's been taking the teenage girls. Get this out to all neighbors and state police forces. When you're done with that, call Roscoe Perry at the Sun Herald and tell him to put the alert on the front page with a file picture of Jacqueline from our wedding. You getting all this, Jenkins?"

"I'm with you Sheriff Cooper, anything else?"

"Yeah, I want you to call the TV station and arrange a press conference as soon as possible. We're going to catch this fucker!"

My second call was to New Orleans. I reluctantly dialed the number that I knew by heart. Frank answered right away.

"Frank, it's Sheriff Cooper. We have a problem."

There was a pause on the line before Frank replied, "What's that?"

"I found a listening device planted in my hat today, by accident."

There was another long uncomfortable silence. "In your hat? How stupid do you have to be to let someone put a bug in your hat?"

"Franklin's kid was in my office the other day and he's the only one that had the opportunity to do that."

"You think Franklin's talking to the feds? I thought he was one of your best men."

"I thought so too."

"Okay William, I'll take care of it."

He rarely called me William; I decided to get all the dirt out on the table. "There's one other thing Frank, Jacqueline is gone. I don't know where she is, but I'm concerned. So you might hear about this on the news. There's nothing for you to do on this one; I'll take care of it."

"You sure it's safe William? She might be talking to the feds too." I could sense that my life was being considered as he weighed the risks.

"I'll take care of her," I said vehemently.

Chapter 49

Gabriel – Friday Morning, Day 12

It was now Friday morning, and I'd woken up early. The memory of last night flashed back to me in a blaze of Technicolor. I looked over and saw Jacqueline curled up, every bit as beautiful in the morning light. She must have sensed my gaze as her eyes drew open. She smiled in contentment, mirroring my thoughts.

"Good morning folks, if it isn't the winner of Final Jeopardy! You get to return tonight for a repeat performance."

She laughed and said she couldn't wait, and then gave me a stern look. "After my shower, you need to take this old Pakistani woman for some breakfast." As we got dressed, we listened to the morning news before heading out. There was no update on last night's late breaking story. I looked over at Jacqueline with all but her eyes covered in the black niqab. "How do I look?" she asked.

"You look fantastic and surprisingly sexy."

"I guess you had better stay away from Muslim countries."

We headed out shortly before 9 and drove south into Ocean Springs. On the way, I suggested that Jacqueline practice her Pakistani accent just in case she had to speak to someone. It would lend even more credibility to the disguise.

"I don't know how?"

"It's very simple. There was a Pakistani family who owned the neighborhood variety store when I was growing up in Detroit. They tend to over-pronounce syllables and end their sentences on a high tone. Pronounce V words as if they started with a W. Oh and be overly polite. Women from Pakistan who would be visiting our country would be higher class, so be snooty, confident and make good eye contact."

"Give me an example."

"Ok, try this, Tank you wery, wery much, my name is Yasmeeen and I am from Kahrahchi, Pakistaaan. Drag Pakistan out like you're calling someone to come in for dinner."

She tried it a couple of times and forgiving the overacting, she did pretty well. It was another 80 plus degrees outside, the fifth day in a row without rain in the forecast. Giant puffy white clouds lumbered across the blue sky like gobs of marshmallow fluff. You could feel the heat bounce off the road. As we arrived into the downtown area, we were both impressed. There was something quaint about a little town where people parked diagonally along the main street. The historic buildings were all well maintained. It reminded me of a scene from a Norman Rockwell painting. We parked on a side street lined with tall oaks at created a beautiful tree tunnel.

As we made our way to the main street, Jacqueline, in her best accent, pointed to a nearby eatery, "Please to stop at that restaurant."

The sign in front of the building announced Henrietta's Café established in 1943. I put an arm out and held her back looking left and right for policemen. I didn't see a soul. The town looked like it was still asleep.

In contrast, Henrietta's was fairly busy, full of folks starting their day with a home-cooked breakfast. The waitress, a young brunette wearing a white uniform with a "Midge" nametag on her left breast, showed us to a table. Midge complimented Jacqueline on her beautiful outfit. "Are you visiting from Arabia?" she asked.

"No, thank you wery much, I am from Karahhhchi Pakistaaan." I think she overdid the Pakistan bit, as people in the restaurant looked over at us.

"Well, golly gee, y'all the way from...where?"

"Pakistan," I interjected "it's near India." I could have said South America and she wouldn't have been the wiser.

"Well…welcome to America!" gushed Midge, handing us laminated menus and taking our coffee order.

When she left, I noticed that an older lady at the next table continued to stare. I said in a voice loud, "Yasmeen, your English is getting very good. Tell me do they watch Jeopardy in Pakistan?"

I saw her eyes trying to contain her laughter, "Oh yes! Very much so, Yeppardy is wery popular. I think I plan to watch it tonight."

"That's great Yasmeen. Maybe I will watch it with you."

The older lady got up to leave and stopped on her way. "I just think you are the loveliest, most delicate person, and I love your accent."

"Oh, werry nice of you fine lady. Thank you." Jacqueline replied, doing some sort of Chinese bow.

Midge came back with our coffees and asked for our order.

"I shall have the eggs and sausage with a side order of toast." said Yasmeen, forgetting about her accent.

Midge wrote this down and said, "The cook said to say that we are so sorry, we just have pork sausages."

I watched as Yasmeen's eyes darted back and forth like frightened fish. I jumped in, "if they're pork sausages, than Yasmeen will not be able to have them. But I can, so you can add them to my order."

"Good catch on the pork Gabriel," she said once the waitress left. "Are there any other rules that I should know?"

"Probably, your guess is as good as mine though."

"Since you're so smart how do I eat and drink with this thing on?"

"I don't know, but I guess when you want to drink your coffee, put it under your niqab and put the cup to your lips." She tried it with the coffee, lifting the bottom up and putting the coffee under. She ended up spilling coffee on her clothes. It was hard for me not to break out laughing. "I can't wait to see how you manage the eggs."

The meal came, and she managed okay. At one point, she dropped the toast from the top of the niqab into her mouth. I noticed a few people watching the show. By the time she was finished her meal she had smeared her black veil with egg yolk and coffee stains. Yasmeen decided to use the washroom to get cleaned up. While she was gone I took care of the bill. There was something bugging me. It was at the edge of my mind; at the back of my brain; something that Jacqueline had said. I couldn't get it.

When Yasmeen came back, she saw that we were once again free to speak and said, "So you are quite the Casanova in bed, Mr. Fleming. Do you have a long list of conquests from when you were younger?"

It took a moment to register that she was calling me Art Fleming, the moderator of Jeopardy. "No, just the opposite I was pretty much a late bloomer."

"I find that hard to believe, you seem to know your way around pretty well."

"I'll tell you a true story from back when I was a kid in high school. I was maybe 14 and like all boys that age I was obsessed with boobs. I had a buddy who had a lot more experience than me and one day I asked him what it felt like to touch a woman's breasts. He said they were kind of spongy, like jello. Well to make a long story short, my Mom had just made a bowl of green jello and had put it in the fridge for dessert that night. At the supper table that night she asked about the mangled jello. I'll always remember my dad laughing when I told her that I groped it."

"Oh my God, you really are twisted, taking pictures of me sunbathing and now this."

That's when it came to me. "You said something the other day about the sheriff's deputy, the guy with the orange hair…."

"What, that he went to college with Will?"

"No not that, something else."

"I'm not sure what I said. They live one block over from our house. They have the cutest little boy, named Travis."

Chapter 50

Gabriel –Friday Morning, Day 12

Now that I put it together, Travis being Deputy Franklin's son made sense. Not only did they both have the red hair, but what ten year old kid would be that comfortable walking into the Sheriff's office with a listening device? I had to think that Travis could have given me up easily, but for some reason had kept my surveillance of Sheriff Cooper secret.

Jacqueline gave me Franklin's address on the way back to the motel. I dropped her off, telling her that I would return as soon as possible. I stopped at a pay phone and called Ben. When he answered, the first thing he wanted to know was whether I had seen the news bulletins about Jacqueline Cooper.

"Yes. We're keeping a low profile, but she's worried that he's going to find her."

"I put the word out to Greenlaw that she was staying at a hotel in Gulfport, but I haven't heard anything."

"Could we get a US Marshall to provide 24-hour protection for her? She could become a material witness against her husband."

"I can speak to Ricketts about that." I brought him up to date on Travis Franklin. "Wait a minute, who's Travis Franklin?"

"At first he told me his name was Jimmy Carter, but then he confessed that his name was Franklin. I just put it together this morning; he's Deputy Franklin's kid."

"Well, guess what? We just got the fingerprint analysis on the locket. There's a partial print on the back of the locket, and it's a pretty good match for what we have on file for Franklin."

"You had his prints on file?"

"He served in the National Guard briefly when he was on summer break. The feds keep a database."

"Is the partial enough to arrest him?"

"Chief of Police Ricketts is working on the warrant as we speak; I expect we'll have it signed by a judge this afternoon."

"What did Ricketts say when you showed him Dermody's written confession?"

"He was very upset; he feels the letter is enough to bring Sheriff Cooper in for questioning. Without any corroboration though, we'll need him to confess."

"Listen, did Mrs. Carson call you about her husband?"

"Yes, I spoke to her last night. As of this morning he still hasn't shown up. We have an alert out. You don't have him stashed in a motel somewhere too do you?"

"Funny man."

Before ending the call, he said he would be back in touch once they got the warrant and had picked up Franklin.

Driving into the office, I wondered how angry the Hulk had been when he finally got out of that elevator. I needed to make sure that I kept an eye out for him. I didn't know what to do about Travis. I decided to head over to Cooper's house and do a quick drive by Franklin's house to see if Travis was around. It was near 11:00 am when I pulled up down the street from Franklin's house. There was a Jeep Cherokee parked in the driveway. It was a Friday so I would have expected Travis to be at school. The door to the house opened and I saw Franklin carrying a box to the jeep. Pumpkin Hair was yelling, telling Travis to hurry up. Something told me I had better park and observe. If I had to guess, I would say someone tipped Franklin off, and he was planning to run for it. I watched as the two of them went back into the house, Franklin shoving Travis from behind. I made up my mind to follow Franklin when he left. At least until I could either safely get Travis away or notify the cops of their location.

It had been 10 minutes, and the two of them were still in the house. All of a sudden a sedan pulled up in front of the house blocking the driveway. I recognized it from yesterday. Mr. Green needed a lesson in parking etiquette. First double parking, now he was blocking a driveway. He stepped out of the car, accompanied by a large black man wearing a purple three-piece suit. His name was probably Mr. Purple. I watched as they approached the house. Green pulled a revolver with a huge barrel out of his jacket. It had to be 12 inches long. I reached under the seat and retrieved Ben's '38 special. Why you ask? I don't know. At the sight of Green's gun, I looked down at my little snub-nosed and it appeared to shrink. I watched the two of them enter the house.

I still didn't know what to do. I looked around the neighborhood to see if anyone else was watching and could call for help. No one. Thank you Ben for the lesson at the gun range. I checked to make sure I had loaded the gun. I couldn't have given a rat's ass about Franklin, but I was hoping that we could at least squeeze him for a confession. My thoughts went to Travis' safety, when all of a sudden I heard a PAAP, PAAP, like the sound of firecrackers going off from inside the house. The PAAPs were followed by a large BOOM.

Taking the safety off my gun, I stepped out of the car. I still didn't know what to do. I didn't know if I had it in me to shoot someone. All I cared about was saving Travis. Crouching, I ran across the street, the '38 cocked and loaded at my side. I heard more PAAPs followed by another BOOM. Gunfire was erupting faster than a bag of Jiffy Pop at a wiener roast in Hell.

Reaching the veranda, I looked around to see if the sounds might have alerted the neighbors. The door to the house directly across the street opened, and an old white-haired man came out holding a shotgun. I waved to him to go back inside, using my thumb and pinkie to make what I thought was the universal signal for phoning for help. He yelled out to me to get away from there, or he was gonna shoot my ass. Continuing the pantomime, this time I made out that I was dialing the phone. I heard a screen door open, and slam closed, followed by the sound of running feet. A moment later Travis came running from the back of the house crying. Quickly I picked him up, throwing him onto my shoulder like a sack of potatoes. I ran as fast as I could back to the Pinto, hoping the old coot across the street wouldn't shoot me. Another BOOM came from behind me.

Back in the car, I put Travis in the passenger seat and jumped behind the wheel. I turned the ignition only to hear the dreaded 'aeheheheheh' noise. "Found on road dead", might just have multiple meanings in this case. I looked across the street to Franklin's house, and I saw Mr. Purple at the screen door. 'Ehehehehehe' as I tried the ignition again. "You're flooding it", yelled Travis. Now Mr. Purple was pointing at me, and Mr. Green appeared, holding up his cannon. I waited a moment then tried the ignition again. Finally, it caught, and I quickly put the car in gear, flooring it. In my side mirror, I saw them coming down the stairs running to their car. The little sewing machine maddeningly lagged, its transmission sluggish. I got out of the subdivision and pulled onto the main road heading for town. I didn't slow down until I got into city traffic.

"It's fine; you lost him," said Travis, looking behind him. I took a deep breath, and I realized that I was driving with the gun still in my hand. "Can we go back and check on my Dad?"

"We're going to find a phone and call this into the Biloxi police. Once they get to the scene we can go back. Right now I want you to be safe."

"Is my Dad dead?" Travis asked, his voice cracking with emotion. "I'm scared."

"I don't know; we'll have to say a prayer for him. So what happened this morning, where were you guys going?"

"Dad got a phone call before going to work and then he told me I wasn't going to school. He didn't say why. He said we were going up north to see my grandparents."

I looked over at Travis and tears had started to roll down his cheek. I pulled over at a pay phone. I told Travis he was a very brave boy and gave him a hug. The kid had been on a roller coaster over the past two weeks and had probably just witnessed his father being shot. I chastised myself for using Travis for my own purposes without giving a thought to what he must be going through. I asked about his mother and he said she left a couple of weeks ago to live with her parents up north. This brought on a fresh round of tears. I guess it was possible that this was a vacation but somehow his tears signaled that there was another reason. I suspected that Travis was unaware of what his father was involved in.

I drove until I found a pay phone and dialed Ben's number. Once again Greenlaw answered. When I asked for Ben, he launched into his normal, "he's not here-I don't know where he is-I don't know when he's getting back" routine. "Listen Greenlaw, my name is Gabriel Ross, I'm a private detective working with Ben and there's been a shooting at 1412 Stampede Drive. That's Deputy Sheriff Franklin's house." I lowered my voice, "You guys are working on an arrest warrant for the guy." I looked over at Travis sitting patiently in the car. "You need to drop everything and get there right away. It may already be too late."

"I don't know what you're talking about. There's no warrant for anyone named Franklin."

"Can't you use your radio and contact Ben?"

"He's not answering his radio. Oh and by the way some friend of yours, a hysterical Irish lady named Carson, has been calling every five minutes. She just hung up on me after calling me a gombeen."

I didn't know what a gombeen was, but I'd bet Greenlaw was the poster child. I asked to speak to Ricketts. Apparently he wasn't available either. I started yelling at Greenlaw, "Listen you had better get someone over there right now, there's been a shooting. If someone dies, then I'll make sure everyone knows you're responsible."

"Okay, okay settle down. I didn't say we wouldn't check it out. What's that address again?"

I gave him the address again and hung up. I didn't know what to do about Travis. I couldn't leave him. I suspected that Mr. Green and Mr. Purple had taken care of his dad. My collar started getting tight with the reality that they now knew what kind of car I drove, along, of course, with where I lived and worked.

Not long after hanging up from Greenlaw, I saw Biloxi police cars with sirens screaming and lights flashing, heading towards Franklin's. I waited another fifteen minutes before following along.

When I got to Franklin's house, the place was packed with cops like ants crawling on candy. The neighbors were out in full force watching from behind a perimeter established with yellow crime scene tape. I parked in the street and rolled down my window to a patrolman doing crowd control. "My name is Gabriel Ross; I'm a Private Detective working with Ben O'Shea. I called this in. Is Greenlaw here?"

"Yeah, he's the tall guy on the porch; pull your car in behind that cruiser." he said, pointing to a police car parked in front of the house. As we got out, the cop waved to Greenlaw to come over. Greenlaw was a tall man with dark hair and a hawkish nose wearing a grey pin-striped suit that was so wrinkled I bet it doubled as pajamas.

"I'm Gabriel Ross, how bad was it?"

He peered down at me, his face a mixture of annoyance and amusement similar to when you slap a mosquito by killing it on your arm. "Who's your partner?" gesturing at Travis.

"He lives here; he's Deputy Franklin's son."

"So what went on here Ross?" Deliberately not answering my question. The guy was as big a dick in person as he was on the phone. I gave him a quick rundown of what happened and the people involved.

"The big guy's name is Mr. Green, and the other is Mr. Purple?" he asked skeptically, writing in a little notebook.

"Well, that's just what I called him."

"Dressed in purple was he?"

"No, never mind, it's not important. What happened to Deputy Franklin?"

Greenlaw looked over at Travis then said, "Who else lives here?"

"Just the Deputy and Travis. The mother is up north with her parents."

At this point, he gestured for me to come with him, and he told a nearby patrolwoman to look after the kid. Greenlaw and I went up to the house, and he said, "There is a guy inside with red hair with two huge holes where his eyes used to be."

"Shit, I was afraid of that."

"After we take a statement from the kid then I will have someone drive him up to his mother and notify her of what happened."

"All right, I need to go tell him about his dad."

"Ross, what's all this business about... Mr. Green, Mr. Purple, some bullshit about an arrest warrant.....spill the beans."

I told Greenlaw about the ongoing investigation into the missing girls and how we had connected Franklin through the locket. "That's quite the story Ross. We'll need a full statement. Will O'Shea corroborate it?"

"Yes he will. Where is he?"

"Listen, I don't know where he is, where he went or what time he'll get back."

Chapter 51

Gabriel – Friday Afternoon, Day 12

I broke the news to Travis about his Dad. There wasn't much to say other than "I'm very sorry." He took it as well as one could expect. He asked me a lot of tough questions that I was poorly equipped to answer, the toughest being whether his Dad did anything wrong. All I could manage was that there was a lot still unknown. Travis deserved to know the truth. It just wasn't my place to tell him. He asked whether what he did, putting the bug in the Sheriff's hat, somehow got his Dad killed. "No, what you did will end up helping us catch those who did this to your Dad." He looked unconvinced, so I added; "Some bad men killed your Dad because they want the truth to stay hidden. The police will catch the killers and bring them to justice."

"Can I come and live with you Gabriel?"

I gave this a moment or two to consider. One day I would love to have a Travis of my own. For now, the kid needed to be with family. "I think those same bad men might want to find me, so the safest place for you to be is to be with your family up north. Once the police have arrested the bad guys, you and I will see a lot of each other. You are a very brave kid Travis. You'll make a fine Private Detective someday."

I left Travis in the hands of the policewoman. She was going to drive up north and notify his family. Watching them leave, I was lost about my next step. It was almost one in the afternoon, and it would be dangerous to either go home or to the office. I decided to grab some lunch at the Friendship Restaurant and trade the Pinto in on another car.

Tweedy gave me a big smile when I walked into the restaurant. I used the pay phone by the cash to call the office for messages. There were a couple of hang ups that I attributed to Mr. Green trying to find me, and a message from Mrs. Carson from earlier in the day saying that she wanted to hire me to find her husband. I decided to spend another dime and tried Ben again. After five long rings, the line was answered by a nasal-voiced lady handling the switchboard. "There doesn't seem to be anyone answering at the moment, would you like to leave a message?"

"Yes please tell Detective O'Shea that he needs to call Gabriel Ross as soon as possible."

My mind was reeling like the tilt-a-wheel at the amusement park. I had a lot of questions. Mr. Green worked for Frank, who was part of the Mafia. Why would the Mafia decide to kill Franklin? Who tipped him off about the arrest? Was it the same guy who tipped off Boone Cooper? Why didn't Greenlaw know about the warrant? Where was Ben? Were Mr. Green and Mr. Purple out looking for me? I had better start finding the right answers before the wrong people found me.

Tweedy brought me the bill, and I don't even remember eating my food. I gathered my gear and walked over to the Hertz office. The same young girl was behind the counter. I explained that I needed to rent something a little bigger for another week. She pulled my rental agreement and asked me if I was happy with the Pinto.

"Sure I just need something a little bigger, maybe a pick-up truck or something."

"You all have some hawlin' to do?"

"Yes, nothing too heavy."

"I have a 1978 Ford Ranger. Think you can handle that?" Before I had a chance to respond she added, "Seeing how you've been driving the Pinto."

"That will be fine."

Once I got the Ranger on the road I noticed a significant difference in pickup. Instead of a vacuum cleaner, I was now driving a tank. It was already 2:30 and I figured a safe place to go would be back to the Sheriff's office. As I pulled into the drug store parking lot, I could see that the listening post was still on the street. I plugged in my recording equipment, but there was nothing, not even white noise. The situation became weirder when the Sheriff appeared at the front of the building talking to a couple of businessmen types. There must be something wrong. He was wearing his hat, but there was nothing coming through on the receiver. Could he have discovered the microphone? If so, could Travis be right and did this somehow explain what happened earlier today? So many questions. Was all the Jeopardy talk starting to get to me?

I put the truck in gear and drove to a phone booth. I tried Ben again and once again got Greenlaw. I couldn't stomach his usual routine, so I hung up. I called Mrs. Carson who was frantic about her husband not coming home.

"I called that Detective you suggested and he said he would get a report out right away. He asked me for some information on Bud's car. I didn't have that with me at the time, so I called back this morning, and they told me he was out. He hasn't called me back. I don't know what to do Mr. Ross, so I called you. Maybe you can take the case."

"Yes Mrs. Carson, why don't you give me the information. I'll share it with Detective O'Shea and see what I can find out for you." She gave me the information about his car, and I asked about other family that he might have gone to visit, friends who might have seen him, etc. "Do you know if he's used his bank account?"

"No, I don't, but I can go to the bank today and let you know." I thanked her for working with me and said I'd get on the case right away. In the back of my mind, I wondered if Bud was already dead. The term dropping like flies seemed strangely appropriate for a strip club owner.

I stopped on the way to Ocean Springs at the Veiled Doll, a local store specializing in Islamic clothing. The slogan caught my eye; "Don't delay, call Allah today." Walking into the store, I saw many colored print fabrics. The store had set up dozens of tables layered in shawls, abayas and niqabs. A girl dressed in a fancy black gown wearing a green silk hijab approached.

"You decided to return," said the girl, who looked to be in her mid-twenties and was very attractive. The girl had helped me pick out Yasmeen's outfit yesterday.

"Your guidance was very helpful. She was very appreciative of the outfit." The memory brought a twinkle to my eye.

"Thank you, what may I show you today sir?"

"I need another outfit like you gave me yesterday, you know, that covers the face."

"You mean a niqab?"

"Yes," I replied, and she brought me over to a rack filled with beautiful fabrics.

"We don't get many such as you in our shop. Most of our business comes through the mail. Is this for your wife?"

"Yes, she's from Pakistan."

"That's lovely. You don't find many women from Pakistan who wear the niqab. Most would wear a simple hijab like I am wearing. She must be very religious."

"Yes she is." I started to feel like I was stepping in quicksand.

"And are you a follower of Allah?"

"Yes, I'll take a couple of these outfits," trying to change the subject. "She probably wears a medium."

"The niqab only comes in one size sir," she responded quietly.

"Oh, I know that. I'll take a couple of these."

"Of course, and we have some beautiful thobes for men. Perhaps with a Kufi?" For a moment, I was about to tell her that it was too late in the day for coffee.

She was quite the sales girl and I suspected she had picked up on my charade, using it to sell me more than I'd intended to buy. I walked out of there wearing a long flowing brown gown and a white beaded skull cap, carrying a number of parcels for Yasmeen. We should make quite the pair at dinner.

Chapter 52

Gabriel – Friday Afternoon, Day 12

I arrived at the motel around 4:30. I parked the truck, and immediately saw there was a problem. The Bug was no longer in the parking lot. I got out of the truck and knocked on the motel room door. After a couple of minutes of knocking and calling out to her, I started to think the worst. Jacqueline had the only key to the motel room, so I ran frantically to the office. The same clerk was behind the desk, probably working on the same jumble puzzle. I would have thought it impossible to get a rise out of him, but when he saw my outfit he stood up and said there was no vacancy.

"I already have a room. My name is Gabriel Ross, and I rented Room 16 from you a couple of days ago."

He looked me over, unsure; "You ain't the same guy that rented the room. That guy was an American."

"Listen buddy," I started to say impatiently; I was about to call him a racist, but decided instead just to show him my identification. I reached into the side pocket of my thobe and pulled out my wallet, showing him my Driver's License. He made a point of looking at me then back to the picture a couple of times.

"Whatcha wearing that getup for? You off to a masquerade party or something?"

I decided to ignore his question. "I think I locked my key in the room. Can I borrow your key for a minute?"

He continued to look at me as if I offended him, and then slowly pulled out a drawer and gave me a key. "You know we haven't been able to get in there and do any house cleaning. Every time I go, there's a do not disturb sign on the door."

"Don't worry about it. I'll be right back with your key." I raced back to the room praying Jacqueline was alright. I opened the door and found everything as it was left this morning, except my Jeopardy partner was gone.

I wasted the better part of an hour pacing the floor of the room debating on whether I should go looking for her, or stay put waiting for her return. I went out to the payphone by the office and called both my number at the Trade Winds, and then at the office. No answer. I tried Ben at home and at work before slamming the receiver down in frustration.

My attention was diverted as a deputy sheriff's cruiser pulled into the parking lot. As the car came to a stop by the office, I turned my face away, acting like I was on the phone. Out of the corner of my eye, I could see two deputies getting out of the cruiser. I concluded that somehow, the cops had arrested Jacqueline. The two deputies ambled into the office. I left the payphone and went to sit on the bench outside of the office. I could hear their conversation pretty clearly.

"We're looking for this girl who disappeared a few days ago in a possible abduction. Do you have someone like her staying here?"

"I haven't seen her, Deputy. We have a handful of guests, but nothing that looks that good."

"Can we take a look at your register?"

I let out a gasp at that point, wondering if the name Gabriel Ross would mean anything to them.

"Knock yourself out. The newspaper said she was from Biloxi, what makes you think she might be on this side of the bridge?"

"We got a report that she was in Ocean Springs this morning."

My fault, the niqab hadn't fooled anyone. I took consolation that they hadn't picked her up yet. She must be out on the roads somewhere in the Bug. I needed to find her before they did. The deputies left a few minutes later and stopped at the door, looking over at me. I looked up at them and smiled, "Greetings Officers, can I be of assistance?" I said using my best Pakistani accent.

From my seat on the bench, the two deputies looked like giants. The taller of the two responded, "What's your name sir?

"Gabriel Ross." I replied quickly.

The deputies looked at each other than the shorter one said, "What's with the getup…you doing a Mohammed Ali?"

"I am a follower of Allah, and this is a traditional thobe, and I wear the Kufi out of respect." I prayed that they wouldn't ask me anything else.

The tall one was carrying a picture of Jacqueline and handed it to me. It was a picture I had seen when I was in Cooper's bedroom. "Have you seen this woman?"

"Oh, what a lovely woman, no, no, no…I have not seen her. She is so beautiful; I would certainly remember if I saw her. Oh look at the way the light shines on her soft face. Her hair is lustrous, look how it glows. Her eyes are the most captivating brown. They are shaped like almonds and are full of laughter. And look at the wonderful gown she is…."

"Can we have the picture back?" The short one interrupted, looking down at me with a pitying look.

Once they left I changed back into my jeans and a t-shirt and headed out in the truck. It was about 6:30 when I got to Ocean Springs. I drove up and down every street looking for signs of Jacqueline or the car. Had she driven further away, clueing in that the cops were onto her disguise? I knew she wouldn't have gone to Biloxi, unless she was trying to find me. Would she have gone to my office or my apartment? She knew those two places were being watched. By 8:30 pm, I had thoroughly searched every street in Ocean Springs as well as Pascagoula and decided to head back to the office. My little ruse with the niqab had backfired on me.

When I arrived at the office there was no sign of Mr. Green lurking about and my office was empty. I was about to leave when I noticed the blinking message light on the answering machine. It said I had two messages. The first was from Mr. Jackson, Rebecca's teacher. The message was to the owner of the Eye on You Detective agency and it went on for an agonizingly long time about how rude he found Mr. Gabriel Ross to be. He was still making accusations and insults when I pressed the delete button. The second message sent a chill down my spine.

"Gabriel if you're there, pickup, pick up. I'm in trouble. I think they're on to me." The message ended abruptly and had been left on the machine at 5:00 pm that afternoon. I was frantic; the love of my life was reaching out to me and I was incapable of helping. I couldn't help imagine what the Sheriff would do to her if he caught her. Last time she'd said he put her in handcuffs for a day and hit her. It sounded like he planned to take her to New Orleans and have his pal Frank finish her off. I was starting to regret not having encouraged her to make a run for it.

I paced back and forth wearing a hole in the floor. I tried Ben again and again, getting nothing but the stale voice mail which had now become imprinted in my brain. I let Bourbon in and put him on my desk. He sat there looking at me intently, giving an occasional meow. Bourbon, if only you were a real partner and could tell me what to do. I gave him some food and a stroke under the chin in his favorite spot. He ignored the food and continued to stare at me as if he sensed my anxiety. I decided to go over the details with him and see if we could piece this together.

Speaking to Bourbon, and pacing the floor, "The deputies came looking for her around 5:45 and they clearly didn't have her at that point. Right? It's now almost 11:00 pm. If they had caught Jacqueline when she left that message at 5:00, then why would they still be looking for her at 5:45? Do you see?" That made sense and we both felt better. "I searched all through Ocean Springs for her and nothing. She wouldn't dare go to my apartment so where else might she go?" I decided I was going to give myself an ulcer waiting around this office hoping for Bourbon to come up with a bright idea. I put Bourbon back on the fire escape on my way down to the car.

My first stop was the Trade Winds. I was almost hoping to find a bad guy waiting for me, but no such luck. I then drove the Ranger by Cooper's house. The Cadillac was still in the driveway where I parked it, but there was no sign of the sheriff's cruiser. Could Jacqueline have had a change of heart and gone back to Cooper?

There were no lights on so my guess would be no. I sat in front of his house deciding what to do and listened to the local radio station as they broadcast the regional news. "There's nothing new to report on the case of Jacqueline Cooper, the young wife of Harrison County Sheriff William Cooper. With every passing minute, concern grows about her well-being. Sources in the sheriff's department report that the search is being directed towards the Ocean Springs area." I felt sick at how powerless I was. "In a related story, continued the reporter, "the body of a Harrison County deputy sheriff was found in a local suburban home today. Sources inside the investigation are speculating that Detective Barry Franklin may have been the victim of a robbery gone wrong. Police from both Biloxi and Harrison County are working hard to investigate this crime. And this just in, a neighbor living across the street from Deputy Franklin has made a statement about having seen a short man with a gun, fleeing from the house with a sack of valuables."

The newscast cut away to the old coot with the shotgun, "I saw him, he had a gun and was runnin,' I gave a description to the police. He was a real short one. I was goin' to blast him, but the little bugger was too quick. He drove off in one of those crappy little Pintos."

I subconsciously slunk down in my seat as the reporter continued, "Sheriff William Cooper, whose wife may have been the victim of abduction, offered this to reporters earlier today: There have been reports of gangs coming down from up north being involved in the drug trade in our city. We are following up a number of important leads. I can't say much more, but one avenue of investigation is that Deputy Franklin's killing was payback for some of the fine police work he had done in this area."

I felt like throwing up. How could anyone come up with this crap? I got out of the car and decided that if Cooper had Jacqueline in the house then I was going to go in and get her. When I got to the top step, I pounded on the door. If Cooper answered, I wasn't going to waste time with words. I pounded again and again. I tried to look in the window, but the drawn curtains blocked my view. In frustration, I yelled out "Cooper, open up." As soon as I yelled, the neighbor's porch lights came on. Rather than having to explain myself, I decided to get out of there. The steam must have been visibly coming out of my ears as I drove away.

I drove back to the office and checked for messages. There were none. It was 2:00 am now and I was still spinning my wheels while Jacqueline was out there. I tried Ben a couple of more times with no luck. I called the Good Night Motel and spoke to the desk guy. He sounded angry when he heard who it was; I had probably interrupted his jumble.

"Listen buddy have you seen anyone go into Room 16 in the last few hours?"

"Yep." He was clearly trying to do his puzzle.

"Can you tell me who?" My frustration was showing.

"Why it was you. Don't you remember you came in here all dressed like an Ayerab and asked for the key? You still have it. I said, are you going to a masquerade party or something…..don't you remember it was just a few hours ago."

"Very funny, I meant someone other than me?"

The guy chuckled into the phone and said, "No one other than you. There were two sheriff deputies here looking for that sheriff's wife. You know, the Chinese one that got took."

I slammed the phone down in frustration and rested my head on the desk. I must have fallen asleep from sheer exhaustion. The shrill of the phone next to me woke me. It was almost 6:00 am. I lunged for the phone. "Jacqueline! Is that you?"

The voice that came back was almost that of a little boy. It took me a moment to recognize Mr. Green. "Mr. Ross, have you lost someone?"

"What do you want?"

"We have some unfinished business to attend to. I'd like to be stranded in that little elevator with you, just the two of us. You had your fun. I'd like to have mine. Maybe I should come down right now…we could sing that stupid Copa song together." He started to laugh like a kid playing in a sprinkler. I waited him out and he eventually stopped and got serious. "I'm sorry Mr. Ross, maybe you have lost someone?" Getting no response, he asked, "Are you sad Mr. Ross?"

"Let me make this simple for you, you big idiot. Fuck off!"

"I think Frank suggested you should be more polite. Regardless, I would like to offer you a little present. Out on the beach strip just to the west of the Gulfport pier there's a navy blue Caprice with a little surprise in the trunk for you."

Chapter 53

Gabriel –Saturday Morning, Day 13

I must have set a speed record driving the Ranger to Gulfport. There was very little traffic this early on a Saturday morning. The sun had just come up, and it was going to be another hot one.

I was dreading what I might find in the Caprice. Trapping Mr. Green in the elevator had pushed things a little too far. I pulled into the parking lot next to the pier. There was not a soul on the beach. I thought about my parents and what they would say about the mess I had created. No matter what had happened at school or at work, they had always supported me. Would they still? I sat in the front seat of the Ranger contemplating what was about to happen. I could see the navy blue Caprice waiting in the lot.

There was a bunch of pelicans sitting on the pilings looking down disapprovingly at me as I climbed down from the Ranger. I imagined hearing one say to the other in a Jimmy Cagney voice, "You're a real smart little boy, and I know how to deal with smart little boys." The bird beside him said in what I imagined was a Humphrey Bogart voice, "Listen to me – I'm giving it to you straight. I got plans see, and there's no room in them for you." A big bird on the last piling spoke in a young boy's voice, "You ruined my shirt with those jelly donuts." I picked up a pebble off the asphalt and wound up like I was going to throw it at them. They continued to just sit there looking at me.

I made the short walk to the car, the only one in the lot. The Louisiana plates had that Sportsman's Paradise saying on it. I knew right away that I was not going to like Mr. Green's little surprise. A spray of bullet holes reminiscent of Swiss cheese decorated the trunk. I moved to the driver's side of the car looking for a way to pop the trunk. The car looked pretty clean, except for some files in the back seat and of course the revolver in the front seat. It looked like the cannon Mr. Green had been using yesterday. Definitely not a sportsman's gun. I opened the door and picked up the gun, checking the barrel and seeing that someone had recently fired the weapon. I sat in the front seat and rifled through the glove compartment, finding nothing of value. Whoever left this little present for me thought to leave the keys in the ignition. There was a rotting smell emanating from the car that made me gag. I suspected it came from whatever was in the trunk. I guessed I was supposed to use the keys to open the trunk and find my "surprise". As I was about to get out of the car, I heard sirens approaching. Looking in the side mirror I saw four cruisers pulling into the parking lot, lights flashing. I got out of the car with my hands up, still holding the cannon.

"Drop the gun" commanded a deputy, getting out of the car and pointing his weapon at me. Before I knew it, the Caprice was surrounded by a half dozen cops, all with guns drawn.

"My name is Gabriel Ross, and I'm a Private Investigator. I can explain."

"Put the gun on the ground, I won't tell you again," shouted the deputy.

I bent over, gently putting the gun on the pavement. "This is all a mistake. I got a message from Mr. Green to come to the beach and collect a surprise."

I saw William Cooper get out of one of the cars and move to the front of the deputies. "You better not make any sudden moves. My men are a little trigger happy with one of their own being gunned down yesterday." He signaled one of the deputies to collect and bag the cannon.

"What's that stink? You wearing some special kind of Yankee cologne?" said the sheriff, chuckling.

"Hahaha," I gave him my best fake laugh. "You're hilarious!"

He told another deputy to frisk me and yet another to check the Caprice for clues. Once the deputy was finished frisking me, the Sheriff approached with his arms folded. The deputy handed him my wallet. Opening my wallet, "Mr. Gabriel Ross, from Dee-troit, I think your license is out of date. You know that is against the law here in Mississippi?" He looked over at the Ranger and said, getting very close, "You like cars Mr. Dee-troit? I hear you drive one of those bugs, not even a fine American car? Then I heard you were driving a Pinto, now I see the pickup truck. I also hear you like to ride in Cadillacs….that right Mr. Ross?" He punctuated this last question by slamming his night stick into my stomach, causing me to fall to the ground gasping for air. "How-ya like that Mr. Yankee Private Investigator?"

"Great, that was fun, how about I frisk you now?" I gasped in pain.

"He also had these keys on him," interjected the deputy who had frisked me.

"Looks like these keys are for this here Caprice. Let's see if we can use them to open the trunk without messin' up Mr. Ross' fingerprints."

I slowly rose to my feet. Looking over at the trunk, the deputy inserted the key. The moments following seemed to pass in slow motion. I closed my eyes and prayed that it wouldn't be Jacqueline. The deputy raised the trunk lid and immediately stepped back holding his nose. The smell was overpowering, too much so. The body had to have been in the trunk for at least a day. We all approached the trunk like a funeral procession.

"Looks to me like Mr. Carson," said Sheriff Cooper looking over at me. "What you say Mr. Private Investigator? Do you think this might be Bud Carson?"

I knew it was cruel - Mrs. Carson seemed like a nice lady, and Bud did try to help me - but at that moment I was silently thanking God that it wasn't Jacqueline or Ben.

The deputy searching the Caprice spoke up saying, "There's some paperwork in the back seat with The Eye on You Detective Agency on it."

"When you just need to know, isn't that how it goes Mr. Ross?" The Sheriff smiled. He turned me around and told me to put my hands behind my back. The lonely sound of the click of handcuffs resonated across the empty beach.

"Gabriel Ross, you are under arrest for the murder of Bud Carson." Before the deputy read me my rights, Cooper said under his breath, "You know, we'll find your fingerprints all over this. And once we check ballistics, how much you want to wager that we'll be adding a second murder charge for what you did to Deputy Franklin?" With that he spit on the ground.

"You seem to be very well educated on your own bullshit." I replied.

Chapter 54

Gabriel – Saturday Morning, Day 13

The deputies drove me out to the county jail, and I was processed with pictures and fingerprints right away. By 9:00 am, when most people were just getting to work, I was sitting in a ten by ten interview room waiting for God knows what. The walls were plain grey brick redundantly painted with plain grey paint. I wondered how many psychopaths had sat in this very room. I looked up into the corner near the ceiling and noticed a camera. There was probably a guard watching me on a television monitor. I had read somewhere that a popular police tactic to weaken you was to make you wait hours without asking you anything. For kicks, I put my feet up on the table and gave the camera the finger. Other than the metal table which was bolted to the floor, the room had three cheap metal folding chairs. The room smelled of antiseptic desperately trying to mask the odor of desperate men.

I was wearing a striped uniform that said property of Harrison County Correctional System. I guessed that would be in the event someone would ever try to steal it. The outfit came complete with paper slippers and a wonderful cold shower with a fire hose. I hadn't been put in a cell yet, but I knew my time was coming.

It was over an hour since the deputy had put me in the room. There was no clock, but I'd developed a routine to help me keep track of time...twenty paces down one wall, then 20 paces down the next. I repeated this for each wall, which I figured equated to 2 minutes. After five trips around the room, I flashed a finger at the camera.

After they had read me the Miranda, I was asked if I understood my rights. I told them that I understood they were a bunch of inbred yokels. The business of being inbred might have been a bit, much judging by their reaction. I demanded my phone call, although I wasn't sure who I'd call. It didn't matter because apparently the phone system was broken. They took my wallet, my watch and all of my possessions. I paced and paced, I couldn't bring myself to sit and relax even though I knew I should be conserving energy. At least I'd be able to say to Mrs. Carson that I had found her husband.

I was on my 50th tour of the room, and my little paper slippers were black from the dirt on the floor. My boredom was broken when Sheriff Cooper came in and told me to "Sit my ass down." I pulled out a chair and maintained eye contact with him as he sat down across from me. I could see why people said he was handsome. He was tall and slim with dark hair and an air of self-confidence. He had a folder with him that he opened up. The inside cover contained my recently taken mug shots. "I've spoken to the county attorney and the case against you is very strong."

"Horsepucky." I feigned disinterest while trying to read the notes upside down.

Cooper looked at me and shook his head, "Keep it up, and I'll just leave you in here to rot. As I was saying, we've already dusted the car and have your prints on not just the car, but also the keys and the gun. We're still waiting on ballistics to come back but there is a pool out there." He gestured to the hall. "Odds are that it will prove you killed Deputy Franklin yesterday with that gun."

"Bush-wah."

"Okay, Mr. Ross you might think you're pretty tough now, but if I left you in lockup with the right guys, then they'd change your tune. They love little guys with faggoty haircuts."

316

"Sheriff, there's a tape recording on my office phone that will prove that I was set up to find that body."

"Well then, I will personally go over there and check. But even if that was true, and I suspect it isn't, it doesn't explain why your files were in the back seat."

"I went to my office a week ago and your pal Frank was sitting in my office chair picking his big nose and snooping through my files. If he didn't plant the files, then his trained chimp Mr. Green did. All of this is a bunch of flap-doodle and you know it. What motive would I have to hurt Bud?"

"Well, I have a statement from a Miss Amber Pirelli, who works at the Rockaway bar. Do you know her?" Not waiting for an answer he ploughed on, "She said you had words with Bud about being thrown out of there last Saturday. Interestingly, he disappeared shortly after that. Smells like motive to me," he said with an air of smugness.

"I want to speak to a lawyer. And I want my phone call."

"Fuck you and your phone call. As for the lawyer we can go that way, but I'm giving you the opportunity to get things off your chest."

"Fuck you, shit for brains. Oh, I feel so much better getting that off my chest."

He stood and took his nightstick off his belt, putting it on the table in front of us. "Sounds like you've got some hostility issues to resolve as well. Want to take them out on me?"

"Yeah, you're so tough with a bunch of deputies behind that door ready to pull me off you and beat me senseless. Listen, let me ask you something "Mr. Mud for Brains." I could tell I was starting to piss this guy off. "What was the time of death, or are you in-breds down here so backward you can't tell?"

He looked in the file and proudly said "Thursday evening around 11:00 pm."

"Ok, that would explain why the body was so ripe, but it couldn't have been me."

"Yeah, why is that?"

"Because I was busy at that time. I have an alibi."

"Yeah? What were you doing at 11:00 on Thursday night?"

I gave him my best Sylvester ate Tweety Bird smile and said, "Sufferin Succotash, I'm Desthpicable, I was fucking your wife."

Chapter 55

Gabriel – Saturday Morning, Day 13

I knew I had needled him pretty hard. It was like toying with a lion in a cage by jabbing him with a stick. You don't tell someone that you're having sex with their wife without expecting a physical response. Cooper didn't disappoint, his face contorted with rage, he leapt across the table at me. Now I should explain that I have lived all my life at a disadvantage in physical confrontations. I have suggested that people be fair and get on their knees to fight me, but no one ever agreed. So when 6 foot 2 inch William Cooper slid across the table at me I saw an opportunity to right many injustices. As he came at me, I kicked my chair out and used his forward momentum to land a hellacious right cross to the side of his face. I heard the sound of bones cracking as he slid off the table onto the hard concrete floor. As I watched him fall, I heard the clang, clang, clang of an alarm. This was followed by the door opening and two guards rushing to the sheriff's rescue. I immediately put my hands up and got down on my knees. I still suffered a couple of bruises from their night sticks but the sight of Cooper lying unconscious on the floor overshadowed the pain.

The deputies handcuffed me again and pushed me down the halls to the cells. I was put into a holding tank with about a dozen cell mates. The deputy pushed me in, commenting that I was going to regret what I'd done. I didn't care; I was bouncing on my toes like Mohammed Ali, I held my hands high like I had just knocked out Joe Frazier. I was the only white guy in the small cell.

The other inmates didn't know what to make of me. When they asked me why I was celebrating being put in a cell, I said...because I just knocked out Sheriff William Cooper, out cold, flat on his ass. They let out a cheer as if my deed somehow cast a blow for all of the scumbags everywhere. I was asked to explain how I did it and decided to embellish a little to fan the flames of my legend. "He came at me with his baton. I circled and feinted to my left. He took a swing at me, but I used my agility to duck. He came closer to me again waving the baton like it was a machete. He swung again, a blow that almost got me. I knew if he hit me, I'd be a goner. He made a fateful mistake; he let me get too close to him. You see, tall guys have the height advantage but we little guys have more agility. He swung again boxing me into a corner; on his last swing he kind of lost his balance. That's when I hit him with a right cross, an upper cut, and then finished him with a left to the body. About 10 deputies came in to subdue me. They were lucky there were that many of them because when I get going, I'm a tiger."

I was in that little holding cell for about an hour holding court with my fellow criminals. The cell door opened and the two deputies said "Ross, get over here." I walked to the front of the cell, shifting my weight from left to right like I was a career tough guy. "Give him another beating!" my cellmates yelled as I was escorted back to the meeting room. This time they left the cuffs on. Cooper came back in with a guard by his side. The right side of his face was all swollen as if he'd been stung by a thousand bees.

"I don't believe you," he said sitting in a chair a few feet away from the table.

"Well what do you want to know Will?" I asked, using the name that she liked to call him. I put my feet up on the table. "How about that little heart shaped birthmark on her inner thigh....did you really think it had anything to do with you?"

"Shut the fuck up." His expression was a mixture of anger and disbelief.

"No?" I put my feet down and stood up. "I want you to visualize everything. I slammed her like a screen door." I made a humping motion at him.

I could see he was getting upset again. "Where is she?" he asked in a monotone voice, trying to control his emotions.

Okay that was a relief; he didn't know where she was either, so she must still be hiding somewhere. "She's probably talking to the FBI as we speak, telling them about Mr. Brown, your little guns for drug deal, the business with the missing girls, all of it you sick fuck."

Cooper waved the guard out of the room and stood by the door. "Listen asshole, I don't know how you know what you know, but you best keep your trap shut. You don't know who you're fucking with. If what you say is true about you and my wife, you'll never see the light of day. And after I catch her, they'll find her body floating face down in the Mississippi."

There was a knock on the door and Cooper stepped into the hall. He came back in looking a little too smug. "A couple of things my little Private Dick, we went to your office and, we couldn't find an answering machine." His voiced dripped with sarcasm. "Second, the ballistics report is back and guess what? Your fingerprints were found on the gun used to kill Deputy Franklin yesterday and we have a neighbor who is willing to testify that you were seen at the house with a gun in your hand." He started doing a stupid little jig.

As he turned to leave I called to him, "Cooper, why do you keep referring to your little dick? From what Jacqueline tells me I'd think you'd want to keep that to yourself."

The deputies came back to escort me to a regular cell. I asked about my telephone call and this time they took me to a private area with a black rotary phone. I was allowed no more than two minutes. I decided to call Ben at his office. My voice dropped in disappointment when the phone was finally answered. "Inspector Greenlaw, please hold."

Oh my God, what a jerk. When he finally picked up the line again I blurted out, "Greenlaw, it's Ross - don't hang up. I need to get an urgent message to Ben; I've been arrested and framed for Deputy Franklin's murder. I need you to find him and get me some help. I'm at the county lockup."

Greenlaw didn't get a chance to say anything as the deputy hung up the phone. I was led to a cell with two beds. Yeah, bunkies! I winced as the steel door slammed behind me. On the bottom bunk there was no linen and the mattress was covered in unknown stains. Next to the bed there was a small table which was attached to the wall. Something brown and disgusting appeared to be swimming in the toilet bowl. The only saving grace was that I had no roommate.

The euphoria over laying out Cooper didn't last. Eventually the reality of my situation hit me like a ton of bricks. I thought Jacqueline might be ok but I needed to be sure. Would she go back to the motel in hope that I would be there? I should have known better than to tell the sheriff about the message on my tape machine. They had a mountain of evidence against me. If Jacqueline didn't come forward to alibi me, I could see myself going away for a long time.

I was wallowing in self-pity when I heard the sound of boots coming down the hallway. Stopping in front of my cell was Sheriff Cooper. "Hey Ross, I thought I'd stop by and make your day."

"Yeah, are you finished flossing your teeth with your tiny dick?"

His face reddened at the insult, "I wanted to tell you that I'm heading out to Ocean Springs." He pulled out the motel room key and dangled it in my face. "I wonder what I might find there. Maybe I'll have a little fun with her."

"Pretty big talk for somebody hung like a hamster."

"And here's the really great news, I arranged for a special roommate for you tonight. He has…unique tastes."

Chapter 56

Jacqueline –Yesterday Morning

When Gabriel dropped me off at the motel, I was congratulating myself for pulling off the disguise. I wasn't looking forward to another day in this motel room, waiting around for Gabriel to get home. I was starting to go stir crazy. Before he left, Gabriel had filled me in on Travis Franklin and how the boy had helped him with the investigation. He told me about how he had arranged for a listening device to be put in Cooper's hat, and that from the recording they had been able to get a good idea about the scope of the corruption inside the Sheriff's Department. Gabriel seemed very concerned about Travis in light of the arrest warrant being issued for his father. We had no sooner said goodbye when he got into the Pinto and headed to Biloxi.

By 11:00 am I was tired of the Beverly Hillbillies. I knew Gabriel would disapprove but I thought a little shopping trip into Ocean Springs might be safe, considering how well the disguise had worked at breakfast.

For transportation there was the VW. Gabriel had left the keys on the night stand. Sure there was a risk to Jacqueline Cooper getting caught, but I was now the beautiful Yasmeen. Besides, the Yasmeen character was kind of fun. At 11:05, I grabbed the keys to the VW and headed out. Someone had done a number on the seat, cutting the cushions down the middle and ripping out the stuffing. The car was still drivable and maybe I could get some tape in town and mend things for him. Driving down the main drag, I was taken with all of the quaint shops. The tourist crowd was out in force which would help me blend in. I parked along the main drag and strolled leisurely in and out of the stores. The people were all very friendly. I think I was the first woman they had ever seen dressed up in a niqab.

When we got married William had insisted we open our joint accounts at the Hancock Bank, because he was good friends with the owner. I thought it would be foolish to go in and present myself as Jacqueline Cooper and try to cash a check. The bank, however, was advertising their new automated teller machine. The bank manager had arranged for us to have a client card so that we could access our account. It worked like a charm, and I used the machine to take out a couple of hundred from our joint account.

From there I went into a ladies store and looked at some of the fashions they had for the coming season. I purchased a few items including some lingerie. An older lady at the checkout didn't know what to make of me. "Where y'all from?" she asked. When I said "Pakistaaaaan" she nodded her head as if she had heard of it. She leaned in conspiratorially and asked "Are y'all really allowed to wear these frilly garments under your robe?"

"Of course," I said. "If you ever see any other women dressed like this, you should recommend these silky pieces. They will thank you."

"Uh okay dear," she thanked me for the tip.

I checked out a couple of other shops, one that sold arts and crafts, and another that sold beautiful paintings. The young lady in the arts store was very helpful when she found out I was visiting from Pakistan. "You must go visit the Gulf Islands National Reserve. There are miles and miles of beach and trails, all kinds of wildlife and really fantastic views of the ocean."

"Thank you oh so very much madam, I will go visit your reserve today. My homeland in Karachi is also well known for its wondrous beach land." I began to realize that I could say almost anything about Pakistan and people would just accept it. For example, I found an Ace Hardware store nearby and went in to buy tape to repair the car's cushions. The clerk in the store, trying to be helpful, asked why I needed the duct tape. I told him that tape was in short supply in my country because it is used so commonly in making houses. The clerk looked back at me in awe.

I drove out to the National Reserve and it was every bit as breathtaking as the lady in the art store had promised. There were miles and miles of white sandy beaches, plam trees and all kinds of wildlife. There was an ice cream truck near a park and I stopped and bought myself a treat. I ended up eating the ice cream in the car as the Niqab was just impossible to deal with. Finishing the ice cream I decided to take a stroll along the beach. I spent a good hour walking along the trails and running in the surf. The few people out walking the beach saw something they didn't see very often - an Arab woman wearing a Niqab covered in ice cream building a sand castle.

I was walking back to the VW in the parking lot when I noticed a Jackson County Sheriff's cruiser blocking it in. Hiding behind a tree I saw the two deputies looking at the smashed driver's window and the ripped cushions. One deputy appeared to be writing the license plate on a clipboard. The other deputy was talking on a radio. The deputy who was writing on the clipboard opened the driver's side of the door and started looking in the shopping bags I'd left on the front seat. I heard him whistle to his partner as he sashayed his body back and forth holding up my lingerie. All men are assholes.

I realized that I was in a bit of a fix when the tow truck showed up. Gabriel had said they knew about the Bug, so no doubt these two just happened to be trolling the parking lot and found it. The Motel was a good 10 miles away. I could start walking towards the major road and maybe flag a cab or find a phone booth to call Gabriel.

I started the long trek at 4:00 pm, and was quickly overcome by the heat. Sitting down beside the road I just had to pull up my skirt and let some air flow. I couldn't imagine how people could wear all this stuff. I was sweating like a whore in a Baptist church. It suddenly occurred to me that the bank might have notified my husband of my ATM withdrawal. It would be just like Will to have the bank flag our accounts. If that's the case, he may have figured out that I was in Ocean Springs. Add that to the report on Gabriel's car, he'd be all over this place looking for me. I kicked myself for leaving the safety of the motel.

I started to walk again, determined to get back to the motel and Gabriel. I contemplated hitching a ride but I didn't have the energy to concoct another believable story. Gabriel was going to panic if he returned to the motel and found the room empty. He'd probably think that the disguise didn't work and that I had been caught. Or with the car missing, would he think I'd gone off on my own?

There was no phone in the motel room, so even if I came across a pay phone what could I do? I made it to Bienville Blvd, a major east-west road, by just after 5:00 pm. It took me a long time to flag a cab, something I attributed to my attire. Finally a Confederate Cab stopped and I got in.

"Evenin' Ma'am, where would you like to go?" asked the cab driver, turning around to give me a once-over.

"The Good Night Motel, please driver." I noticed a picture on the back of his seat saying he was Mr. Robert Lee.

"Very well Ma'am, you in town visiting?"

"Yes, my husband and I are enjoying your beautiful town."

"That's great Ma'am; we have a growing Islamic population. We even have special clothing stores. There's one called the Veiled Doll in case you happen to be in Biloxi."

"Thank you Mr. Lee."

We drove in silence for 10 minutes. As we neared the motel I told Mr. Lee to drive by it slowly. It was 5:30 so I was sure that Gabriel had to be there, but I didn't see the Pinto as we drove past. There were however, a couple of pickups and a sheriff's cruiser. "Keep driving, keep driving." I shouted, my worst fears realized. Hopefully Gabriel had gotten away and not fallen into a trap. An idea came to me and I asked the driver to take me to a pay phone.

My first call was to Gabriel's office. The phone rang and rang before the answering machine picked up and I heard the "Eye on You" recording. "Gabriel if you're there, pick up, pick up. I'm in trouble. I think they're on to me." I ended up leaving the message on the machine.

I didn't know what to do. I paid the cab driver and let him leave. I could try to check into another motel, but chances are they'd want to see identification before renting me a room. With my name plastered across the front pages it wasn't worth the risk. I made another call, this time to a number in New Orleans.

The phone rang a number of times before a young woman answered. "Chevon? Is that you?"

"Jackie? Whoa it's been a long time girl. I haven't heard from you since the wedding."

"It's so great to hear your voice. I really need a friend. I need help."

"Sure, what can I do for you, is everything alright with Mr. Dreamboat?"

"He's not a dreamboat, he's a sociopath and if he catches me, I think he's going to kill me."

"Oh my god Jackie, are you kidding me?"

"Totally serious. My life is in danger. He's not the man I thought he was and he's involved with some awful people. Can you come down to Ocean Springs and I'll meet you in front of the … ACE hardware on Bienville Boulevard? We'll need to rent a room somewhere and hideout for a while."

"Oh my God Jackie! What the hell is going on?"

"I'll explain everything when you get here. You may hear something about it on the local radio station; he's set up a bulletin to arrest me. Please say you'll come Chevon, please!

"Jackie, Jesus on a stick girl. I'll be there as fast as I can. You stay right there girl, the cavalry's coming!!!!!!"

Chapter 57

Gabriel – Saturday Afternoon, Day 13

When Cooper finally left I sat down on the bed and tried to think of my options. I had none. My pity party was interrupted by something coming down the hall. I went to the cell door and tried to look down the hall. I couldn't see anything but I heard the shuffle of shackled prison feet making their way towards me. A shadow approached from my left. I looked around the cell for something I could use for a weapon. My search was interrupted by a deputy banging on my cell bars. "Oh, Mr. Ross, I have someone for you to share your cell with. Please meet John Lee Pettimore. Old John Lee here is serving time for buggering little boys. The sheriff thought you two would get along real fine."

I looked at the creature. He was wearing the standard prison stripes, but on him they barely stretched to cover his massive gut, making him look like a pregnant zebra. He had to be over 6 feet tall, with a shaved scalp and a neck that was covered with prison tattoos. I looked at him and gave him my best grin. His head was big and round like a Wal-Mart happy face but without the smile. He had a large veined bulbous nose. The only thing small about him were his eyes. They were small beady eyes, looking at me with anticipation like a hungry man eying his first meal.

I decided on a Hail Mary pass as the deputy unlocked the cell door. "Deputy, when will the doctor get here? The infections are getting worse. They're all puss-like and there's this drip. I think I might have gonorrhea."

"Nice try Mr. Ross," said the deputy laughing. "But old John Lee already has gonorrhea and a few other disgusting things as well." The deputy chuckled again as he removed John Lee's leg shackles and hand cuffs and pushed him towards the cell.

Pettimore had to move sideways in order to fit through the cell door. As he lumbered towards the bed where I was sitting, he cast a huge shadow.

"Did you want the bottom bunk? Sure you want the bottom bunk," I said, standing up then climbing onto the top bunk. He continued to look at me like a depraved madman, inching closer to the bed. "Listen John Lee, whatever you think is going to happen isn't, so you might as well just lie in your bunk." He was right beside the bed and reached a hand out for my leg, which I quickly pulled away. "I don't want to hurt you Mr. Pettimore, I'm sure you're a nice guy." He reached again for my leg. I was now plastered against the wall. "Seriously I'm going to lay a beating on you." I said threateningly, my voice not quite as confident as I wanted it to sound.

"You want to wrastle?" These were the first words he'd spoken.

"Sure, Pettimore let's wrestle." An idea came to me as John Lee stepped back a bit, expecting me to get down from the top bunk. The big lug's head was even with the bed, his bulbous nose hanging like a huge ripe strawberry. Before he could react, I kicked him square in the face with as much power as I could muster. Pettimore staggered backward, at which point he realized that his nose was gushing blood like a water fountain. He started to yelp, and squeal, and then cry, his hand trying to staunch the blood flow. I jumped down as he staggered to the bottom bunk, crying openly. I debated kicking him in the nuts, but he looked so pitiful, his whole body shaking. I grabbed some toilet paper and handed it to him.

He was still crying when the deputy returned. The deputy looked at Pettimore blubbering on the bottom bunk. I gave him a smug look and raised my arms in victory yelling out, "It's your fault Deputy, your fault! You made me hurt this man."

There was some commotion behind the deputy and I was never happier to see Ben's grinning face come down the hall. "Thank God Ben, I've been calling and calling."

"Let's get you out of here." There was another man standing next to Ben as he spoke.

Once out of the cell, we were ushered into the interrogation room. As I passed by the deputy on my way into the room, I pretended I was going to hit him. I saw fear in his eyes as he flinched. Using my best Three Stooges voice I said, "Why I oughta."

Ben introduced the other gentleman as Agent Graham from the FBI field office in Jackson. Graham was a tall man with a firm handshake and a friendly smile. "Agent Graham and I have been collaborating on a multi-jurisdictional investigation into Sheriff Cooper and some gangster types in New Orleans. Your information has been invaluable in getting us pointed in the right direction."

We shook hands and I said, "It's great to meet you Agent Graham, but we need to get out of here right away." I brought them up to date quickly on Jacqueline's disappearance, the motel in Oceans Springs and the news that Cooper had left to go there almost an hour ago.

"Okay, we can fill each other in on the way." As we got up to leave, Ben asked the deputy to return my belongings.

"Wait a minute, we have murder charges against Mr. Ross, plus the sheriff was assaulted and now we have a cellmate who won't stop crying because Ross hit him."

The FBI agent stepped up and responded, "Listen Deputy, here is a court order for the release of Mr. Ross into my custody. If there are outstanding charges, then we'll guarantee that he'll appear before the courts."

We got out of there by 3:00 and piled into Ben's cruiser. Cooper had at least an hour head start. I brought them up to date with the gun battle at Franklin's house, Jacqueline's disappearance and frantic message, then the anonymous phone message and the setup.

"What evidence do they have against you?" asked Ben.

"Well I was pretty stupid. When I was checking the abandoned car I touched the keys to the trunk and a revolver that was sitting in the seat. The rest is just bullshit."

"Don't worry about the Carson murder, we've already determined that he was killed in Louisiana and then someone drove him to Harrison County, presumably so that Cooper could pin it on you," said Agent Graham.

"How do you know that he was killed in Louisiana?" I asked.

"The car he was in was stolen from an old lady in New Orleans on Thursday night. Since the time of death was also Thursday night, then he had to be killed in Louisiana," said Agent Graham.

"Ben, where've you been? I was frantic when I couldn't reach you."

"I followed your suggestion and I let it slip to Greenlaw that Jacqueline was stashed in Gulfport. When I was talking to Ricketts I told him that she was at a motel in D'Iberville. When the motel in D'Iberville was raided it confirmed a suspicion that I'd had for quite a while. Ricketts is now in custody. One of the detectives actually heard him call Franklin and warn him to get out of town."

"Do you have an alibi for Thursday night?" asked Agent Graham.

"Well, I might if you speed up a little." I told them about the interrogation with Cooper. I only hoped Jacqueline hadn't gone back to that motel.

Chapter 58

Cooper –Saturday Evening, Day 13

It felt like the blood inside my body was boiling. I looked in the rear view mirror and caught sight of my swollen face. It was one thing to let that little jerk get the better of me, but what he'd said about Jacqueline was too much for me to take. I was running lights and sirens, weaving in and out of traffic like a punch-drunk fighter. Well, that little smart-ass would be begging for mercy when Pettimore was finished with him. Then he could look forward to a nice long stay courtesy of the State of Mississippi. I wondered whether Jacqueline was really talking to the FBI. I could still salvage everything. Franklin and his sick little abduction business was over with no loose ends. It was a shame about Jacqueline, such a good piece of ass. But her self-righteous, Yankee attitude was just too much to take. Now the ultimate betrayal had signed her death certificate. I turned off the lights and sirens as soon as I crossed the bridge. I pulled into the Good Night Motel and thought how fitting…a dump for a slut.

The clouds finally burst open as I got out of the cruiser. It was the kind of storm that came up from the Gulf once every few years. The wind was howling and the rain appeared to be falling sideways as I approached Room 16. I moved quietly, wanting to catch the little slut by surprise. As silently as I could I turned the key in the lock and swung open the door. What I saw was Jacqueline wearing some ridiculous gown like she was an Arab, sitting on the bed with a little colored girl. "Well, well what do we have here?"

Jacqueline's screams were enough to wake the dead. I was across the room in two strides. I slapped her hard, taking out my building frustration. She flew off the bed and landed on the floor in front of the washroom. "You might want to keep that little tramp mouth shut!" I said to her, my voice menacing.

The colored chick looked familiar. She charged me, nails scratching, going for my eyes. I struggled with her and finally threw her off me. She came back kicking, connecting with my nuts. Little bitch! I faked like I was hurt, then when she let her guard down I hit her with my nightstick. I heard the sound of bones breaking. She landed on her back, blood pouring out from her nose. I looked down at her; she was kind of hot. I remembered her now. She was one of the little bitches that came down here ten years ago. Jacqueline's friend from New Orleans.

I took my handcuffs off my belt and approached Jacqueline. She was crying like a baby in the corner. I slapped her hard again. All of a sudden the little nigger girl grabbed my leg, trying to trip me. I used the nightstick again, this time connecting with a solid shot to the head that made her fall back to the floor. I turned back to Jacqueline who was cowering in the corner, turning her over and cuffing her hands behind her back. Pulling her up to standing, I pushed her towards the door. "If you cooperate Jacqueline, then I might not hurt your little nigger friend."

I pulled her out to the cruiser and pushed her violently into the back seat. "You aren't going to get away with this; other people know what you did," she babbled.

"Shut the fuck up. If you're thinking about your little detective friend Gabriel, don't bother. Right now he's in my jail, most likely being raped for the tenth time." The news about Gabriel shut her up. Only the sound of the wipers trying to keep up with the torrential rain broke the silence as I drove across the bridge. Eventually, curiosity got the better of me, "So Gabriel tells me that you've been a bad girl. Do you know what Arabs do with a whore who cheats on her husband?" Not getting a reply, I continued, "No? You don't know? I heard they stone them to death. I bet you think that sounds pretty bad huh? Well, when you see what I have in store for you, it might not look so bad."

We passed the street leading to the Sheriff's office. "Where are you taking me?"

"Somewhere special my dear."

I drove for another five minutes before pulling onto a country road heading north. Another few minutes and we were in a heavily forested area. I turned onto an overgrown dirt road. "I hope you feel energetic Jacqueline. You have a little digging to do."

I continued down the country road until I stopped the car at a deserted clearing. "This is a little spot I like to use for my private meetings. Only the most trusted and loyal people get invited. That is, until you." Getting out of the car, I pulled her out of the backseat and threw her to the muddy ground. I opened up the cruiser's trunk and grabbed a shovel. "Okay my dear, it's only about a hundred yards that way. Watch out for snakes, this area is known for cottonmouths." I had her lead the way and used the shovel to prompt her every once and a while.

"Do you have anything to say Jacqueline before I announce your sentence on charges of adultery, treachery and all around bad house-wifing?"

"Who are you to talk, I've seen the pictures of you and the stripper."

"Oh, that was you or your little midget friend outside the window last week. Pretty hot pictures I bet. She's a much better fuck than you. Since we're chatting let me tell you something. I might not have taken up with Angela if you weren't such a lying whore about the birth control."

"Only a crazy person would want to have your child. You're really sick." That remark got her the edge of the shovel jabbed sadistically into her back, knocking her to the ground. "Now you know that's not true. As Sheriff of Harrison County, I am loved by everyone."

Chapter 59

Gabriel – Saturday Evening Day 13

We arrived at the motel in Oceans Springs around 9:15. Ominously, the door to Room 16 was wide open. I raced from the car to the motel and found a black girl struggling to get up. Someone had done a number on her face. I helped her onto the bed and told Ben to call for an ambulance. Turning to the girl, "My name is Gabriel Ross; can you tell me what happened?"

She was in a bad way, fading in and out of consciousness, and unable to speak. "Ben, better tell that ambulance to hurry!" I yelled. I covered her with a blanket and held her hand. At one point, she gathered enough strength to mumble, "He took her."

Agent Franklin came in and announced "The guy in the office said he saw the Sheriff push a woman into the back of his cruiser about 15 minutes ago, and then take off towards Biloxi."

Ben and I were out the door in a flash, calling to the office guy to stay with Chevon until the ambulance got there. With Agent Graham driving, we peeled out of there with lights flashing and sirens blaring. The clouds had burst earlier, and we were dealing with a torrential downpour.

"I doubt he'd take her to the jail or to the Sheriff's office," said Agent Graham as he zigzagged in between cars on the bridge. "He has nothing to charge her with and there are too many witnesses."

"He could be taking her back to their house." My hands were shaking with fear. But would Cooper take her back to his house? His rage and humiliation might just be enough to want her to disappear. He probably still thought that with me in jail, he would be in the clear if

Jacqueline were to disappear. He could then say she was abducted. Going to his house might be wasting valuable time. After a couple of minutes I suggested, "Can we send a squad car to check his house? I know another place that I think he might take her."

I gave Agent Graham directions, and he turned north on Debuys Road. I had only followed Cooper to this place once, and in the dark and with the rain it was hard to spot the dirt road. "I think this is it, can you pull over to the side and we can hoof it from here." The three of us got out in the rain, Graham and O'Shea with their guns at the ready. We made our way through the forest under a full moon. We approached the clearing and sure enough I saw the sheriff's cruiser. I only hoped we were in time. When we got to the cruiser, we found it empty with the trunk open. I thought I heard something to our left and quietly pointed in that direction. Agent Graham took the lead as we started into the forest. After a few minutes the voices became clearer. Agent Graham held me back from going closer. There appeared to be two people about 10 yards up ahead. One had their back to us; the other had a shovel and was digging.

"How can you expect to get away with this?" My heart leaped as I recognized Jacqueline's voice.

"I told you I can do pretty well whatever I want."

"There are other police forces. They'll stop you."

"Are you talking about Ricketts? Chief Ricketts' head is so far up my ass it's starting to hurt. I own this town; I make it possible for the right people to do business here, all the while making sure that our good citizens feel safe to walk the streets at night. Notice I said "feel safe" not be safe. Keep digging Jacqueline, I want it to be nice and deep when I bury you alive."

"How many other people have you buried here?"

"Not many, but if you get lonely it may help to know I buried old Artie a few feet from you. Little bastard reneged on selling Boone the business, so brother dear took a hammer to him."

"Did you bury those missing girls here too you freak?"

"No I think they probably suffered a little worse. But I can't take the credit for that. That was wacko Franklin's little scheme. Some rich millionaire comes to New Orleans every year; Franklin and Boone get paid handsomely for delivering the right merchandise to the sicko's yacht. From there who knows, who cares what happens to them. Now quit yapping and dig. Maybe I should get you to dig a second grave for your little colored friend. Would you like that, ole Jackie Poo?"

"I hate you, you're crazy … and fuck you and your shoveling." She threw the shovel into the mud. Jacqueline's outburst resulted in Cooper striding to her and slapping her with his gun. She went down like a bag of rocks, into the grave that she had dug for herself.

Instinctively I jumped from my hiding spot and crossed the 10 yards like I was O.J. Simpson. Cooper had just started to turn towards me when I tackled him with everything I had. We rolled around on the forest floor before I kneed him in the nuts. I punched him over and over again, my fists growing numb. I was a crazed as a rabid Chihuahua after a mail carrier. Agent Graham eventually pulled me off of him. Ben had gone to Jacqueline and was holding her up.

Chapter 60

Gabriel – Saturday Evening, Day 13

Sheriff Cooper was taken into custody while Jacqueline and I were taken to Memorial Hospital in Gulfport. My hands needed attention; the beating I'd laid on Cooper had turned them into hamburger. The doctor gave me a sedative because my heart was racing like I was on a track in Indianapolis. Jacqueline was kept overnight for observation. She had contusions to the right side of her face and was suffering from exhaustion.

I went to see her as soon as they released me. When she saw me she started to cry. I held her until she stopped. It took a long time. Cooper was behind bars, kept in solitary in his own prison. Ben stopped by, wearing a black blazer with a brown shirt and grey stripes. He told me that with Jacqueline's alibi, I was no longer being charged with Bud's murder. As for Deputy Franklin, a young witness named Travis came forward to corroborate my story. I was still in trouble for breaking Pettimore's nose; however, even if it got to trial it would be my word against that of a convicted pedophile. Ben mentioned that Chevon had suffered a serious injury and that she would be in Ocean Springs Hospital for a few weeks.

Jacqueline told me that she'd waited outside the Ace hardware store for the better part of 2 hours before Chevon drove into the parking lot. They'd gone to grab a coffee and after Jacqueline told Chevon her story, they decided to go back to the Good Night Motel.

"Why didn't you just have her book a room at another motel under her name?"

"We were going to do that but then she convinced me to go back to the motel because that would be where you would find us. Chevon was very brave. She went after him like a wild

342

animal to get him away from me. I sure hope she's going to be okay". I said I would find out about her status over at Ocean Springs' hospital.

Ben asked me how I wanted to handle notifying Mrs. Glaswell and Mrs. Carson. I wasn't looking forward to it, but I knew it came with the territory. I had already told a ten year old boy that his father was dead. Telling Mrs. Glaswell her daughter wasn't going to be coming home would be worse. Rebecca hadn't done anything wrong. She had done nothing to deserve this. You could say Bud Carson had taken a risk by running the strip bar and that he could have picked up stakes and got out of there. Still, what did Mrs. Carson do, other than to stand by her man?

"I'll do it," I said.

Ben didn't stay much longer but invited us out to a meeting the following day once the hospital released Jacqueline. "There are things to discuss," he said ominously.

Chapter 61

Gabriel-Sunday Morning, Day 14

I picked Jacqueline up at the hospital when she was discharged and took her out to breakfast at the Friendship restaurant. Tweedy was our waitress again, and she seemed happy to see me. I introduced her to Jacqueline, who she recognized from that morning's Sun Herald. There was a front page story on the arrest of Sheriff Cooper for conspiracy to commit murder, kidnapping and attempted murder. A follow-up piece on page 2 showed a picture of Mrs. Cooper and quoted anonymous sources saying that the alert issued last week was an attempt by Cooper to capture his runaway wife, whom he had routinely brutalized.

We were halfway through our meal when we were interrupted by a tall man wearing a sports jacket and bowtie. "Mr. Ross, it's great to run into you again. Are you and your missus ready to start looking for a home in Biloxi? There're so many exciting things to do here you know. There's virtually no crime and the beach is wonderful."

We simultaneously broke out laughing. I apologized to Pat and suggested that we'd need to have more time to finalize our plans.

We got to my office shortly before 11:00 for my meeting with Ben and Agent Graham. As we were getting on the elevator, I saw Larry mopping the lobby floor; I waved to him and told him not to play around with the elevator. I hadn't heard what became of Mr. Green or Frank Galliano, and I was hoping we would get some news in a few minutes. The elevator was packed and once again I thought about getting new premises. I looked over at Jacqueline, who like everyone else was looking up at the floor indicator. I started to sing "At the Copa, Copacabana, and the hottest spot north of Havana". A bunch of people joined in. I moved closer to Jacqueline and touched her shoulder. Jacqueline turned to me and shrugged off my arm mouthing the word "pervert".

We walked down the hall to my office door and I saw that the paper sign that said "Eye on You Detective Agency - When you really have to know" had been replaced by a black metal plaque with gold embossed letters.

"Do you like it? "Asked Ben, standing in the doorway wearing a tweed jacket with a polka-dot purple shirt and a brown tie.

"It's beautiful Ben; it's about time we start spending a few bucks on this place."

Seated behind my desk was Agent Graham. He welcomed us and thanked me for letting them use the office. On the desk, I saw a tape recorder and a file folder. The investigation and my role in the process were still being kept under wraps. Otherwise, the meeting would have been held at police headquarters.

"First of all I want to thank you Gabriel for what you have done. Detective O'Shea and I have been talking about the situation down here for at least a year. The only real break we got on the case was when you came on board. I think with what we overheard in the forest than we have enough to put Sheriff Cooper away for a long, long time.

He then turned to Jacqueline, "I'm sorry Mrs. Cooper, that we couldn't prevent all this from happening to you. We just didn't have enough to move on Sheriff Cooper and his friends until recently. With Gabriel finding the safe deposit box and the letter from Dermody, we knew we had them." He then pulled out a sheet of paper from a file folder on his desk. He handed a copy to both of us and asked us to read it through fully before asking any questions.

These are the notes from a psychiatric assessment Sheriff William Cooper, on May 20th, 1979 at the Gulf Oaks Psychiatric Hospital in Biloxi Mississippi.

Preliminary diagnosis: There is little doubt that William Jefferson Cooper is a sociopath. At times in the interview he demonstrated exceptional charm and charisma. At other times as you will see from my notes, he was prone to outbursts of anger driven by arrogance and a warped view of his omnipotence. I found that when discussing relationships his answers were driven mainly by his need and right to possess versus any true caring for the other person. I asked him to explain his feelings to me and in my opinion he was unable to do any self-reflection or appreciate the impact he made on others. At times I found him demonstrating compassion, but only as a tool of manipulation. While delusional in many aspects, I believe he was rational in making his deal with the prosecution.

Dr Jeffrey Gillies, M.D., Psy.D

Background information: Sheriff Cooper has been charged with conspiracy in the murder of strip club owner Bud Carson. Evidence has been presented that Cooper conspired with known members of a prominent member of the Dixie Mafia to move the body of Mr. Carson from where he was murdered, to Harrison County where it would be discovered. The purpose of this subterfuge was to ensure that his Sheriff's Department could work the case and either bury the crime or implicate someone other than the perpetrator. In response to the overwhelming evidence, Mr. Cooper has decided to turn State's evidence in return for the witness protection program. The court has ordered this examination to assess his fitness in making this decision.

"What, he is being offered a deal?" yelled Jacqueline.

"We have a solid case against him but without his testimony it would be hard to convict those who are truly responsible. Unless we offer him a deal, they'll just get another William Cooper to do their dirty work."

Jacqueline started to cry and held my arm so tightly it hurt.

"There is something else that we shouldn't be sharing with you, but feel that we must under the circumstances. The tape recording you are about to hear is a partial of the session that was held with Cooper and the State-appointed doctor. I could lose my job if it got out that I shared it with you." Agent Graham pressed play on the tape player.

A voice I figured was the psychiatrist said, "Thank you for agreeing to sit with me Mr. Cooper."

"It's Sheriff Cooper."

"Okay Sheriff, please call me Dr Gillies. Are you nervous?"

"Not at all."

"I would like to delve briefly into your personal relationships, how you see your role as Sheriff and then to discuss how you are feeling about the charges against you. Would that be alright?"

"Go ahead and ask your questions, I have nothing to hide. "

"Tell me about your relationship with your wife Jacqueline."

"We met some seven years ago when I rescued her and some of her friends along the state highway. We got to know each other and then things developed and we decided to get married."

"Were you happy?"

"Of course, she's a beautiful young woman and I gave her everything, money, status a home, family..."

"Were you always faithful to her?"

"Absolutely!" There was a pause on the tape before he added, "Well, a man like me you know, in my position gets his share of offers. I may have messed around a bit to relieve the stress, but nothing serious."

"There's been a suggestion that she might have been unfaithful to you with Mr. Ross the Private Detective, how do you feel about that."

"That's what that little pisshead said, but I don't believe it. She would never betray me."

"How would you feel if she did?"

"LISTEN, I already said she didn't, so move on."

"If she didn't cheat on you why did you try to hurt her in the woods?"

There was silence on the tape. I could hear rustling as if someone was moving in their chair. "I wouldn't have hurt her. I just wanted to teach her a lesson about loyalty."

"Loyalty?" There was a pause on the tape before the next question came.

"Ok let's change topics to your role of Sheriff, how did you feel about your role in keeping the peace?"

"I was elected Sheriff by the folks of Harrison County in 1971 and they chose to re-elect me again in 1975. I am the most important person in the county in terms of protecting our good citizens from some of the scum that come here from up north."

"How do you feel about the progress you have made in reducing crime?"

"What's with all these feely type questions? I feel just fine about it; I got the streets cleaned up and business is booming. All kinds of people would like to live here because they know that I've made it safe to walk the streets at night."

"How would you describe your relationship with Bud Carson?"

"He was scum. He allowed underage drinking in his bar, and some of his girls were no more than 15."

"Why do you think someone killed him?"

"I don't know."

"But you've already admitted to state investigators that you moved the body from the crime scene so that someone would discover the body in your jurisdiction."

"Look, there is a group of businessmen - some from New Orleans - which have some control over what happens here. They ensure that things happen in an orderly manner. I can tell you Carson was scum. And I wasn't surprised when I was asked to move the body and hush up the investigation."

"So who asked you to do that?"

Once again there was another pause. I could almost sense Cooper weigh his options. "It was a contact that I have named Frank Galliano, he represents a Mr.Castolonatto in New Orleans."

"So you are telling me that Carson was killed on orders from a Mafia kingpin because he allowed under aged-drinking to take place in his strip club?"

"NO! WHAT ARE YOU STUPID? I'm sure that Carson did something else to piss off the guy."

"So why did you decide to turn state's evidence?"

"It doesn't matter what I do. Just because I'm here, arrested, they're going to think I talked. They have people in Angola Penitentiary and up in Parchment. I wouldn't last a day. This way we can start over somewhere else."

"Do you feel any remorse over what happened?"

"Why? I said he was scum, and he's off the street."

"So you are turning state's evidence because you have no other option?"

"Well...I want to do the right thing."

"Do you think you're thinking clearly about what transpired in your marriage or at work?"

"Of course."

"A moment ago, you said, "we" can start over. Who were you referring to?"

"Jacqueline of course."

Agent Graham pressed stop on the cassette player and looked over at us.

"That interview suggests that he still wants to be with Jacqueline. A couple of days ago he was making her dig her own grave. The guy is clearly demented." I said, standing to show my concern.

"He will remain in lockup until he is finished testifying and at that point he will be relocated to another part of the country, where he will continue to be locked up and under care of a doctor.'"

"How can you make a deal with a sociopath?" I said, my voice rising.

"Mr. Ross, please sit down." Agent Graham waited a few minutes until I sat back down. He stood up and looked out the window at the red brick building and said, "Not much of a view. Mr. Ross you would be surprised how many sociopaths there are walking the streets out there. They run companies, become professional athletes, musicians and for the most part under therapy and with the proper medication, they can be some of the most productive citizens in the country. We'll make sure that Cooper gets the treatment he needs before we let him loose."

Chapter 62

Gabriel-3 years later

More than three years have passed since the day that William Cooper made his wife dig her own grave. It was the same kind of night tonight. After five days of sweltering temperatures, the clouds had erupted in a torrential downpour earlier today and the storm had been raging all day. The gutters and potholes swelled and overflowed. Winds reached gale force and Palm trees were bent in half.

It had taken a long time for the scars to fade and the nightmares to die out. Jacqueline had moved up north at first to live with her parents. They were better-equipped to help her come to grips with what happened. Initially, we just stayed in touch by phone, like survivors of terrible tragedies.

William Cooper had kept his word and turned state's evidence. Convictions were obtained against Mr. Brown, Mr. Green and Mr. Purple, as well Frank Galliano. Cooper refused to admit guilt when it came to Alex Dermody's accident. He'd said this was all Franklin's idea, spurred on by Dermody finding the locket in his desk. Through his cooperation, the authorities were able to identify a rich millionaire wacko who had a thing for young blondes, but he was able to slip away before police could arrest him. Through Ben I learned that Michael Glaswell was picked up by the California State Troopers. He had been living on the beach near Malibu.

I spent time with Mrs. Glaswell, who I believe knew that her daughter was never coming home. I also spent time with Mrs. Carson, who upon inheriting the Rockaway, had torn it down and converted it to a parking lot. Boone Cooper, who was Franklin's partner in the abductions, disappeared without a trace. As for ex-Sheriff Cooper, after he finished testifying, the US

Marshalls took him away. According to Agent Graham, who I still occasionally saw, he was responding well to therapy and wanted only to put the past behind him.

As for me, the business had grown. The Eye on You Detective Agency received excellent publicity during the trials. A day rarely went by without an inquiry from a prospective customer...someone who just needed to know. Bourbon and I moved to a bigger, much nicer office. We also hired a receptionist named Rachel, who had previously worked as a nurse at Gulf Oaks. Bourbon and I were sold once we found out she could make coffee and tuna casserole. Ben was offered the Biloxi Chief of Police position once Ricketts went to the big house. He turned it down. According to him, he didn't want to give up the best job in the world so that he could push paper around and report to assholes.

About 18 months ago my life had taken a turn for the better. Jacqueline began to come back for short visits. She reconnected with a recovered Chevon, claiming that it was the Southern charm that brought her back. I had bought a small bungalow, not far from the place she used to live. Jimmy, I mean Travis' mother had moved back into the family home once Franklin's funeral was over. Travis was a regular visitor now. He still acted like he was President and had gone back to calling me Tab. On one of her visits Jacqueline announced that her divorce was final and that she was going back to her maiden name Chen.

I don't remember when she decided to move in with me. Seemed like she just came visiting and never left. I encouraged her to accept a position with the Biloxi Cultural Centre and to develop her career as an art historian. We still play Jeopardy. We regularly play, so regularly we are expecting a little Gabriel in a few months.

I looked down at the Sun Herald in my lap. John Hinckley was found not guilty by reason of insanity in the shooting of Ronald Regan. Anyone can walk into a pawnshop in Biloxi and buy a deadly handgun for $10. No questions asked. I still have Ben's snub-nosed '38. I keep it in the night stand, but I've never fired it, still not sure that I could. Like Rockford said, a good detective doesn't need a gun.

The wind outside howled. Flashes of lightning would periodically illuminate the night, followed by the boom of thunder sounding like a bass drum in a marching band. I looked over at Jacqueline and moved in for a kiss, saying that I was very happy. She asked me if I could put that in the form of a question. We were interrupted by the ringing of the phone in the kitchen. As it rang I put my arm around her and said, "Who's the happiest man alive?" The call went to the machine.

After my voicemail greeting, I heard a familiar voice. "Gabriel if you are there, pick up it's important."

Reluctantly Jacqueline pushed me away and said "Go answer the phone." I got up and crossed over to the kitchen picking up the receiver.

"You really have horrible timing Agent Graham," I said.

"I'm sorry, my apologies to Jacqueline for the interruption. It's probably nothing, but I thought I should call just in case."

As I listened, I looked over at Jacqueline. She already sensed something was wrong. "You have my full attention."

354

"A week ago William Cooper missed a regular check-in with the U.S. Marshall responsible for him. Like I said he's probably on vacation and just forgot to check in. He hasn't mentioned either of you in about a year."

I was aware that Cooper had recently been released to a Los Angeles halfway house. "Okay, we'll be on the lookout. Is there anything else John?" I gestured to Jacqueline not to worry.

"No just wanted to give you a heads up, there's no reason to believe he's in the area."

I thanked Agent Graham for the call and told Jacqueline that it was nothing. People miss check-ins all the time. I sat down next to her, hoping to get back to Jeopardy, but she had already gone to a commercial. "Did you hear a noise just now coming from the bedroom?" she asked.

I took my erection and went to check the noise that Miss Sensitive-Ears must have heard. As I walked into the bedroom, my nerves made me jump. She had left the back door open, and the wind was blowing the curtain inward like a woman wearing a sheer negligee. Taking a breath, I noticed that the wind was also causing a knocking sound as the screen door opened and closed. I went to the door and closed it, using the latch to lock it. That's when I heard the breathing.

"Hello, rat fuck" the voice was behind me. I turned; that's when everything went black.

Chapter 63

Jacqueline – A few minutes later ...

"Gabriel? Gabriel?" I called out. I heard what sounded like a bag of potatoes falling to the floor in the bedroom.

When I didn't get an answer, my niggling fear from the phone call earlier turned into an avalanche of panic. I struggled to get my bloated body off the couch. I made my way to the kitchen looking for something to protect me. My senses were alert to every little creak coming from the house. Keeping my eyes trained towards the hall and the bedrooms I reached into the pantry for a weapon.

A shape entered the dark hallway. It was tall, taller than Gabriel. A flash of lightning illuminated the enraged face of William Cooper. "Hello baby, I've come for you. OH, what do we have here? Has my little slut got herself preggers with a little bastard?"

I screamed as loud as I could, which just brought him running towards me. My hand gripped the can of chili, and I threw it at him, hitting him in the forehead and momentarily stunning him. I reached for something else and threw a box of hamburger helper at him. He blocked that throw with an arm, the pasta scattering all over the floor. "Stop throwing food." I hit him right in the temple with a can of Green Giant peas. He started making this "ow, ow" noise, but I knew he was faking it as he inched closer. My hand found the can of Pam cooking spray. When he got close enough, I took the cap off and let him have it in the eyes. He bent over rubbing his eyes. "You bitch". That's when I closed my hand around the Bush's Baked Beans.

I used it in my fist to deliver a crushing right to his jaw. "That's for Chevon you sick fuck!" Cooper went down. I wanted to make a run for help, but his body was blocking the door. The beans had only stunned him and he started to move. He had his nightstick in his hand. Getting to his feet, he slapped it against his hand. Cooking spray dripped off his face. Using his shirt sleeve, he wiped at his face. I reached back into the pantry; this time I came up with a pack of Twinkies. I threw them at him and he laughed at me. His right fist connected with my jaw, knocking me to the floor. He stood over me, his foot raised ready to stomp. I begged him; "Please Will, whatever you want...I'll go with you. It can be like it used to be."

"Hey, little dick remember me?" Gabriel's voice sounding from down the hallway! Cooper turned towards the sound. "Put down the nightstick and I might let you live." A flash of lightning illuminated Gabriel holding the '38.

"Go ahead and shoot," said Cooper, moving back down the hall towards Gabriel.

"Don't make me shoot you." Gabriel's his voice was almost pleading.

"I don't think you have it in you."

"Put the baton down and get on your knees." This time Gabriel was shouting.

Cooper moved closer; Gabriel cocked the gun. A moment went by. You could almost hear Cooper's mind measuring, weighing the risks. Finally, he dropped the nightstick and got down on his knees. "You know shrimp; they'll just put me back in the program."

"Shrimp? Well, maybe so, but you'll be dead." A gunshot rang out, and Cooper fell flat on his face. "No one calls me a shrimp!"

The End

Made in the USA
Charleston, SC
07 December 2014